Portia Da Costa is one of the most internationally renowned authors of erotic romance and erotica, and a *Sunday Times*, *New Y̶o̶r̶k̶ ̶T̶i̶m̶e̶s̶ ̶a̶n̶d̶ ̶U̶S̶A̶ ̶T̶o̶d̶a̶y̶* bestseller. She is the author of eighte̶ ort stories and n̶o̶

Jani f fantasy, horror

Oliv sity and a teache ike Phillip Pullman. She is an enthusiast for old religions, folklore and mythology. Her unique blend of fantasy and reality, of science fiction and magic, makes her the new name to watch in erotic romance.

Magic
and
Desire

PORTIA DA COSTA
JANINE ASHBLESS
OLIVIA KNIGHT

BLACK
LACE

1 3 5 7 9 10 8 6 4 2

Black Lace, an imprint of Ebury Publishing
20 Vauxhall Bridge Road,
London SW1V 2SA

Penguin
Random House
UK

Black Lace is part of the Penguin Random House group
of companies whose addresses can be found at
global.penguinrandomhouse.com

First published in 2008 by Black Lace
This edition published in 2015

www.eburypublishing.co.uk

A CIP catalogue record for this book is available from
the British Library

ISBN 9780352347848

Printed and bound in Great Britain by Clays Ltd, St Ives PLC

Penguin Random House is committed to a sustainable future for
our business, our readers and our planet. This book is made from
Forest Stewardship Council® certified paper.

MIX
Paper from
responsible sources
FSC® C018179

The House of Dust

by

Janine Ashbless

The House of Dust

by Janine Ashbless

I've never been to the King's bedchamber; he has always come to mine. But this day is not like any that has gone before it. A priestess shouldn't hurry; she should always retain the dignity of her office, but I pick up my fringed skirts and run down the long palace corridor and my handmaidens fall back behind me, squawking in alarm. Guards and servants haunting the dim rooms gape as I flit past, my gilded sandals snapping on the mudbrick floor – the royal palace is not so grand a building as the temple of Inanna, for all its size; there we have limestone paving.

As I run into the private audience chamber, Emmer, the King's chief scribe, comes to intercept me and I slow. Emmer was born to a priestess of Inanna and is still loyal to the temple; he often keeps me informed of happenings in the palace just as he did my predecessor on the *huluppu*-throne. On this occasion neither of us can waste time being discreet.

'Emmer – the King?'

'This way.' He beckons me towards a door and I jog after him into a courtyard garden. Emmer is portly and getting on in years and can't run as fast as I can.

'Is it bad?'

Emmer shoots me a look and I know from his refusal to answer exactly how bad that is. In the palace, to say 'The King is dying' would be to invite disaster not just upon the monarch but also upon the speaker. To say something is to wish for it; to be heard invoking demons like that would be to sign one's own execution warrant.

'What happened?' I catch him by the arm, bringing him to a halt. I have to know.

He wriggles uncomfortably from my grasp. 'Great Lady . . .' His gaze sweeps the date palms and the fig trees anxiously.

'What happened?' I drop my voice to a hiss. 'I saw the King yesterday and he was well. Now he's sick?'

Emmer's voice is barely audible. 'After his meal he complained that his feet were cold and numb. He tried to stand up from the couch but he fell. Servants carried him to bed. He said he could feel nothing in his legs. Now . . .'

He doesn't need to finish. A thick knot forms in my throat. 'Inanna preserve him,' I mumble, but my tongue feels like leather, an alien thing flapping in the dry vault of my mouth.

'You should hurry.'

We set off again. As we scurry beneath the cedar lintel of the King's quarters, past guards who shrink away bowing their heads, I remember the first time I met King Tamuz face to face. It was on the night of the Spring Equinox, the first night of the nine for which the Great Marriage is celebrated and the beginning of the New Year, and it was my first time in the role of Inanna, Queen of Heaven and Earth. I was no maiden of course, at nineteen years old – no priestess of Inanna's is – but I was just as nervous as any bride. There's a hierarchy among the priestesses, and those of the grade of *nu-gig* such as was I, a daughter of princes, do not have to work the common chambers of the temple unless the goddess moves us. Perhaps I'd had less experience of men than I assumed. Certainly I hadn't yet realised that in public rituals such as the Great Marriage it's never the woman who needs fear she will not acquit herself properly.

The high priestess then, Gushea, should by rights have been playing the part of the goddess as she had done ever since I could remember, but she was ill that year with a hot fist of pain in her belly, the first sign of the sickness that eventually took her, so she'd nominated a lesser priestess as was her prerogative. I don't know why she chose me, only that it was the beginning of the period of her favour that was to end in my ascension to the *huluppu*-throne.

My first good look at Tamuz's face was as he climbed the steps to the bridal platform. It was a breezy night and the torch flames were flapping and hissing, threatening at every moment to go out, sending shadows dancing all across the great open square. But as he reached the foot of the bed the wind suddenly dropped and everyone, not just the drummers and the timbrel- and the sistrum-players but the whole crowd – the whole city of Uruk from nobility to slaves – gathered on every balcony and roof and step for a good view, fell absolutely silent, holding their breath. Their King and their goddess were bathed in a nimbus of golden light as the torches renewed their vigour; I remember thinking that it was the best of omens. I remember the way his long hair gleamed in oiled ringlets upon his shoulders. He wore no crown that night of course; he approached the goddess Inanna in humility, as a mortal man, though his cloak was of the finest, most heavily worked embroidery. The bed beneath my bare feet was spread with sheepskins to represent his status as the shepherd of the people, to represent the flocks and herds of Uruk whose fecundity for the coming year depended upon the heat of our passion. Over the fleeces were strewn seeds of flax and lettuce and barley, which could not germinate unless quickened by our desire.

I remember how he paused to look me over. It was the lift of his eyebrows, the slow appreciative grin – so entirely unexpected – the unmasked and unforced pleasure in his eyes that somehow invited me to reciprocate: those were the things that lit the flame in my belly. There'd never been any question that the goddess would move in me; my body was trained to be her vessel. But I'd never expected my heart to jump like that.

Clearly, so that all could hear, we spoke the ritual verses. Then he slipped off his long cloak and he was naked beneath it, naked and muscular and golden under the torchlight except for the dark hair at his groin, black and oiled like his beard, and his duskier phallus already heavy and pendent with anticipation.

My honey-man, my honey-man sweetens me always,
He is the one I love, sang the women.

Tamuz took me without hurry into his arms, drawing off my fragile nuptial gown and caressing me tenderly. 'Oh . . . my holy jewel,' he murmured as his lips stooped to my breasts and grazed my nipples. 'Oh, my wondrous Inanna.'

The words were as familiar as my own heartbeat, but for the first time I heard them as if they were truly meant for me. In those moments Inanna did not simply fill and inhabit me; I felt as if I were really her: the goddess who moved the world to love. We spoke the verses as our hands moved to explore and arouse one another, skin on oiled skin, everything smooth and slippery. His phallus was soon as hard as *huluppu*-wood under my fingers. And there, in front of all the people, on that bed smelling of fleece and cedar oil and scented resins, he covered me and entered me and moved upon me with sweet unhurried joy, his fullness my delight.

That was the first time. Afterwards we attended the wedding feast in the palace and I sat regally clad beside him upon his throne, as all the luxury of Uruk was laid before us in a feast of roasted meats from the fields and the steppes and the far mountains, fish drawn from the Two Rivers, almonds and dates and honey and cheeses and soft bread, wine and beer both dark and light. Musicians played their stringed instruments and sang for us and dancers displayed their lithe and naked bodies up and down the room, the whole assembly loud and relaxed and joyous. As the night wore on many guests slipped away to couple in the shadows behind pillars; such things were expected on this night. The harsh hungry days were over; the parched fields would soon be green again, the thin herds fat, the ewes giving milk as they dropped their lambs. Soon the god Enlil would unleash the Two Rivers from their sources in the distant mountains and their flooding would fill the canals and ditches that would water our fields all year. The King had wed the goddess and her blessings would shower upon his land. And I sat in the middle of it all, the radiant ornament of the assembly, the toast of the land of Sumer, my fingers twined with his. They sang in celebration and in praise and I accepted it as the goddess's due, all night until dawn, and then I went to greet myself, the Morning Star, shining upon the horizon.

There on the balcony Tamuz found me in prayer, my hands raised to the heavens. Softly he dismissed the company and came up behind me. I faltered in my words as he slipped his hands about my upper body, cupping my breasts as he pressed up against me.

'Don't stop,' he murmured, kissing my neck.

Such informality was permitted during the time of the Great Marriage, so I carried on praying while he rolled my nipples to points of exquisite frustration between his fingers and bit softly at my ears, tugging at the clusters of golden balls strung from my pierced lobes. I made it to the last verse in a stumbling rush, my spine arched so as to press my shoulders and my buttocks back against the hard wall of his body. I could feel little bolts of lightning chasing across my breasts and down to the wellspring of my sex, as if great Enlil himself were playing with my nipples. When Tamuz laid a firm hand upon my navel and slid it down to cup my pubic mound I gasped out loud. I wanted so much for him to set me face down over that low wall and root me there high above the flat roofs of Uruk, now touched with faintest pink from the approaching sunrise, so that I might encompass the whole of my realm with my eyes as he filled me, so that Utu the shining sun might blind me with his glory as I was made incandescent from behind and within. But Tamuz turned me instead and sat me upon the edge of the wall, lifting my skirts over my knees to reveal my smooth thighs and sliding his hands up their inner surfaces, all the way to the mound of my delta. I put my arms around his neck and drew him closer, my legs encompassing his. Gently, with the tips of his fingers, he stroked my purse until he broke the fragile seal of flesh and let the moisture within seep out.

'Daughter of the Moon,' he whispered, his eyes shining, 'we've hardly met and yet I have wounded you sorely.'

'You did,' I breathed. 'The pain is unbearable. My whole body cries out.'

'Forgive me. I thought you might be healed by now.' He circled the pomegranate-pip of my clitoris expertly, making me shudder. I dug my nails into his skin.

'This is a wound that can't be healed. You hurt me too deeply and now I must live with it forever.'

'Can I make reparation?'

'You might, if you are brave.'

His fingers were slippery now to the root, moving slickly in and upon my sex, stirring me beyond endurance. 'And how shall I do that?'

'You must staunch the wound,' I said, parting the layers of his long kilt to reveal the length of his prick, the skin already taut and glistening, 'with the weapon that made it.' I took hold, and Tamuz's expression made it clear I had his undivided attention. 'It's an ancient magic,' I confided, my eyes wide and serious. 'Only by wounding me again can you ease me of my pain.'

'Then,' he said, his voice hoarse, 'I see you're skilled in the magical art.'

My hand was working his copper to harder bronze. 'Oh yes, my King.'

'And it is my duty to help you.'

With infinite care, both of us breathing shallow and quick, he nudged into me, sheathing perhaps two-thirds of his length. The wall held me at just the right height for him.

'Don't let me fall,' I whispered.

His arm tightened about my waist. 'Never.' And as he pressed into me with long firm thrusts, taking his time, I gave myself up to his arms and his lips, letting my head fall back until I hung over the dizzying drop and the city below. The stars were fading overhead into a pale and cloudless sky but within me whole new constellations were exploding into birth.

That was the first night. Eight more days and nights we spent in each other's company, and Tamuz hardly left my side. For eight days and nine nights the cares of rulership were taken from his shoulders. He was forbidden to make war or sit in judgement or to slay man or beast in all that time; his only duty was to bring pleasure to his divine wife. Willingly, I think, we both played the part of young lovers, rapt in our first all-consuming passion – though for neither of us was this the first, or anything like. By day we walked hand-in-hand, and lost ourselves in foolish games, and sailed upon the river listening to songs of desire. At night we lay together in the pavilion in the temple garden, denying ourselves sleep, hunting each other fervently across the bed. Then the ninth morning came and Tamuz returned to his palace, to his wives and his concubines, and I returned to being a priestess of a high, but not the highest, rank. For a time.

Years have passed since then, ushered in by the scorpion-men that open the Gate of the East, and ushered out through the Gate of the West into the darkness beneath the earth.

As I hurry through the palace at Emmer's side, it seems to me that the colour has drained from the red and black and yellow zigzag patterns on the walls, from the lapis lazuli of the stone mosaics, from the gilding on the carved beams, until everything looks grey and brittle. Fear and fury twist like wrung linen in my belly. Tamuz is a king in his prime; for him to die now is an affront to the gods. It is also, it transpires, a public spectacle. His bedchamber is filled to the door and overflowing with officials and noblemen, slaves and guards and priests of every one of the gods. Everyone is talking and pushing and arguing; women are already wailing, and the air is sour. Emmer has to hammer on the backs of those who cram the doorway: 'The First Daughter of the Moon! The Lady of the Morning and the Evening! The Queen of Heaven! Stand aside for the High Priestess of Inanna!'

They part reluctantly, but they let me in. I push my way to the bed, tiny in that great chamber but far too big for the lone figure which occupies it. Positions immediately round the bedside are taken by physicians, and by Tamuz's four noble-born queens and his family. He has no sons for all his vigour, but I recognise his sister Geshtinanna, his half-brother Nergal and Nergal's son. Kneeling by the bed, weeping and clinging to Tamuz's hand which hangs limply over the edge, is his senior queen, Ninsu.

'Get off him!' I order and she shrinks away. Then I hoist my skirts and climb on to the bed to kneel over him.

It's a shock. When last I saw him only yesterday, returning from a lion hunt in the steppeland beyond the Euphrates, he was in the fullest health. Now, covered to the waist with a sheet, Tamuz looks like he's already a corpse, his strong frame almost flattened against the bedding and his skin as grey as salt. His eyes are only half-open and under the lids they still move in their sockets, but his chest is hardly rising at all. I touch him and he feels cold and clammy. I lay my fingers to his throat but his pulse is barely there, as slow and muddy as the Tigris in late summer. Kneeling forwards until my face is right over his, I call his name.

The King's lips move, but no sound issues forth. Only his eyes turning to mine under their lowered lids show that he is conscious of my presence. I have to swallow my tears. It's far too late to save him. If news had come to me earlier, if the malady had not been so rapid, then I'd have had time to make him an amulet that would restore his strength or cast the poison from his body by prayer and rite. As it is, I'm barely there in time to bid him farewell. 'My face covers your face like a mother over her child,' I whisper, my voice cracking. 'I will place you like a jewel between my breasts; during the night I will give you covering, during the day I will clothe you. Fear not, oh my little one, whom I have raised.' A tear slips out and splashes on to his cheek. 'Tamuz . . .'

Softly a sigh escapes from his lips. I am close enough to watch as his eyes darken, the pupils dilating in death. My own eyes I have to close, and for a moment the roar of blood in my ears is so loud it drowns the gabbling of the crowd.

'The King is dead,' I say, when I can find my voice.

As I sit back people start to scream and I shut my eyes again. All around me I hear the sound of the rending of cloth. They will all tear their garments and their hair; they will rip at the skin of their faces and their thighs with their nails until the blood runs; they will pour ash over their heads. And, when they grow too tired to carry on, the mourning will be taken up by the professionals from the Temple of Ereshkigal, the Queen of the Dead. That is the way of it when someone dies.

I feel for a moment that I'm going to be sick. My own saliva has turned so bitter I can hardly swallow and my eyes feel like they're burning. It isn't sorrow. A creeping paralysis that begins at the feet and spreads up the body until the heart and lungs give out – I know those symptoms. Tamuz has been poisoned. Somebody has fed him the oily distillate of the hemlock weed that grows on the banks of ditches and rivers. It gives an easy death, they say; painless so long as you have the courage to face it.

But who has done it?

Then I look around and in the midst of that wailing, hysterical crowd I meet the cold black eyes of Nergal, brother to the late King. And I know.

Tamuz's funeral rites take seven days. On the last of those I linger in his shrine when all others have finished and gone. A part of me does not wish to face the world outside that simple room. The bare mudbrick walls enclose a square space open to the overcast sky, and as I kneel before his altar the first sparrows flit cautiously in to inspect the feast laid in offering there; food provided for his sojourn in the House of Dust. Buried with Tamuz, deep beneath my feet in his burnt-brick vault, are more precious gifts and possessions: the gold and the silver, the harps and the chariots and the thrones.

The boldest of the sparrows is pecking at a loaf of barley bread when movement in the doorway behind me puts it to flight.

'Still here, Daughter of the Moon?' says Nergal. 'You're taking your time.'

'Tamuz was a great king,' I say, getting to my feet; I don't like being on my knees before this man. 'Mourning him is not swiftly done with.'

Nergal's hair is worn unbound and uncombed in sign of mourning; it gives him a wild look that matches the glint in his eye. 'I think your attendants wish you grieved him less.'

He has a point; the chanting of my entourage, waiting outside in the royal cemetery grounds for me, has sunk to a mumble. They are not comfortable out there: even the best woollen cloaks are little use against the biting winter winds and the sacred harlots of Inanna are used to a life within sheltering walls.

'My women are as loyal as I am.'

'But not so grief-stricken, I think. Nor so bitter.' His smile does not stretch further than his lips.

I look him in the eye steadily as I acknowledge his words. I am oddly relieved. There is between us an honesty of a sort: each of us knows where the other stands.

'The gods dispense joy and woe. We must endure both.'

'Yes. And tomorrow there will be a new king upon the throne of Uruk, and then of course you will rejoice, Lady Ishara.'

'Of course. Tomorrow.'

'And are you looking forward to the Great Marriage?'

I don't hide my coldness. 'Naturally I look forward to the return of spring.'

'Will you take the role of the goddess yourself?'

'Should I not?' My voice is husky; I've already considered that point.

He folds his arms. 'The first time you played the part of Inanna, I remember I thought you perfect in your beauty. I was an ardent and romantic youth then. I came to the temple the next month and asked for you in person – do you remember?'

My eyes feel like stones in their sockets. 'How could I forget the brother of the King?'

13

'And you were . . . most beautiful. Most accomplished. The goddess shone in you, Lady.'

'She blesses us.'

He puts his hand on my waist. I stiffen. That hand makes me too conscious of the sweep of my hip below it, the curves of my thighs and buttocks. It makes me conscious that he is not curvy at all; he is all blocky mass and hard lines.

'Don't touch me.' I try to retreat.

'Oh come, Lady.' He backs me up against the altar, so I'm nearly sat upon the lip. 'Aren't you a courtesan of Inanna? Why refuse me?'

I grit my teeth. 'You are not yet king, Nergal – and I am in mourning.'

'Love is the balm for grief, isn't it?' Without effort he bats away my protesting hands and cups a breast, kneading it through the fine wool of my dress. I bite the inside of my lip to stop myself gasping; despite my anger and my loathing my nipple responds to the masterful sureness of his touch, rivulets of hot sensation pouring across my skin. There's no hesitation in him, no need for exploration; he knows what to do and my treacherous body melts like clay under a winter storm.

All I've wanted for this last week is to feel Tamuz's arms around me, to relax in his sheltering strength, to hear his reassuring murmur in my ear. My body aches for comfort and for release – but this is the last man I should take them from.

'Of course . . . You're not so young now, Lady Ishara. These breasts are not perfect any more.'

Blood burns in my face but his hands give the lie to his scathing words.

'Hardly fit for a king. There are a hundred women in my palace more beautiful than you and as many in the temple of Inanna, no doubt. Just on the way in here I noticed one of your maidens, with a face as sweet as that of a newborn calf and breasts that stand in perfect cones . . .'

'If your taste runs to virgins then you will have every chance to satisfy it when you are king,' I say bitterly, but I can't drag my attention from the touch of his hands, the pressure of his body, the way he's turning my insides upside down.

'Hm. Has the part of Inanna ever been played by a virgin?' he muses. His caresses are ruthless.

'Don't be a fool –'

'Better the King beds a young beauty than a worn-out harridan, don't you think?'

'Don't mock the gods,' I groan. 'The Great Marriage is not about your desires or your pride. Even you must come before the Queen of Heaven in humility, or bear her curse. The King needs Inanna, Nergal. Inanna does not need the King.'

His eyes look like pools of bitumen in the dim light. 'We'll see,' he says. He pulls up my skirt and sinks a hand between my thighs. I gasp and twist, then I grab at his forearm but he is too strong for me to shift.

'Would you have me call my women so all know of your shameful behaviour?' I hiss in his ear as he leans into me, his body hard.

He grabs the hair at the back of my neck, pulling my head back to stretch my throat. '*My* shamefulness?' he mocks, his fingers moving in their tight slot. I can't force my thighs together hard enough to keep him out. 'What about yours, Ishara?'

The edge of his hand is grinding right up against my mons, bruising my clit. His fingers are finding wetness. Inanna is a bitch: she loves the strong man, the forceful man, the one beautiful in his power and confidence. She moves in me like a flood-swell and I am borne up, helpless. Nergal hears my gasp and laughs, then kisses me punishingly, his tongue invasive. I can't keep him out. The goddess in me doesn't want to

15

keep him out. I yield to his hot wet mouth and as his tongue goes in deep his fingers enter me too. My hips buck.

'I bought your favours when you were younger,' he whispers, biting my lips. 'Now you give them to me for nothing.'

'Inanna!' I gasp, calling on my goddess to have mercy, to get out of me, to let me hate what this man is doing to me with the hands stained with his own brother's death; to hate it as I ought to. I can hear the moist noises as his fingers work my wetness, twisting and flexing within me.

'Yes,' he says, 'call her. I want her to see this. I want her to see her whore giving herself up to me. I want her to see you loving this. Loving my hand in your wet hole. Loving your King. Loving your King's cock.'

He pushes me on to my back and I go down among the roasted fishes and the glazed ducks and the cakes. He hoists my knees up and wide, splaying the gash of my sex and parting his kilt he pulls out the thick prick I remember so well. Its blunt head stretches me and he's inside me with one thrust. And then he lays his hand back on my swollen mound.

This is the cruelty of the man; he doesn't just intend to fuck me. He's going to make certain that I want what he's giving. He's going to make sure that I taste the dregs of humiliation, needing to be pleasured by the man who slew my King and my lover. So he takes his time, sliding his whole length in and out of me in measured, perfectly timed strokes, sometimes withdrawing altogether so that he can have the pleasure of penetrating me again and finding on each occasion that I am wetter and wider and more ready for him. He lifts my breasts up through the deep neck of my dress so that they are held squashed together by the fabric and he slaps them with his big hands to make them quiver, sharply enough to make me see the stars. And all the time he stirs my clit, slippery with my juices, until I despair of my soul and my sanity and remember only what it is to want.

As I start to come, he leans over me and grips my jaw in his hand, grinning into my face, forcing me to meet his eyes and confront myself there as I dissolve into the ecstasy of Inanna.

When my stifled cries have made it clear how I have surrendered myself unreservedly to him, he takes his own pleasure, gripping my hips as he thrusts fierce and fast in a breathless race to his climax. His rhythm sends my breasts slamming back and forth and the harmonies that sets up shake my whole body and send it tumbling to a second crisis, just as he reaches his first and fills me with his seed.

'Good!' he roars triumphantly, slapping my arse hard. 'Good! Yes!'

He braces himself on his arms when he's done to look down at me. There's a puddle of spilt wine under my left shoulder and a soapstone bowl is digging painfully into my hip.

'That was what you wanted,' he observes. 'Where's your loyalty to Tamuz now, Lady Ishara?'

I pull him down so I can speak in his ear. It's better when I don't have to look at myself reflected in his eyes. 'You first wanted me when you saw Tamuz love me in front of all Uruk. Tamuz fucked like a king. Tamuz fucked like a god. Let me tell you this, Nergal; never *once* were you as good as your brother.'

That kills his smirk. He pulls away, leaving me both relieved and in torment. I sag, gasping, and tug at my clothes with clumsy hands.

'Bear in mind, Lady, that I have one great advantage over Tamuz: I am alive, while he dwells among the worms in the House of Dust.' He picks up a loaf and wipes the juices from his fingers thoroughly on to the bread before tossing it back on to the slab. 'That's the only way he will ever taste you again. But, given that you fucked me in his tomb before the funeral feast got cold, I doubt he'll have much stomach for it.'

I flinch as his words stab deep, and watch with burning eyes as he leaves.

Smoke coils in the still air of my bedchamber, illuminated by a single lamp. The smoke stinks; I've been burning a hank of my own hair. It makes the familiar pieces of furniture seem less solid, the shadows deeper, the walls further off. I drop another sheaf of henbane on the smouldering embers in the brazier, and speak the words one more time.

In a corner something moves, uncoiling. My first impression upon glimpsing its long neck is that it is a serpent, my second that it is a vulture. It cocks its head from side to side as it looks at me and its eyes glow dull red like the underside of the charcoals. It is a *galla* – a demon of the Underworld.

As it creeps forwards, I see it better, though it remains as insubstantial as dirty smoke. Its body is that of an old man emaciated to the point of starvation, but there are great grey wings springing from its bare shoulders and its head and feet are those of a carrion bird. All four of its arms end in ragged claws.

I motion towards the dish of blood I have set out. 'Drink.'

The blood is mine, and my arm aches as it stoops and laps with a pallid tongue at the dark liquid. It seems to grow a little more solid after its repast and sits up, regarding me with flickering eyes. It speaks without moving its mouth, its voice a dry whisper in my head.

What do you wish for, Priestess of Inanna?

'I want you to go to the royal palace. I want you to kill a man for me. It must be tonight.'

That is easily done. What is his name?

'Kill for me Nergal, son of Enmerkar, father of Gilgamesh. Turn his bowels to blood. Fill his flesh with gnawing worms. Take his soul to your mistress in the deep places under the earth and let him stay there forever.'

The demon is incapable of facial expression but somehow conveys a wary surprise.

You wish me to slay the King of Uruk, Priestess of Inanna?

'He is not king until he is crowned tomorrow. Slay him tonight.'

And what will you pay me?

'A black lamb sacrificed at the dark of every moon for a year.'

It nods.

It is agreed.

Like smoke the *galla* drifts across the floor and dissolves into the wall.

Geshtinanna, sister of Tamuz, half-sister of the new King and high priestess of the god Enki, comes to my room at the worst possible time: just as I am being prepared for the Great Marriage. My cosmetics lie scattered about the table: kohl and malachite for my eyes and red earth for my lips and nipples, rosewater for my skin and perfumed unguents with which the black curls of my hair have been oiled, bronze tweezers and razors with which my body has been smoothed to silky perfection. I've crunched crystals of frankincense between my teeth to perfume my breath and more resins burn in the brazier to further scent the air because this is a holy occasion. My bridegroom awaits. Crowned, he still needs the goddess Inanna to seal his authority. In her keeping are all the attributes and gifts of civilisation and only by her blessing can a man reign in any of the cities between the Two Rivers.

Nergal has taken the throne-name of Lugulbanda – 'ruler of

all the land' – but he is still the same man. As my serving women tilt the copper mirror before me I look at my stony face and wonder if I will be able to fool the city into thinking I am opening with joy my arms and my thighs to him. In the dim surface of polished metal my kohl-rimmed eyes look like black holes in a beautiful mask.

I could choose another priestess to take the role, but that would be an act of cowardice. Either the goddess blesses the city of Uruk through its king or she does not; Inanna does not count out half-measures of her love like a housewife giving grudgingly to a beggar at her door. She loves as a young woman does, fiercely and unstintingly, with passion and without reason. That is why she is titled Maiden as well as Lady.

I hold out my arms and my women slip over me the gown that I will wear to my bridal bed: a net of gold thread. My rouged nipples snag upon the weft and poke out through the holes of the weave. Though ankle-length it is shaped to my frame, and there's no disguising the lines of my body within this glimmering sheath.

It's at this moment that Geshtinanna enters my room. She bows her head simply, as one high priestess to another. 'Ishara. Let us talk.'

I have to tell myself to close my mouth. For a moment I'm angry at her intrusion; my mood is bleak these days and I'm quick to snap. Then I hold up my hand to my women. 'Leave us.'

'Great Lady,' says the eldest, 'you've little time before the ceremony.'

Geshtinanna's eyes are bright and hard; she says nothing. 'A few moments,' I order. 'The moon hasn't risen yet.'

'But your hair –'

'Out!' I snap my fingers and they withdraw, leaving me alone with the sister of a murdered man. 'Let's talk, then.'

Geshtinanna comes closer, and when she speaks it's in a low voice. Her gold rings glitter as she reaches to touch my arms. 'Ishara. Please. I came to beg you not to wed that man.'

'Not wed him? It's too late for that. None of the other *nu-gig* have been purified.'

'No. I mean, not you. Not any of the priestesses. Please – refuse him the love of the goddess.'

'Why?' I ask, though I cannot bring any sense of shock to my voice.

'You know why. You know what he did.'

I can't hold her gaze. 'I know. But there's nothing I can do about it.'

'Denounce him, Ishara. Do it in public before all the people.'

'Without proof? Nergal has already executed those who confessed to the plot.'

Three servants of an inconvenient nobleman had been beaten into loquacity, and then impaled with their master on stakes at Uruk's rubbish pits, to rot unburied. Their ghosts will whine among the stink and the smoke forever.

'You believe they were the ones?'

'Of course not!' My rage, clamped for weeks in my breast, threatens to flare up like burning pitch. I can feel a great black cauldron of it boiling under my ribs.

'In the city there are those who say that the goddess Inanna discarded the King because he fathered no sons. They say it is your decision that he died. That Nergal is your choice.'

I clench my fists until my nails slice the skin. 'I've heard that.'

'Then prove them wrong. Reject Nergal.'

'I can't!'

'You can refuse the Great Marriage.'

My tongue feels like it is drying up inside my mouth. 'There would be famine,' I grate. 'The people would suffer and die.'

'Haven't we got grain and hay stored away for such a time?'

I back away from her and sit on my bed. I want to bury my face in my hands and weep, but I can't afford to smudge my make-up and I haven't cried in many weeks. Not since Tamuz died. Every woman in the city wept except me – whose tears are dammed up like the Apsu, the ocean of water that lies under the earth. Sometimes I cannot breathe for them filling my throat. 'I can't,' I repeat. 'He is the King.'

'I worked a magic against him.' Geshtinanna's voice is hoarse. 'I tried to slay him, for what he did.'

I look at her sharply. 'You shouldn't tell me that.'

Of course, Enki the Wise is the god of the magical arts – but, even for his priestess, to use magic against the King is to seek death.

'It didn't work. He surrounds himself with sorcerers and they ward off all attacks.'

I nod. I can't tell her that I'd tried it myself, equally in vain. 'He's blessed by fate. Geshtinanna . . .' For a moment I weaken, wanting to confess and rage and hear my words echoed by hers – it would be such a relief to weep in each other's arms. But it would achieve nothing. 'Geshtinanna, I can't act against Nergal. He is the King. He is the might of Uruk. The Queen of Heaven always desires a strong consort, a warrior, who will love her well and fill her to overflowing and guard his people. It's not my job to choose the King. It's written by the gods who lives and who dies. It's written who rises and who falls.'

Geshtinanna clasps her hands together. Her face is flawless under her heavy make-up but her hands are beginning to look old. 'Then be careful the gods haven't written about you on the Tablets of Fate, Ishara. Nergal wishes to offer me in marriage to the king of Nippur.'

I frown. 'What? But you're the wife of a god.'

'Not for much longer. Priestesses can fall too.'

'He can't do that!'

'He feels someone younger and more comely would please my Lord Enki more.'

This is the moment that my women come back into the chamber, apologetic but determined. 'Great Lady?'

Geshtinanna bows. 'Forgive me for wasting your time, Ishara.'

I'm trembling with suppressed anger as they complete my toilette, painting my eyelids green and braiding my hair into place before arranging upon me the jewellery of Inanna – the delicate crown of golden leaves, the heavy earrings that brush my neck, the agate necklace, the belt of precious stones, the spiral bracelets and anklets. The other priestesses notice my discomfiture but mistake it for the impatience of a goddess eager for her bridegroom; I see the glances and little smiles they exchange.

Then all of a sudden there is no more time for combing and painting because the blowing of rams' horns signifies that the moon has risen. I make my way to the front door of the temple, hemmed by all the temple priestesses as I walk. Next to the door is the pen of the sacred bull. Hearing us pass he snorts and bellows, clashing his horns against the wooden bars that confine him. I know how he feels; my heart howls for release too. Then the doors swing wide and I step out alone on to the platform before the temple courtyard and raise my arms.

The roar of the crowd strikes like a stormfront. They are there, waiting for me; all of Uruk. They are waiting for their goddess to bless them. And with that roar, that endless deafening cry of delight and need, she comes to me. The gaze of the multitude draws her down from heaven and incarnates her in my flesh. I feel her stir between my thighs, and in the pit of my belly and in the orbs of my breasts. I am lifted up on a wave of worship and I feel my skin come alive, tingling. Pulling down the neck of my nuptial gown I reveal my breasts, cupping them as I draw them from out of the fabric, holding them for everyone to see. My red-stained nipples look very dark under the torchlight and are stiffly erect. The crowd screams its appreciation.

There is a throne waiting for me on a bier, and as I step on to the platform male priests take up the poles and lift me to shoulder-height. But I don't sit down; I brace my legs instead and balance as they walk me down the steps into the courtyard. We must make one circuit of the crowd and I must be seen by all. I stand with thighs parted and back arched to show off my breasts, my hands hefting those golden treasures, my rear in that clinging dress as round as the full moon overhead. I accept the adulation proudly, as the due of the goddess Inanna. People hold up their hands to me and weep and shriek with joy, trying to catch my eye, only held back to the edge of the courtyard by warriors of the Royal Guard. All around my bier the sacred harlots of the temple clash tambours and shake sistrums and chant my sacred names. Morning and Evening Star; Queen of Heaven; Life-giving Goddess of Goddesses; Whore of the Gods.

Once around the courtyard and then we reach the temple façade again. This time we ascend the outer stairs to the bridal platform over the door. Even on the ascent I make sure I stand triumphantly, and my bearers are well trained. Only when we get to the sacred bed of the Great Marriage do I step lightly down. The mattress beneath the sheepskins is of fresh rushes soaked in cedar oil and the smell is pungent; it is a windless, sticky night.

Last time I underwent this rite it was with Tamuz. For a moment the memory threatens to swamp me, but I push it back. For Inanna there is no past or present, and every one of her kings is a husband beloved above all others. The waves of adulation beat upon my body like caresses, stoking the heat in my flesh. I am Inanna: I am all love and all sex and all joy; the giver of life, the source of plenty, the flame in the heart of all that lives. I dance for them, undulating my hips and caressing my body. They love me and I love them. I wish I could have every man in that crowd, and every woman too. I want to feel a thousand cocks in me, I want to plunder a thousand cunts – the source of life and pleasure, they are mine and I want to rejoice in every one of them. I can feel the slippery melt of my excitement sliding on my thighs.

All along the edge of the crowd my priestesses dance too, writhing against and teasing anyone within reach.

Then trumpets sound – brazen ones, martial and commanding. The crowd falls silent. Into the empty space reserved in the centre of the courtyard steps King Lugulbanda, resplendent in his embroidered robe. Down the length of a hall roofed with stars we stare at each other, and all eyes are on us.

'The bed is ready,' I say, and the wall behind me takes my voice and throws it out across the crowd so that everyone can hear. 'The bed is waiting. My sex, the Boat of Heaven, is full of eagerness like the young moon.'

They roar. Nergal steps forwards. He has relatively few words in this ceremony; others take the burden of ritual incantation for him and leave him to concentrate on the physical. My eldest priestess steps out to his side. She looks even frailer than normal beside him, but her voice is clear.

'My Queen, behold the choice of your heart: the King, the beloved bridegroom.' She leads him forwards. 'May he pass long days in the sweetness of your holy loins! Give him a glorious reign! Grant him a royal throne, firm in its foundations! Grant him the sceptre of righteous judgement! Grant him an enduring crown!'

So it goes on as they approach: she asking for blessings upon the city and the people, the fields and the land about: he saying nothing. And I watch him, torn. The goddess in me sees his comeliness: he is a big man, even taller than Tamuz was, and he is muscled as a king should be in his prime, fit for hunting and for battle and for love. If his face is naturally stern then it is a sign that he has a king's wisdom. If he walks with an arrogant set to his shoulders then it is a sign that he has a king's greatness. The goddess Inanna wants him. She roils in my belly, hot and wet. She is breathless with desire for his long limbs and his heavy hands, for the bronze pillars of his legs and the proud jut of his prick.

If only I could forget how Tamuz died.

As Nergal mounts the flight of stairs to our bed, the musicians strike up one last wild fanfare, shaking and drumming until the sweat flies from them. They fall exhausted and silent as he steps up on to the bed itself, and all the city holds its breath.

'My untilled land lies fallow. Who will plough my high field? Who will plough my wet ground?' My voice is clear and confident, my words a challenge as well as an invitation. This is the bridegroom's moment to speak.

Nergal says nothing. A fire burns in his black eyes and I think that fire would consume me if it could. I reach out and draw the cloak from his shoulders to reveal the body beneath. He's naked of course, and my heart jumps in my breast to see that even so he is unimpeachably regal in form and proportion. His cock, heavy though not yet fully erect, jerks a little. Turning, I rub myself against him, my shoulders to his chest and my buttocks to his crotch. I find it easier if I don't have to meet his eyes, and there is genuine pleasure in the undulation of my spine and the writhing of my hips. I like it that the people of Uruk can see the best of me like this.

Lazily, Nergal reaches round and cups one breast. My nipple responds to his touch instantly, like a slave to its master. The rouge will rub off on his fingers. His pinch would be cruel in other circumstances but right now it only inflames me and I press my rounded rump into him with a cry. With his other hand Nergal pulls off my gown, baring me before the courtyard. I hear a sigh go up. His fingers find the cleft between my legs and enter just far enough to sample my wetness. Then suddenly he lets me go, spinning me back round to face him. There's a half-smile on his lips. Hands on my shoulders, he pushes me to my knees. His prick kicks restlessly as he urges it to my lips, but it's no more impatient than I am. I long for that thick sceptre. I take him in my mouth and lave the royal crown with my tongue, causing his hips to surge. He tastes salty. He's hot and hard already, his erection thickening with each beat of his pulse. I consume him, taking his length right down my throat until my nose is buried in his oiled hair. It's no mean feat and I hear the collective inhalation of the multitude watching. For a moment he holds me there, unbreathing, his hands tight in my hair. Then I pull away from him, slow and sweet. His cock sways, glistening with my saliva. His face is pulled into a grin that is almost a grimace.

'Who will plough my wet ground?' I gasp, part of me wondering if he has forgotten the words, while the goddess simply mews with desire.

'Not I,' he says clearly, and steps off the bed.

There is deathly silence across the square.

For a moment I do not understand what I've heard. 'What?' I hiss through my teeth. Mentally I chase the words of the ritual through my head as if I might say them for him. It's only the sight of him retrieving his robe and furling it about him, hiding that kingly body, that brings it home to me what he has done. 'What?' I squeal, and I don't sound very divine. 'What are you doing? This is the Great Marriage!'

His erection is clearly giving him trouble but he masters himself enough to announce, 'There'll be no marriage between us, Lady.'

'I am Inanna! I am the Prosperity of the Palace!' My voice is harsh.

'Then, Great Lady,' he says with a frigid bow, 'I shall be pleased to deliver to your temple gifts of gold and wool and copper, that in your divine generosity you may continue to inspire and enrich the city of Uruk. But I will not wed you.' His eyes are like stone. 'I have no wish to wed you. What good would it do me, after all?'

'How can you say that!'

He grins. Every word he speaks is enunciated clearly, intended for our audience. 'Consider your history, Lady, and how your lovers fare. Your favour is short-lived, and little good does your love bring anyone. You've loved the lion, so say the poets, and pits are dug for the lion without number; my bed is spread with lion-skins. You've loved the stallion, and destined him for the bit and the whip and the bridle. You've loved the eagle and broken his wings. You loved Tamuz, the shepherd of his people.' He pauses to let the words sink in, and sweeps his arm in an arc. 'Where are his children that will bear his name? Where, Great Lady, is he?'

He might as well have struck me in the face.

'Your lovers, Lady, have found you worse than useless. You're like a back door that doesn't keep out the wind, a leaky water-skin that drenches the carrier, a broken sandal that trips up the wearer. If I wed you, wouldn't I be served in the same fashion?' He laughs. 'I'd rather stand on my own, Great Lady. I don't need your help to rule this land – and I don't need you to make me king.' He raises his fist, displaying the muscles of his arm. 'I am king by right of this.' He thumps his breast. 'And by this. Not by bedding you. Find some other man to rub your itch, Lady – and let him sleep in the wet patch left by your old lovers.'

He walks away, and as he starts to descend the stairs the silence swells to a moan of anguish and outrage and fear. I clamber to my feet. I think they expect me to curse him dead on the spot – and, believe me, if I had the words I would do.

What Nergal has done is unforgivable.

'Great Lady!' The steward of the temple lands is the first to come forwards to the bed, his eyes as round as his shaven head. 'My Lady –'

Nergal reaches the bottom of the stairs. The moaning of the priests rises until, when I finally speak, my words to the steward are inaudible.

'What?' He's forgotten all honorifics.

'Release the Bull of Heaven!' I roar. 'Now!'

Ducking his head he scuttles back into a doorway to descend the interior stair into the temple. I step to the edge of the bed, steadying myself with one hand upon the carved pillar. My chest is heaving. I watch Nergal make his way across the court-yard below, head high, glancing commandingly to the soldiers on either side. The people watching seem stunned: except for that noise of dismay, they do nothing. My priestesses are all looking up at me, waiting for some sign.

I give them one. From the main door of the temple the Bull of Heaven plunges out into the sanded arena. Dark as a storm-cloud and with horns plated in gold like the lightning, the sacred bull is tame to the hand in the summer months when he dwells with his cows in the lush fields along the curve of the great canal. But during winter he is taken from his women-folk and kept penned on his own, and his rage grows monstrous. He charges out snorting and ramping around and heads straight for the nearest target, one of the guards. People start to scream as the man is hurled into the air with a toss of that horned head, and they do not quieten when the bull turns from over-running him and goes back to stamp upon the prone figure. The great beast's bellows mask the smack of hoof upon skull, but they do not disguise the blood and when the bull wheels away looking for the next victim it leaves a dark trail in the sand.

Everywhere people are trying to climb up on to roofs and retreat down alleyways. The Royal Guard waver but hold their line – at least until the Bull of Heaven charges into it, scattering bodies and goring anything that stands up to it. I see priests and spectators go down, people falling over each other as they try to flee, the weak being kicked to the floor and trampled.

I see Nergal run into the fray. He has to, of course: a king without courage is no king at all: the king is the guardian and the champion of his people. He snatches a sword from one of his guards and, dropping his only garment, runs up and grabs the Bull of Heaven by the thick of its tail. The animal leaves off trampling the crowd and whirls, blaring. Nergal holds on grimly, hauling to slow the beast, and they pirouette into the centre of the square. The bull is not quite able to reach him with its horns but Nergal is not able to keep his feet under him long enough to do more than cling on.

If he trips, if he lets go, then he is dead. I rake my nails down my arms, shedding blood as I urge Namtar the god of fate to cast his doom.

Then another figure enters the arena. It is, I realise, Gilgamesh, Nergal's eldest son and a tall well-knit youth for his age. If he lives he'll be as big as his father one day. He doesn't attack; he runs in and snatches up a handful of grit and pebbles from the ground, hurling it at the beast and shouting, waving his arms at it. The Bull of Heaven is confused.

It stops for a moment, pausing in its tail-chasing to turn and glare at the boy, trying to decide which is the worse irritant. That pause is long enough for Nergal. He sweeps back his sword-arm and plunges the blade round and up, deep into it, into the fold between haunch and belly.

The bull roars and buckles. It tears out of Nergal's grasp and flounders away, but there is something wrong with its back leg and it staggers as it rounds on him, allowing him to keep just out of its reach. It's confused by its own weakness as much as it's enraged by the pain, and when it turns its neck and tries to nose at the wound Nergal seizes his chance. He's no coward. He steps in, grabs a horn with his offhand arm and, clinging to that huge head with all his might as the animal slews about, reverses his grip on the sword and plunges it down through the nape of its neck, severing the spine. It's a heroic blow even for a trained warrior. The bull drops to its knees, taking Nergal with it.

In the roar that follows I jump off the bed and step up to the edge of the temple wall, tears and kohl running down my cheeks. My people – all the dancing and singing girls, the priests and the courtesans – cluster at my back.

Arising from the steaming carcass, Nergal raises his arms in triumph. The crowd thunders his name, then falls slowly silent as it sinks in what they have just seen him do.

I take advantage of the hush to spit my curse. 'Woe to you, Nergal! Woe to you and all your line! For you have scorned the gods in killing the Bull of Heaven!'

Nergal looks up at me once, eyes blazing, then turns back to the bull's corpse with a roar. With hacks of his sword he finishes what he's started, severing the animal's right haunch. Taking it up in both hands, he spins around and launches the limb into the air, straight for me. He's so strong it nearly makes it, but I stand my ground even though my retinue flinches away and the bloody trophy smacks into the wall just below my feet before falling back.

'If I lay my hands on you,' Nergal shouts, 'I'll do the same to you – and truss you with your own guts!'

I have nothing to say. I turn away as my women begin the mourning song for the Bull of Heaven, their voices bleak and harsh with anguish.

The only place Geshtinanna considers that it's safe for us to talk in her temple is right within its holiest shrine, the chamber of the god Enki himself. So we kneel side by side before his statue, under the gaze of those staring lapis lazuli eyes. Beyond the statue I can just glimpse his couch where Geshtinanna sleeps every night, ready for her divine husband to join her.

Even here we speak in low whispers. Nergal has paid agents in every temple.

'This is what I am intending to do,' I tell her. 'At the dark of the moon I shall go to the royal cemetery and open the gate to Aralu.'

Geshtinanna's eyes flash. 'And you said you would not act against the King!'

'No. I will not.'

'Then . . .'

'I will descend into the Land of the Dead. And I will bring back Tamuz, the true King.'

For a moment only her breathing is audible in that windowless, stifling room. 'That isn't possible.'

'Inanna once descended to the Great Below; we know the story.'

'Ishara . . .' Her face is lined with doubt. 'Inanna is a goddess, not a mortal woman.'

'Inanna will go with me. Where she goes, I may go.'

'And she was killed when she tried to conquer her sister! Only my Lord Enki's intervention restored her.'

'That's why I need your help, Geshtinanna. I need you to pray for me. I've already sent word to the other temples of Inanna in Ur, in Kish, in Lagash. I need you to watch for the signs of Inanna's death, so that you may petition your husband on her behalf. His cunning is my last defence if all else fails.'

She stares. 'I've never heard of anyone trying this.'

'Nor I. But I will not let Nergal mock the gods as he has done. He must be stopped.'

She nods. 'Then I'll aid you in any way that I can.' But she doesn't sound confident.

'You know the signs to look for?'

'Of course.' She folds her hands and quotes:

'Since Inanna has gone down to the Land of No Return,
The bull refuses to cover the cow, the ass no longer
*   impregnates the jenny,*
In the street the man no longer approaches the maiden,
The man lies down in his own chamber,
The woman turns her shoulder and lies alone.'

'Good.' I feel dizzy. Speaking my plan out loud has made it seem both more real and more impossible.

'You really believe you can do this?'

'I believe it.'

She takes my hands in hers and looks me in the eye. 'Then whatever you need of me, I will do it. If it will bring Tamuz back to life, I will do anything you ask.'

At sunset at the next dark of the moon, I ride out in my chariot through the great gate in Uruk's walls. I'm wearing the regalia and ornaments of the goddess, though I take with me a minimum guard and only two handmaidens. The guards on the gate step out to bar my way, but they look uncomfortable and do not touch the bridles of my white onagers. All Uruk knows of my quarrel with the King, but he has not yet issued any orders that I am to be deprived of my freedom.

'We only need to know where you are going, Queen of Heaven,' says the guard apologetically. Married or unmarried, he knows it is unwise to antagonise the goddess of desire.

'You may report that I am going to the tombs,' I say, hoisting two black cockerels by their trussed legs, 'to make sacrifices for the shades of King Tamuz and the Bull of Heaven.'

They insist on sending an honour-guard with me. I don't care. I leave those to wait and bicker with the temple guards outside the tomb. I station my women on watch at the curtain wall of Tamuz's shrine, and I enter alone.

It has sadly changed since I was last here for the funeral. Then there were sheaves of wheat and jars of wine, food and garlands piled high for a magnificent feast. Now everything has fallen to decay. Bones are the only solid objects jutting from the crumbled mould lining the platters of wood and soapstone and woven reeds. The sheaves and the joints of meat have been scattered and stripped and gnawed by scavenging animals. The great jars of drink have had holes knocked in them – by the cemetery guards, I suspect – and the contents are gone. There's nothing but a faint musty smell left; that and the statue of Tamuz, the size of a child and with the forlorn look of all funerary statues, standing over the decay and the neglect. It's a poor memorial for such a great king and I feel anger move in my guts.

Kneeling on the floor, I make a prayer to the man buried far below me, but my words die to bitter silence. He lies down there upon a golden bed, at his side Ninsu his Queen, who volunteered to follow him into the afterlife. And in the second chamber rest my loyal Emmer and four other scribes, and those of the royal concubines whom Nergal did not wish to retain, and the charioteers and the guards and the musicians – who had not volunteered, but had laid themselves down obediently and gone into Aralu by the same route as their master: hemlock poisoning. My resolve hardens to a keener edge.

Swiftly I make my preparations. Shedding my woollen over-mantle, I reveal to the watching sky a dress of linen so fine that it is translucent. I wear the Crown of Inanna and all her jewellery. I speak with her voice as I scribe the circles and the sigils on the dirt floor in salt and in my own blood. I speak the words of power. I invoke the gods. I slay the birds one after another and offer them to Neti the gatekeeper. The sound of murmured conversation beyond the mud walls is replaced by a thick unnatural silence and when I chant and call out I know my voice will not be heard outside. The light from the lone lamp I've brought grows steadier and more intense but the shadows darken too in the corners of the room. Beyond the altar the outline of a doorway begins to be discernible on the mudbrick wall. Every tomb has this second door, though it cannot be seen by humble eyes: one door leading out, one door leading in – and down.

Dust shivers down from the lintel of the door as the crack becomes wider. It's truly visible and solid now: a single slab of cedar as tall as I, within a wooden frame. The wood looks old, its grain dulled by the years. Falling silent, I take a moment to catch my breath.

'Open,' I say.

The door does not move.

I cross to it and lay my hands upon the smooth surface. I can feel a faint breeze from the crack, but there is no handle or bar of any kind on this side.

'O, gatekeeper, open up,' I call. 'Open the gate so I may enter!'

There is no answer, and suddenly I feel a great rage swell in my breast. To have come this far and no further is unbearable. My frustration heaves within me like the fire that moves my sex during rituals. 'Open for me, Inanna!' I shout. 'Queen of Heaven and Earth!' I slam my fist against the timber and it shakes; the ground beneath me and the shrine about me tremble. Words roar from my throat: 'If you don't open the gate, I will break the door! I will shatter the bolt, I will smash the doorpost and I will raise up the Dead to eat the Living! The Dead will outnumber the Living!' Then I step back, and the door swings slowly open.

Neti the gatekeeper is dressed as a priest in a plain white kilt and with shaven head. He is very pale, paler than any man I have seen. His skin is as white as the linen he wears and smooth, like something polished by sand. He bows politely to me.

'Lady Inanna, First Daughter of the Moon.' His voice is as smooth as his skin. 'Why are you here, on the road from which no traveller returns?'

I take a deep breath, momentarily speechless. My rage has vanished like a campfire flame on the night air. I have to fight my fear in order to tell him, 'I have come to see your Mistress, my sister, Ereshkigal.'

His eyes are white too, like a blind man's, but they are far from blank. A silky malice gleams there. 'You know the rules of the Underworld, Lady Inanna. If you wish to enter this gate while still living, you must surrender your crown.'

Oh, I know the rules. I know this story. I know what it takes for Inanna to descend through all seven Gates to the House of Dust. And I know what fate awaits her there; I have heard the story since I was a tiny child. But I have no choice. This is the only way. Still, I hesitate.

'The laws of the Underworld are perfect, Inanna. Do not question them.'

'As my sister commands,' I say hoarsely. Then I step forwards and bow my head. The crown is the symbol of all my earthly sovereignty; that I am Queen in Uruk and that Inanna is Queen of the Earth. I tell myself that under Nergal's reign my queenly status is empty, a dry husk of my former authority. I tell myself that it is necessary for me to approach my sister in humility, not power, if I am to persuade her to have mercy on Tamuz.

'Kneel,' he tells me.

So I close my eyes and kneel before him, and feel his dry smooth hands upon my head. It is no easy matter to remove the Crown of Inanna: it's not a circlet but a complex net of gold wires and flowers and leaves that coils in and out of my dressed hair. They say there are a thousand petals on this crown, and though I think the tale is an exaggeration I have never counted them. Neti has to unwind the soft gold tendrils from about my braids. He uncoils my hair too, pulling it free. His hands are not rough, but I shiver at his touch. My mouth is dry.

'You have beautiful hair,' he observes. 'Black as the night between the stars.' He drapes it over his hand, caressing the tresses. In itself the sensation is not unpleasant – as the glide of snakeskin on the skin is not unpleasant until the serpent strikes. I hold my breath and wait for him to finish. When he does the crown flares up in his hand like sunlight and vanishes. I gather myself to rise.

'The Lady Inanna will submit herself,' he says softly, his hands descending on my shoulders. 'The Lady Inanna will be humbled before the Great Below.'

I understand, though my heart catches in my breast. He does not wait for my acquiescence, however. Smiling, he draws aside the folds of his kilt even as he reaches for my hair with his other hand. My face is at the level of his groin; I see clearly that he is perfectly shaved, even his soft and rather pendulous stones. And he is already erect, as white and hard as caked salt. The effect is strange but not displeasing to the eye and I am stung to feel Inanna's interest quicken within me. He pulls my face to his thigh and I do not resist. But he doesn't want my mouth. Not even my co-operation is required; he wraps my thick dark tresses about his jutting member and caresses himself with the hair.

'Let me fill your dark night full of stars,' he mocks.

This is an exercise in humiliation, I realise. I have to kneel before him and listen to the small wet noises of his hand upon his member, to the rising tempo of his breath and the gasps he makes as he pumps himself. He works with fervid concentration. My breasts brush his thighs but I cannot see anything except his hip and his flat belly. He tugs my hair, gathering handfuls to rub over his cock, bringing tears to my eyes. I only know he is done when he grunts and shudders against me.

When it is over he wipes his phallus clean on my scalp. He lets me stand, at last. 'Follow,' he orders, and leads me through the First Gate.

Beyond that portal is an absolute darkness through which stairs descend, a narrowing ribbon of rock flanked to either side by a gulf. Within a few steps the way is no wider than my own shoulders. I balk at the path presented, trying to peer into the blackness. The air is cool but dry. There is no sound except those we make ourselves, no draught, no scent except the musk of my befouled hair. The only illumination comes from Neti himself, who gives off a pallid gleam like marsh-light. There is nothing else but the void. As he slips past me and starts down I realise that I must keep up with him or be marooned in the darkness, unable to take a single step and forced to crawl on hands and knees. I follow in his wake down the irregularly hewn steps, sick with vertigo. It's impossible to tell if our path is held up by solid rock or by pillars or by nothing at all; it seems to curve gently to the left but no glimpse can be caught of anything but the worn steps directly beneath our feet. I follow until I lose count of their number, until my thighs ache from the descent and my hips feel jarred from their sockets. He does not flag, and as he pulls further ahead it becomes harder for me to see where I am walking. Suddenly I misstep: my foot slides on the edge of the path and I pitch forwards with a cry.

Neti is there, faster than thought; he catches me by my tangled hair as my knee bangs off the stone, and wrenches me back on to the path. My fingers claw at the rock.

'You must stay on the path,' he says with satisfaction. 'The dead fall – but they cannot take harm from the drop.'

'Wait. Let me rest,' I beg.

'We are here.' He sweeps me with a triumphant smile. 'Behold the Second Gate.'

Before and below us is a patch of red light, hanging in the darkness. I try to nod, but he still has a hold of my hair. He pulls me to my feet by it and leads me the rest of the way bent double in his wake, gasping, his fingers knotted in my locks. There is no chance of my falling now. He leads me on to an island of stone that floats in the void. It is pillared with painted columns and furnished with mounded cushions. The gate in the far wall is of red bronze with two leaves, barred on this side. I realise for the first time that the gates are not there to keep intruders out of the Underworld; they are there to bar the way from below. There is a figure between us and that door and my sickened heart clenches.

'This is the Great Lady Inanna, Queen of Heaven,' says Neti, pushing me forwards on to my knees upon a rich rug. I am grateful just to be still for a moment.

'She smells like a gutter slut,' observes the Keeper of the Second Gate, who gives light to this place. He is taller than

Nergal and built like a warrior. His skin is scarlet and flames burn about his head where hair should be.

Neti laughs. 'She seeks to pass the Second Gate while still living.'

'Then she must surrender her earrings.' He closes until he is standing right before me, his feet nearly touching my splayed knees. I look up mutely, in dismay. His eyes are crimson.

'Must I?' When we write, the word for *ear* is the same as that for *mind*.

'The laws of the Underworld are perfect, Inanna. Do not question them.'

'As my sister commands,' I say.

He unhooks the heavy gold clusters from my ears and they turn to water in his palms and run away over his wrists. I bow my head.

I will do this, I tell myself, for the sake of Uruk, for the sake of my vengeance; I will do whatever it takes. And Inanna is with me. I feel her move more strongly than ever in the heat in my blood, in the pulse that beats at my sex.

Thoughtfully, the Keeper of the Second Gate hooks his bare foot under my skirt. His foot nudges up against my mound and I gasp at the heat of his skin as he plays roughly with the folds below. He does not find me dry. 'So the Lady Inanna is humbled before the Great Below,' he rumbles.

'Yes,' I whisper.

'Yes,' gloats Neti. 'Do with her as you wish. As I did.'

'Do you suck cock, Queen of Heaven?'

'Yes.' I can't keep my voice calm.

'I would have you suck this, little queen.' He opens his kilt. My eyes widen involuntarily: given his body size I should expect a daunting length and girth – but this is a monster. It lolls and drools like a drunk between his thighs. The gatekeeper takes hold of me and rubs my face in his groin, forcing me mouth-to-cock, marking me with the scent of his crotch. The scarlet bludgeon kicks eagerly against my jaw. His skin is hot – not so hot as to burn but uncomfortable on my tongue. It is all I can do to stretch my mouth around his turgid glans. I tongue the slit, tasting his readiness and finding it both smoky and sharp.

'Good,' he says, surprised. 'You are well trained, for a queen.'

Rebellion kicks under my ribs and my eyes flash.

'Thank him,' instructs Neti dryly. 'He has complimented you.'

I pull my lips from his cock, leaving sticky saliva trails. 'Thank you,' I whisper.

Laughing, the gatekeeper turns his back on me. 'Stay,' he orders, and I do not move as he goes to sit upon a mound of cushions. He spreads his knees, opening his kilt so that I can see his huge ruddy erection. Lovingly he strokes it up and down, hefts his balls and preens himself. 'Now come here.'

I gather myself.

'On your knees.'

I flush. Nobody has ever treated me with such contempt. Not even Nergal has dared do that to me. He knows I am a goddess. And Inanna . . .

Inanna loves this. My vulva is soft and wet and swollen.

Hitching up my skirt, I crawl slowly over to the Keeper of the Second Gate on my hands and knees and look up from between his splayed thighs.

He pats my head and strokes my face. 'Lick my cock.'

I lick the hot throbbing column, kissing the pronounced underside ridge all the way to his juicy plum.

'Lick my balls.'

I roll his stones with my tongue, sucking them into my mouth.

He sighs and leans back in the cushions. 'Now lick my hole, Queen of Heaven.'

And I do it, pushing my face down between his spread cheeks to probe that deep hole until the root of my tongue burns and my mouth is filled with the tang of him. He likes that. He sighs and spreads himself for me, jacking his cock with one hand, pushing me deeper with the other. His scrotum has tightened to a mass of wrinkles. Then it becomes too much and he pulls me out and forces my mouth down over his cock-head so that he can stroke off with a last few jerks, filling my throat with a fiery liquor that burns me and explodes behind my eyes like a sunrise. I choke as I gulp it down. Released, I fall gasping against his thigh and he caresses me roughly.

'You liked that, didn't you? Who would have thought it? The Queen of Heaven likes to get dirty for me.' He pushes his bare foot back between my thighs and rubs it back and forth in my wetness, even hooking his toe in my cunt. I wriggle and whimper upon him. 'Like that too? You going to beg me for more?'

'Please . . .'

Without warning he pushes me flat over on my back. The thick carpet cushions my bones if not my dignity: I stare as he stands over me and plants that same foot on my face. I can smell myself on his toes. I lick the salty skin.

'Second Gate,' he says as he pushes his big toe into my mouth and lets me suck it. From somewhere he has brought a red leather collar and leash such as one would use for a hunting dog: he stoops to knot it around my throat and then he drags me to my feet. I'm sick with frustration and physically reeling – his inhuman ejaculate has made me dizzier than the strongest beer. Then he pulls me over to the bronze gate and knocks aside the bar.

The Third Gate is not so far as I fear but the path is the same, steep and narrow, and I am glad that he leads me. I'm grateful for the collar and his strength keeping me safe. Neti does not follow, and the light by which we tread is red as blood.

The place of the Third Gate shines like a dim sun in the black depths. Like the gate itself the floor is made of beaten gold, and upon a fur-draped couch in the centre lies the gate-keeper. His skin is golden and he casts a yellow light. Upon his head he wears curled horns like a ram's and all over his body are studded eyes, as black from lid to lid as those in his head. He rises to his feet and smiles when the Keeper of the Second Gate jerks me to my knees. His teeth are like bronze arrow-heads.

'This is the Lady Inanna, Queen of Heaven. She seeks to pass the Third Gate while still living.'

'Then she must know that she will give up her necklace.'

'She knows that and submits to your will.'

There seems to be no call for me to speak. I crouch at the end of my leash like a whipped bitch, mute with dread, wanting to touch myself between the legs. But, when the Keeper of the Third Gate unties my collar and lifts the broad necklace from my breastbone, I cannot help but whimper. Inanna's necklace, edged in lapis lazuli with a central band of polished many-coloured agates, is the Rainbow itself. It was lifted into the sky when Ziusudra made the first sacrifice after the Deluge, in token that the gods repented their attempt to destroy mankind and would remember their dismay forever. It is the symbol of Inanna's magic at work in the world.

He hears me with disapproval. 'The laws of the Underworld are perfect, Inanna. Do not question them.' Pulling apart his hands, he explodes the necklace into its constituent beads and they bounce across the smooth floor until they drop over the edge into darkness. I take a deep breath.

'As my sister commands.'

The many eyes on his body blink, like black stars flickering in a golden sky.

'She will do as you wish also,' observes the crimson gate-keeper. 'We've made good use of her already.'

'So I see.' He touches my swollen mouth. 'Was she difficult?'

'Surprisingly eager to please. Enjoy yourself.' The red light fades as my last tormentor leaves, and I am left alone with this one.

'Stand,' he orders, and when I do so he walks around me, studying me with dozens of fathomless eyes. My breast feels vulnerable without its heavy necklace and I cross my hands over it. 'You have no idea,' he murmurs from behind me, 'how good it is for those of us imprisoned in this place since the Sweet Water was separated from the Salt to see you in our midst. Such beauty, shining in the darkness. The celestial brought low. The Queen of Heaven humbling herself before the powers of dust.' He slides my robe off my shoulders, then reaches round to prise my hands apart and scoop my breasts out from under the taut linen. He cups them one in each hand, soft orbs quivering with my swift breath. 'We could have been gods like you.'

'You should not have fought us,' I whisper, but my eyes are closed and my attention is all on the way he is playing with my breasts. My nipples mimic the beads of my lost necklace for hardness. He rolls each between thumb and forefinger.

'There is no fight left in you now, I think.' Pinching, he sends radiating shockwaves of sensation through each breast, tightening the skin and swelling the areolae. I moan under my breath. 'Does it please you to be handled thus, by a slave of your sister?'

'It – it does,' I admit, my voice wavering as he tugs upon my teats.

'Did it please you to be used by my brothers?'

Heat fills my moist sex once more. 'It did. Yes.'

'There are seven Gates to the House of Dust, Inanna. Will you pleasure each of the gatekeepers, like a street whore begging shelter on a cold night?'

Inanna is the lowest whore, I want to say; Inanna pleasures all the world without distinction of rank. But all that comes from my lips is a low and broken moan.

'Good,' he whispers. He picks me up and carries me to the couch, where he drops me upon the saffron-dyed sheepskins and straddles me. His mouth descends to my breasts and I arch to meet him. His tongue is very slippery and very muscular and it makes my nipples so stiff they ache. I do not recoil even from those terrifying teeth, though the sweat of fear and helpless lust causes my gauzy robe to cling to me.

His phallus is a painfully hard ridge trapped between us now. He pushes my breasts together and buries his face in the cleft, snuffling his eagerness. I can't reach past his thighs to my clit and I'm in an agony of frustration. I try to grind my pelvis up against him but when he realises what I'm doing he pulls away. Then he sits up.

'I'm going to fuck your lovely tits,' he tells me. He spits between my breasts and then shuffles up my torso to lay his erect cock along my breastbone and smear it in his own lubrication. His weight is not fully on my ribs but still I find the air pressed out of my lungs, and I cannot protest as he slaps my breasts together over his cock, making a sheath for his shaft. My own sex is left utterly bereft, but there's nothing I can do but watch as, grunting and grinding his hips, he fucks my cleavage with the utmost concentration, his multitudinous eyes half-closed, roaring with every thrust as he approaches his crisis. When he finally spends, his semen is molten gold and it hardens upon my skin at once, clinging fast to my breasts and throat: golden beads and splashes to replace my Rainbow Necklace.

I wait till his eyes all open fully once more. My whole body throbs with my pulsing heart. 'Please,' I whisper.

'What is that you want, Queen of the Gods?'

'Touch me. Enter me. Fuck me. I need . . .'

'Your next lover will fill you full enough.' From somewhere among the furs he brings out a golden chain, one end bifurcated and culminating in something I've never seen before: tiny golden jaws. He clips one to each of my bruised nipples and I wince, spasms running down my skin. 'Beautiful,' he says.

He leads me through the Third Gate by my breasts. The ache between my legs is now so deep the sharp pain at my teats is almost welcome as a distraction. Every step sends hot jolts from my nipples right through my body, and my breasts feel heavy, far more so than normal. Demonic eyes in his shoulder-blades watch every limping step I take as I follow him.

The Keeper of the Fourth Gate dwells upon a lapis lazuli floor before a door of smooth and smoky blue; it takes me a long time before I realise the leaves are cast of glass, since I've hardly seen glass in pieces larger than a bead before this day. He gives off an azure light. His grey-blue body ripples with silvery markings, as of scales, down as far as his hips; below that he is an immense serpent.

When my golden gatekeeper removes the tiny jaws from my nipples I gasp at the sudden stabs of pain.

The snake-man does not talk to him or to me: any words between us would be wasted. The Keeper of the Fourth Gate is without ears, though his eyes are like green gems. He simply seizes me and wrenches the girdle of semi-precious stones from about my hips, slinging it out into the void. I watch it vanish, open-mouthed. Inanna's Belt is the Zodiac by which destinies are read. It is the sign of her sovereignty in the heavens.

The gatekeeper lifts me clean off the floor, his thick coils mounding beneath us and around me, sliding between my knees to part my thighs. He holds me about the body from behind, clasping my torso in his hands, and I cannot see his face. A coil is looped under my ribs, another about my shoulders. When something blunt and muscular delves my wet slash I cannot tell if it is some erect cock previously concealed beneath the pale scales of his underside, or perhaps the tip of his tail. I do not care; I am only grateful to be touched at last and I cry out. But the relief does not last; slippery with my juices the member muscles its way between my rump cheeks and probes urgently at my more tender rear opening. I flash hot with shock and squeal as he enters me – not because that aperture is unused to invasion but because he's unhesitating and far too swift. And he's *big*. It's good that I'm used to invoking my dark star, because he pumps me with enormous vigour. He fills me all the way, his bulk both painful and comforting. It can't be his tail, as I feel him come. He keeps thrusting as he fills me with his cream, stone-cold and so slippery and so copious that it squirts out and runs down my crack. It goes some way to soothing the burning caused by his girth and his urgency. But still I find no release. My cunt feels like a wound screaming to be staunched.

When he lets me slip from his coils, I can't even stand upright. He opens the Fourth Gate and carries me through, slung over his shoulders like a bag of meal.

The place of the Fifth Gate has a stone floor and a fawn light. I am too dazed to notice more than that as the serpent-gatekeeper drops me and retires. I lie huddled, my arms over my head, my thighs wet with the serpent's seed and my own unsated concupiscence.

'Lady Inanna,' says a deep masculine voice. 'Why are you here?'

I lift my head dizzily. The Keeper of the Fifth Gate has the body of a muscular man wrapped about with copper chains, but tawny wings and the head of a desert lion. His lip is curled, revealing teeth that could rip my throat out. 'I wish to pass the Fifth Gate to the House of Dust,' I whisper.

'Then you must surrender your armlets and anklets and be humbled before the Great Below.'

'All of them?' I say, dismayed.

'The laws of the Underworld are perfect, Inanna. Do not question them.'

It's the last of my jewellery. Without my golden regalia I will be indistinguishable from any common woman. Already I've been stripped of my titles, no longer Queen on Earth or in the Heavens – yet I am still Inanna. I can feel her, stronger than ever. She drives me on, indomitable; she burns in me like the white heart of the fire. She will not be stopped until she has what she wants. 'As my sister commands,' I whisper.

He pulls off the heavy ornaments from my arms and my ankles, tipping me on to my arse to lift each leg in turn. I see for the first time that the Fifth Gate is hewn of two panels of ivory, each so large they must have come from the mouth of the dragon Tiamat herself. In this place grow trees, though their twisted branches are bare of leaves and they may have been dead for years – or since the dawn of creation. Upon the black twigs sit blacker crows, watching him as he crushes the soft metal in his hands. When he lobs the mangled twists to the floor, the birds swoop down, quarrelling, before the biggest snatch up their prizes and fly off into the blackness.

He growls, 'Now, Inanna, you must prove yourself of use to me.' His breath is hot and smells of fresh blood.

I lick my lips, bracing myself yet eager. At last, I think.

He gestures at a wooden bucket. 'Clean my floor.'

My eyes flash.

'What?' he snarls contemptuously. 'You think I should stoop to rooting a common slut like you? You've been used by every servant, like a kitchen drab; now I put you to the work that best suits you.'

Blood burns in my face. I have the pride of a goddess still. But if it must be done then it will be done; I hitch up my skirt again and crawl over to the bucket. There's a rag inside and some water. I see that the stone floor is all splotched with white droppings from the crows, and after wringing out the cloth I begin to scrub. I'm strikingly bad at it. I've never done such labour before and I'm quickly sweating and panting. I can't keep the slops of increasingly filthy water off my dress, no matter how often I try to tie it up out of the way. And there's no strength left in my arms and legs, though they should be lighter without their burden of gold. My wrists tremble with the strain.

'You need to finish before you pass through the Gate,' the gatekeeper points out, from where he's watching me on my hands and knees, with his arms folded across his chest.

A crow lets fall a white splash on the stone I've just scrubbed clean and I groan involuntarily.

'Hurry up!'

'I can't,' I complain, but he leaps forwards and grabs me by the back of the neck.

'What?'

'I'll try,' I amend hurriedly, but that's not enough.

'How do you address me, slut?'

'Gatekeeper,' I groan through clenched teeth; his grip is harsh.

'Master!'

'No –'

He grabs the stinking rag out of my hand and whips it down over the curve of my behind. I shriek at the sting and try to tear from his grasp. He just knots his fingers in my hair and slaps me again. The crack of the wet cloth on my soft skin is like a thunderbolt, and it sets where it strikes aflame. I scream and try to circle my rump out of his reach but that's impossible; he is the centre of my circle. I fall to the floor and he whips my thighs; I flatten myself as if I could melt into the stone and twist to present a different target; nothing works. He whips my buttocks through my dress and then pulls my skirt right up to bare my globes and whips them again. My arse is on fire. I spread my thighs without thinking and he lands a blow accurately on the split of my sex: I feel like my body is exploding. Everything is swollen, everything is burning. The tears running down my face are like flaming oil. I've lost track of what I'm doing, lost awareness of my body except for that white-hot streak of fire upon which I dance.

'Master! Master!' I scream.

He stops instantly. Then he flicks one more deliberate sting between my legs. My shaking thighs are spread wide, my engorged sex upthrust for his blessing to fall upon. I cry out.

'What did you say?'

'Master,' I sob. My clit is trembling on the verge of spasm. 'Hit me again, Master – please. Please!'

'You are ready at last,' he says with satisfaction.

He makes me crawl the long dark path to the Sixth Gate on hands and knees, walking behind me so that every so often he might encourage me with another flick of that rag. My strength is nearly exhausted and I rely on the pain to keep me going; luckily it isn't too far. There's no blooming of a new light; only the sudden widening of the floor under my hands lets me know we have arrived.

We are in darkness. The dun light emanating from my lion-headed drover seems to be swallowed up by the blackness.

'This is Inanna. She has humbled herself before the Great Below and begs permission to pass the Sixth Gate while yet living. Take from her what you wish.'

Then I see them, because when they move they generate a flickering light like the dance of distant lightning. There are four of them, scorpion-men, bigger than oxen. Their rear parts are the bodies of scorpions and from the front grow the bodies of men. All parts are covered in black chitinous plates, and when those plates rub together the light flickers into being, illuminating their staring faces. Venom-laden tails arc high over my head.

There are no words here. They take me from him and rip from me my torn and filthy dress. They reduce me to a naked body, and then they pass me between them like a doll. I surrender to them gratefully. They have male parts between their front pairs of arachnid legs, and at last – at long last – I am given the satisfaction that Inanna demands. In the clattering, hissing darkness, illumined by staccato flashes, I am filled in every orifice, over and over again, until I am replete and slippery and barely conscious.

They carry me then, quite gently, through the obsidian Sixth Gate.

The place of the Seventh Gate is the first one that is walled. It is lit with a grey light, revealing a round pool of dark water and beyond that a door faced with lead. The gatekeeper here is twice the size of a mortal man and dressed like a king, but he has four feathered wings and the head of a hawk. He stands knee-deep in the centre of the pool, his yellow eyes perfectly round and pitiless.

'This,' whispers the scorpion-man as he lays me down upon the lip of the pool, 'is her.' It's the first time I've heard one of them talk.

I'm parched, and grateful when the gatekeeper eases me into the water. I wonder briefly what it is he has left to take from me – and then he plucks a handful of feathers from his own wing, dunks me beneath the surface and begins to scrub me. He is very thorough. There are moments when I am sure I am going to drown on the very threshold of the House of Dust. I'm too exhausted to struggle, almost too exhausted to care. He scrubs every inch of my skin. He scrubs my hair. He scrubs the inside of my mouth and my cunt and my arse. Then he drops me in the pool and wades out.

I kneel in the water until I regain my balance, then rise to my feet. I'm not thirsty any more – or tired, or aching. I feel almost empty of sensation. The water is curiously heavy, reluctant to ripple even as I wade across it. The black surface reflects better than that of a mirror, and with one glance down I am snared by my own reflection. I stare in horror.

In all my life I've never seen my own face without the temple make-up upon it. My face, even to me, was that of the goddess: dark-eyed, dewy-lipped, smooth and lovely. Without the paint, I have the face of . . . well, I could be anyone. A merchant's wife. A domestic servant. I'm a little paler than average perhaps, through working indoors. My wet hair hangs in black strings. My eyes look small and lack drama without kohl. My lips are less full. Two lines crease my neck and tiny bird-prints bloom at the corners of my eyes. There is no seduction, no fire, no delight in this face. Instead there are freckles across the bridge of my nose.

I didn't know I had freckles.

I close my eyes briefly, searching within. She has gone. I understand what the last gatekeeper has taken from me and it fills me with cold thick despair. I am not a goddess. I am not the centre of all desire, the heart of all love. I am not Inanna any more: I am only Ishara.

Throwing back the bar, the gatekeeper opens the Seventh and last Gate, then turns and looks at me.

'I can't go before her like this,' I tell him. Even my voice sounds thinner.

That hooked beak opens to speak: 'The laws of the Underworld are perfect. Do not question them.'

He has taken from me even her name.

I cannot believe there is any purpose in my going on, but I can't stay here in this pool either. Bowing my head, I climb from the pool and pass through the door. Beyond is a short ramp down on to a grey plain. Slowly I descend, until I sink over my toes into the dust that covers everything, and the great lead doors close behind me.

There is light here, of a sort. I am not sure if it emanates from the dust or from myself, but though there is nothing but darkness above my head I can see the ground a little way about me. It is a circle of nothingness, almost completely flat. The bottom of this cavern is not defined by walls or pillars; if there are any limits they lie beyond my sight. I set off across the plain, keeping the Seventh Gate directly at my back as far as I can. My footfall is all but inaudible, but at least I leave my prints in the dust. There are no other marks upon the floor. It is absolutely still and absolutely silent. I walk for what feels like an hour before I come across my first landmark.

It seems at first like a bird, crouched in the dust – it has feathered wings at least. But as I draw closer I see that its head is human, that of a middle-aged man. He squats with his eyes squeezed closed, his mouth set in a line. There is a thick patina of dust upon him too, greying his hair. I can make out nothing of his body beneath the feathered cloak he wears.

I circle him warily but he makes no move and I don't dare hail him. How would I, Ishara, defend myself against the hungry souls of the Dead? For I have no longer any magic or power or authority; I have given these things up and come into the Underworld alone and more naked than the Dead themselves.

As I move on the bird-people grow more common; first singly, then in scatterings, then crowds that hunch ever more densely together. There are men and women, children and ancients. They do not move except to shuffle a little and settle, and they do not speak; only by their bowed human heads are they distinguished one from another. Some have elaborately dressed coiffures – the sign of the wealthy – some more simple peasant hairstyles, some are shaven like priests. Horror and pity grow upon me as I realise that none of the elaborate arrangements we make for feeding and equipping our beloved Dead has availed them at all. Here in the House of Dust dwell lord and priest, sorcerer and prophet, the very ones whom the gods anointed and blessed in lives long past: without light, without water, clothed like birds with wings for garments, dust their nourishment and clay their food.

What is my hurt pride compared to this? What is my vengeance? I want to tear the eyes from my head.

The path I am upon cuts a pale line through the ranks of souls and the ground to either side sinks away. Eventually I am pacing down a raised walkway between two great pits, and the floors of those pits are crammed shoulder-to-shoulder with the Dead. There finally before me is light, a pale-green light streaming from burning flambeaux. There's a platform and stairs and a raised throne high above – and on the throne is a woman. I stand at the bottom of the steps and gaze up at her. She is crowned and robed and her face is very beautiful, but black tears spilling from her eyes have stained rivulets down her cheeks. She is Ereshkigal, Queen of the Underworld. Her head is bowed, her face still, but even as I climb the tears slip out and drip upon her knees like pitch. Her skirt is stained black; she has been weeping down all the dreary centuries since creation.

She opens her eyes and looks upon me. 'Sister,' she says, her voice cold as water in a dark well.

I wonder why she calls me that when it's so clear that the one standing before her is not the goddess Inanna but a naked, drab and helpless mortal, emptied of all that might be of value. I can hardly look at her, so beautiful is her face.

'Why are you here, Sister?'

I bite my lip. I know this story. I know why Inanna comes to the Underworld: to seize power from her sister, to be Queen of Death as well as Life. This is the moment I should challenge her, if I were Inanna. This is the moment at which I learn the lesson Inanna did.

Without a word I sink to my knees. I crawl the last couple of steps with my hands in the dust, and I lay my head upon Ereshkigal's sandalled feet. Her skin is cold.

'What do you require of me, Sister?' she demands.

'I require . . . nothing,' I whisper. 'Nothing, my Queen.'

I hear the intake of her breath.

'Then why are you here?'

I search all the answers in my heart for the one that is still true. 'I come to grieve.'

For a long time neither of us moves, and it seems to me that in my surrender I have at last found peace. The loss of Tamuz is no longer a stone on my heart. My urgency and anger have withered away. I no longer expect or desire or hope for anything, and with the giving up I realise how heavy a burden it has been to carry.

A black tear falls on the back of my hand. 'Why do you weep?' I wonder.

'Who else can weep down here?' Ereshkigal asks bitterly, and as I look up into her face she wipes at her own cheeks and indicates her subjects. 'They cannot, and if they could it would be dust they wept. All the forgotten and the lost, the dwellers in shadow . . . Who will mourn for them? You, Sister? You who live among the stars? You who feel the warmth of the sun on your skin, the touch of grass under your feet; you who drink wine and lie with the comely lovers of your youth, who sing and laugh – will you weep for those who live forever in darkness and silence, eternally alone?' She puts her hand suddenly over her twisting mouth, black eyes dancing with pain.

Pity and understanding move in my heart, but I have no answers here – no answer except that of Inanna, which is to reach up and put my arms about her.

'You don't know what it is to be alone, Sister!' Ereshkigal cries, pushing off one of my hands.

'No,' I admit, kissing her cold cheeks and her soft lips. 'I don't know how to live without love.'

This time she doesn't fight and I fold her to me, holding her close. I may not be Inanna but I do understand what it is to need love. I run my hands up and down her back as she weeps and spits into my neck, tightening my arms to contain her shuddering sobs.

'You have everything you ever wanted!' she groans.

'I've lost everything.'

'But you had it! At least you had it once!' She pushes her hand angrily into the crease of my sex and I lift her face and kiss her softly, trying to gentle her. Her fingers are cold in my cleft. 'I never had it at all!'

'Shush. Let me see.'

The folds of her robe part easily under my caresses. Her skin is soft and sensitive and she gasps at the brush of my fingertips. She lets me bare her thighs and breasts.

It's strange, but though her face is perfect her body is exactly as mine, even to the mole on her left hip. Her nipple responds to my taking hold of it exactly as mine would, and she whimpers and arches her back. I kiss her shoulder and her breast, drawing the engorged flesh of her nipple through my teeth and rolling it with the tip of my tongue. Then I cup her and concentrate on tantalising the inner slopes of her twin orbs with tender bites and kisses, each wet mouthful an audible act of worship. She scuffs her feet and wriggles clumsily; she hasn't the grace I've acquired through experience. I have to take charge, laying her back upon her cushioned throne. She strokes at my unkempt hair and pulls me hard against her – impatient, or perhaps frightened that I'll stop. I slip one hand down over her soft mound and between her thighs. Her sex-lips are soft, like the cushiony petals of certain heavy flowers. And, if she is cold to the touch outside, that does not hold true for the furrow within. She is hot there and slippery-eager. She moans into my mouth, eyes widening. I spread her with my fingers and circle her clit with a thumb slicked in her own juices. Her sex sucks at my hand like a second mouth, and as I slip my fingertips in and out she pulses and grips at me. She'd eat my whole hand if she could. I've never met anyone so hungry. She heaves under me, her pale flesh craving sensation. I stoop to mouth at her breast again, harder now. She strives to get her thighs apart, pushing down on my fingers. Her breath is coming fast and her eyes are half-closed.

She wants . . .

She needs . . .

She is going to . . .

There. There she is. She turns from solid matter, every muscle straining, to rippling fluid. She's like cream poured out in offering upon an altar, like the smooth slide of the river in flood, like honey oozing from the cut comb. She thrusts her knuckles into her mouth and bites on them, wailing; she laughs and then keens and then collapses in my arms.

When I pull my hand out there's a little blood on the highest knuckles. I wipe them on her dishevelled robe. Then I stretch out beside her, my arms around her, feeling the pulse that makes her whole body quiver, at peace in the sweet-smelling drifts of her hair.

It's a long time before she stirs and sits up. I follow her lead. Her back is plank-straight.

'What is it that you came here for, Sister?' She is composed once more, her black eyes steadier than mine, and for the moment they are dry. 'If not for my throne, then what? To steal from me some subject of mine?'

I let out a long breath. 'No. When the gods created man they gave him Death. Life they kept in their own hands.'

'But you came here because of a death.' Nothing in me is hidden from her.

'Yes.'

'A lover.'

'Yes.'

'You have so many lovers, Sister.' There is a taint of her old bitterness in her voice. 'Why come so far for one?'

I look at the back of my hands. My knuckles are heavily etched in skin no longer perfectly smooth. 'He . . . His name is Tamuz. He was King in Uruk.'

'I remember him. Would you ask me for him back?'

How can I now? That arrogance has deserted me. 'No. He died very suddenly, and I didn't have time to say . . . my fare-wells to him. If it pleased you to be merciful, I might hope to see him one last time.'

'And that's all?' There are knife-edges in her words.

I close my eyes. 'Yes.'

Her hand brushes my knee. 'Then stand up, Sister. If you

can find him, then you may speak to him. I let you do this because ...' She thrusts out her lower lip, eyes glittering. 'Because you mourned with me.'

I look at her with a gratitude that I dare not express, but when I stand to look out across the multitude the sheer number of the Dead makes me quail. There are hundreds of hundreds of souls, and all look alike. 'Will he hear me?' I murmur, half to myself.

Ereshkigal puts her hand upon my shoulder. 'He might. If he remembers your voice.'

I raise my voice and call his name. The word falls into the dust like everything else, without an echo. Beside me Ereshkigal smiles.

'They are no longer as the Living, Sister. They are echoes without a voice. They are shadows without a form to cast them. They are memories given shape by dust.'

Filling my lungs with the dead air, I speak again. I use the words of the Great Marriage, but down here Inanna's voice doesn't speak through me; it is only Ishara's voice, husky and a little uncertain: 'My untilled land lies fallow. Who will plough my high field? Who will plough my wet ground?'

And from the shadows an answer comes, a man's voice speaking the ritual response: 'Great Lady, the King will plough your high field. I, Tamuz the King, will plough your wet ground.'

My heart clenches painfully in my breast. One of the crouched multitude is rising to his feet, lifting his head, moving towards the throne. I take a step to meet him.

'Remember, Sister,' says Ereshkigal, 'he is not a living man.' She releases me.

There are steps out of the pit and Tamuz ascends to meet me on the walkway. I bite my lip as he draws near enough for me to recognise his face. It is Tamuz as he was before he died;

every line drawn in perfection – the strong shoulders, the hard thighs, the fall of his hair about his neck, the arch of his nose, the curve of lips a little fuller than a man's ought to be. But he's the colour of dust; his feathered cloak, his skin, his hair, even his eyes – which don't meet mine but stare blankly at the air over my head. He cannot see me.

'Tamuz,' I whisper.

He does not respond. He is a shape formed from dust, nothing more. But that shape is so familiar, so yearned for, that I feel like something in my chest is tearing in two. Gingerly I reach out and lay my hand upon his breastbone. There is no proper resistance to my palm, though there is some form there. I realise I could drive my fingers into him as easily as into a heap of flour.

'Tamuz?'

He isn't breathing. Of course he isn't. I put both hands softly on his chest and look up at his face, though he will not look down at me.

'Tamuz ... I ...' There are a lot of false starts before the lump in my throat stops choking me. 'I've something I would say. Ten years you loved me – the King loving the goddess. Nine nights each year. Ninety nights in my life. The goddess loved you, Tamuz. You were everything she wanted in her King. But I loved you too, Tamuz. Not Inanna: Ishara. I loved you. It killed a part of me every time you left. It left a hole in my gut all year round.' My voice starts to crack. 'It would make my heart blossom to see you – in the courts, at feasts, at the Royal Council. Every word we exchanged, every glance, the way you'd smile at me across a room ... You don't know how I hid what I felt. I never told you. I never told myself ... I said, Inanna loves him and rejoices in her King ... That's what I told myself: I am the priestess. I am the vessel of Inanna.' My mouth is twisting out of shape, my words almost incoherent.

'Now I tell you. I couldn't tell you to your face. You died and I didn't admit it even then. I didn't know how to. It hurts so much! Inanna is no comfort to me any more: I curse her for betraying you. Nergal took away half my soul, Tamuz. He took away the sun and the moon from my sky, and the water from my earth. I wanted to die myself. I loved you – I love you – I love you ...'

And finally the pent-up waters of the Great Abyss burst from their vaults, and I am weeping so hard it is agony, pressing my face unheedingly to his chest and sobbing into the dust, wracked by the waves of my grief. He slips his arms softly about me and holds me, but that doesn't staunch the tears. I weep until I am too exhausted to sob, and then I close my eyes and rest against him, face cradled in the dust.

'I have never seen that.'

My eyes open blearily. I hadn't noticed Ereshkigal approach. I am half-slumped against Tamuz and his arms are around me, and that is all that matters. His body is neither warm nor cold, just a little darker where my tears have stained him.

'I didn't know the Dead could do that.' Her black gaze dances over Tamuz. His dusty eyes are closed, his expression troubled. 'They are only memories of feelings; they do not feel.'

I do not know what to say.

'He must remember you well.' She takes a step back, furling her robe around her. 'Take him with you.'

'What?' I whisper.

'I will let you take him away. You want that, don't you? I will let you take him back to the world above. If ...'

'If what?'

'If you send me a living lover.' She blinks. Her eyes are swimming with black tears once again. 'The Dead are no use to me, Sister. I want a warm and breathing – a *living* – body in my bed. Young and strong and filled with passion. I need ...' Her mouth works. 'I need what you have. I need *that*.' A jerk of her chin indicates my beloved. 'Give me that and you can have your Tamuz back.'

Wordlessly I nod.

'Of course, his carcass is useless by now: you will have to find him a new body.'

'I can do that.' My voice is hoarse and does not betray the tiny spark of fire that glints like an ember amid ashes.

'Then give me your promise, Sister.'

'You have it, my Queen.'

'Go now then. Don't look back. Don't hesitate. A life for a life, remember; a soul for a soul.' She draws me out of Tamuz's unresisting arms and thrusts me down the path. 'He will follow. So will my servants. Don't look back.'

I ascend from the Underworld with a host of *galla* demons in my train, billowing at my back like an animate dust-storm. They hiss and crackle with eagerness, vulture heads thrust out and beaks snapping, and they sweep me forwards with impetuous haste, my feet hardly touching the ground. I catch no glimpse of Tamuz and dare not look behind me for his face among that crowd.

I must pass through each of the Seven Gates once more to regain the world of the Living. As I approach the Seventh Gate the hawk-headed gatekeeper kneels to touch my feet. When he stands he cups my face briefly in his grey hands. Glancing into the pool I see that, though my face has not changed one whit, though it is still freckled and brown, now Inanna shines out from it again, wild and joyous.

At the Sixth Gate the scorpion-men kneel to touch my feet. They dress me in a new robe of sheer linen, without a stain or tear. I am restored to human dignity.

At the Fifth Gate my lion-headed tormentor kneels to touch

my feet. He clasps about my ankles and wrists intricately moulded bracelets of gold. My strength is restored.

At the Fourth Gate the snake-man abases himself at my feet. He offers up a gemstone belt and glides about me to fasten it over my hips. My status as Queen of Heaven is restored.

At the Third Gate the demon of many eyes kneels to touch my feet. He brings to me an agate necklace glittering with rainbow colours, and fastens it about my neck. My powers of magic are restored.

At the Second Gate the fiery ogre kneels to touch my feet. He gives me pendant earrings of pure gold. My mind is made whole.

At the First Gate Neti kneels to kiss my feet. When I allow him to stand he places upon my head the Crown of Inanna, and my undressed hair streams from beneath the golden flowers like dark water. My status as Queen of the Earth is restored.

Then he opens the Gate. The Underworld exhales dust into the land above, and like a denser cloud the *galla* pour out with me, filling the small shrine, clustering on the roof-edge and hanging like cobwebs in the corners. Their shadowy wings flap and rustle. Even with the shade they cast, it takes a while for my eyes to adjust to the daylight.

'He is yours, Great Lady Inanna,' says Neti with a pointed glance over my shoulder.

Turning, I see Tamuz standing upon the threshold. He might almost be taken for a living man, if he were not so grey. His face is expressionless, his eyes blank.

'Come here,' I say and he steps towards me without hesitation or eagerness.

You owe our Queen! say the demons with one voice. *Waste no time!*

'You will wait!' I reply and they cringe back, fluffing their feathers with resentment. I circle Tamuz once, my mind racing. He isn't going to be solid to the touch, and has no more autonomy than a reflection.

For a moment I cover my mouth with my hands, wondering if I have the skill for what I am about to attempt. Then I go to work. There can hardly be a person in all the Land Between the Two Rivers who does not know the art of weaving rushes – and my first post in the Temple of Inanna when I became a full priestess was as supervisor of the workshops of the basket weavers. I set myself to weaving Tamuz a body, as I might to weaving a basket. I have no good green rushes to work with, though. My materials are the dust on the floor and the detritus of the funerary offerings around me: cracked stems from wreaths and barley sheaves, date stones, bones and mould, the slime from the bottom of the beer jars, wisps of uncarded wool and unspun flax that have been used as packing. I roll them between my hands and chant words of power, moulding the unmouldable and binding the unbindable. Kneeling in the dirt, I weave about Tamuz's still form a framework formed of the humblest materials of life, a basket in the shape of his body. I weave it close enough to be watertight. I twist and twine the stiff fibres until my fingers bleed, and then I sing my blood into the mix too. Where the layers must be sewn together I use strands of my own long hair. From his toes to the top of his head I recreate him – and if I knock off ten years to make him as I remember him the first night we met, then that only brings him down to my own age, and who is there to criticise my artistry?

Finally I reach up to kiss his lips and whisper into his mouth my own breath and the word that seals the magic. Then Tamuz's dark eyes fly open and he gazes into mine; pulling me suddenly against him he groans, 'Ishara!'

My eyes fill with tears and I can hardly breathe. I grab his hair with my hands and press my cheek against his.

Do not delay! roar the demons. *Fulfil your promise or he is forfeit back to our Queen!*

'Yes,' I mumble, my lips lingering upon his skin. 'Yes.' Then I let him go. My woollen overmantle is still lying where I left it before my descent, and I give it to Tamuz so that he won't have to go naked. He looks confused and alarmed by our surroundings, but he nods with determination when I explain where we must go.

It's almost sunset by the time we emerge from the shrine, but the dust pall hanging over the land gives the horizon an unnatural bloody tint. We walk hand in hand toward the walls of Uruk; I will not let him go while the *galla* are threatening to tear him from me. They follow at our heels and billow over our heads; before we even reach the city I see distant figures fleeing and as we set foot upon the ramp the great gates are swung shut against us, guards and farmers falling over each other as they scramble to be on the inside.

It does none of them any good. The *galla* hit the bronze facings of the door and wrench the whole thing straight off its hinges, tumbling in through the doorway and over the top of the walls with hardly a pause to acknowledge any obstacle. People are screaming and fleeing down the narrow streets; a small knot of soldiers is trying to form up inside, raising their spears to throw.

The *galla* overwhelm them and reduce them to bloody rags before I can draw breath.

'Stand down!' roars Tamuz, flinging his hands out at other soldiers running in. Enough of them recognise his voice and face and stop in their tracks, mouths open. 'Stand aside! The King returns to the royal house of Uruk!'

One of the guards shouts his name in shock.

'Harm no one without my command!' I order the demons. 'One life only is forfeit to the Great Below!'

They obey, though hardly willingly. We march swiftly into the open square before the gates of the palace, but there are plenty of people fleeing at top speed to carry the news in advance of our force. Like a filthy cloud the *galla* hover at our shoulders as we face a stunned cohort of the Royal Guard and a retreating crowd of civilians.

'Listen to me, Captain Uait!' bellows Tamuz, but he's speaking to everyone lingering in earshot or hiding in the doorways. 'I am Tamuz, King of Uruk, murdered most treacherously but brought back from the Underworld by the power of Holy Inanna. Bring out before me my brother Nergal who slew me!'

Captain Uait doesn't obey; he just slides to his knees, eyes wide with terror, while his men follow his example or retreat cringing. However, word has already reached the inner courts: the doors are flung wide as King Nergal storms out through them, dressed for feasting. Close at his heels are his senior queen and his family, including the boy Gilgamesh and – my heart clenches as I see her – his half-sister Geshtinanna. She is still wearing the robes of the Wife of Enki.

'Nergal!' Tamuz spreads his arms wide in mockery of a greeting.

Nergal stands at the head of the stairs, looking down upon us. His face is as grey as the dust of the Underworld.

'Brother!' shrieks Geshtinanna. Her face has locked into a grin in which joy and terror are equally balanced. She looks from him to me. Then she takes a wobbly step forwards.

Shall we take her? ask the *galla*.

At the sound of their unclean voices in their heads everyone flinches.

Choose swiftly, Lady Inanna: choose one who is worthy.

'Who else is a worthy substitute for Tamuz, save one of his blood?' I answer.

Geshtinanna gasps, then sets her jaw, the cords standing up on her neck. The demons gather themselves.

'And who else is worthy to serve my sister Ereshkigal, save for a king?' I finish.

I point at Nergal. 'Take him.'

They pour past me like dirty smoke. They seize Nergal's limbs and drag him down the stairs, which shatter beneath their vulture claws, the ground sinking and falling away into a gaping cleft. Tamuz and I both reel back as the earth of the courtyard sags beneath our feet. Into a deep black gulf wider than a chariot the demons drag Nergal, who cries with rage as he falls. The dwindling scream seems endless.

No mortal less than Nergal could hope to satiate my divine sister, I tell myself; anyone else would disappoint her. And if ever a man had the hubris to face that challenge, to match the Queen of the Dead, it would be him.

Under a pall of falling grit Tamuz turns to stare at me, and I brace myself for his wrath. For a long moment nobody moves. Then he lifts one eyebrow and blinks. 'Daughter of the Moon,' he says stiffly, 'as you will it.'

The aftermath goes on deep into the night. I stay while the nobles and the priests of all the temples in Uruk are ordered in to witness the King's return, and I attend for the swearing of the oath of fealty that Tamuz demands from each. During quieter moments I notice how his eyes turn thoughtfully to me, his expression unreadable. I tell my story – or at least a version of it – so that they might all know how he came back. I accept the gifts of gold and oxen and slaves that Tamuz promises the temple of Inanna in gratitude. But I slip out while the priests of Ereshkigal are arguing among themselves as to the correct purification rites for a situation so unprecedented. I have a goddess to thank.

I find her in a courtyard garden of the inner palace: a point of light shining at the roofline. I kneel beside the bathing pool to thank her, knowing I have a terrible penance hanging over me – but I don't dare begin that, so I put it off until tomorrow. After praying I sit with my bare feet in the water and trail my fingers between my ankles, watching the ripples dancing on the moonlit surface and remembering a pool that had no ripples. I should be exhausted: I was in the Underworld for seven days, so it turns out. But I can't even think of sleep at the moment, my mind is churning so.

Tamuz, emerging quietly from the night, finds me there. I hear him dismissing the servants and then he kicks off his gilded sandals and sits down next to me on the stone lip of the pool, shin-deep. It's three weeks since the Spring Equinox and already the nights are swelling with warmth; the tepid water is pleasant on our skins.

'It's all done,' he says with a rueful smile. 'For tonight at least. I sent them all home. Tomorrow there will be ceremonies and envoys and petitions to hear. And a celebration. I've already sent messengers to the other cities. But tonight . . .'

I can't meet his eye. 'You spared Nergal's family,' I say, because that has puzzled me and I have to say something.

'You disapprove?'

I shrug. 'It's the law; a murderer's family must suffer with him for his crime.'

'I'm not in the mood for executions, given what we've been through.' He rubs at his chest self-consciously. 'Besides, tomorrow I will declare Gilgamesh my heir.'

That does surprise me and I stare.

He sighs. 'If I'd done that last year maybe none of this would have happened. It would have given Nergal honour and hope enough to satisfy his ambition.'

'Maybe. Are you sure about this? Gilgamesh is a wild boy.'

'He'll grow out of it.'

I bite my lip. 'He saw me destroy his father. It'll be hard for him to be reconciled with Inanna.'

Tamuz hitches round to face me. 'I watched you destroy my brother and rob me of my vengeance. But I find it easy to be reconciled with Inanna.'

'Do you?' My heart is thumping hard under my ribs; there is so much between us for good and for ill, and I don't know where to start unravelling the knots.

'You brought me back from the Dead, remember?' His expression is warm, but as he looks upon me it grows thoughtful, almost bleak. 'I don't remember anything, you know. Nothing. I mean . . . I remember dying and then . . . nothing until your voice in the darkness. Your tears. Your body warm against me. But, even then, it was like the flickering glimpses of a dream. Nothing seemed real until suddenly I was standing in my own tomb.' He shivers and I want to touch him, but I don't dare. There is horror in his eyes.

'We should put it from our minds.' I'm trying to reassure him; I cannot comfort myself.

'No.' His mouth is suddenly stubborn and he shakes his head as if trying to clear it. 'I've spent all my life in expectation of . . . an afterlife befitting a king. And I've made misjudgements. I've thought . . . I have paid too much attention to certain things in my life. I've not listened to the voices of my heart because I thought they were unfitting, or not politic, or too indulgent. I put off choosing an heir because I thought that I must have a son of my own: I wanted a lineage I could look upon from the afterlife and be proud of. I thought that my military campaigns, my monuments, my treasures . . . that I would find satisfaction and pride in what I had achieved in my life. But it's not like that, is it?' That stubborn mouth twists. 'No ease. No glory. No reward. Nothing at all.'

I grimace helplessly. 'You will be remembered; your name as a great king will be honoured. Your people mourned because they loved you!'

'Ah.' He smiles sadly. 'But I will not know that. All I have is this life. All I have is now. So, it seems to me that I should listen to voices other than ambition and pride. I should have heard the words you carried unspoken in your heart, Ishara. I should have listened to my own.' He leans in and kisses me, soft and warm. I quiver like a girl of fourteen, my heart jumping. As he pulls away he lifts his brows quizzically; I think he was expecting a more passionate response. 'Am I wrong?' he murmurs in that voice that turns me to liquid butter.

'What I said to you in the House of Dust – you remember that?'

He nods, his lips curving. 'It . . . doesn't displease me, Ishara.'

This is what I've dreaded.

'I shouldn't have said it! I spoke in despair – I spoke thinking I'd lost you and my life and everything.' I'm almost tripping over my words. 'It was not proper. I blasphemed against the goddess. Please, Tamuz . . . I've betrayed my Queen; I am polluted by my weakness.'

'Weakness?' He blinks. 'You think you've been weak?' He pulls a face. 'Anyway, the matter of blasphemy is between you and Inanna. Nothing to do with me.'

'But I'm not fit to be her vessel for you. Not now.'

He sits back to give that consideration, his eyes holding mine. 'Tell me if I am right,' he says, shucking off his open robe to bare his torso. 'It seems to me that, as a priestess of Inanna, you can love me – or any man – with absolute confidence.'

'Yes . . .'

'But, as Ishara, though you defied a king and descended into the grave for my sake, though you won me from Ereshkigal herself, you are *afraid* to love me.'

My mouth falls open. He doesn't wait for my response – which will not be forthcoming anyway: he slips down into the pool, still clad in his kilt and, facing me, lifts my left foot clear of the water.

'Well, that we can remedy,' he says, sliding my anklet off and tossing it on to the poolside.

'No,' I whisper, but he moves with calm efficiency to rob me of my other anklet. Then he pulls me into the water with him, hip-deep, and removes my bracelets before placing my palms on his bare chest and drawing me firmly to him.

'Ishara,' he murmurs, his mouth on mine, his breath mingling with mine, his lips teasing mine open with sweet, possessive kisses. 'Hear this: I love you. For what you did; for what you are. Not as my goddess but as mine. I love you.'

It's crazy: I, the high priestess of Inanna, am shaking like a maiden on her wedding night. 'No,' I mouth almost soundlessly, and I don't know whether I'm denying his words or his unclasping of the gemstone belt from about my hips, but he laughs.

'Yes,' he contradicts me, his eyes dancing. He lies back in the water, pulling me with him so that I am half lying upon him, half floating. The water is like a kiss rushing all over my skin, tightening my nipples. He sculls backwards until he can sit with his shoulders resting on the stone edge and he can hoist me up astride his thighs. The wet linen of my robe clings to the orbs of my breasts as they break the surface. 'And this,' he mutters, working the clasp of my broad agate necklace free and dropping the whole thing over his shoulder.

I cannot escape from the memory of being undressed by the gatekeepers. And he is right: I am afraid. Afraid of being stripped of the protection and anonymity of my office; afraid of being Ishara once more, unadorned and vulnerable. Afraid of the intimacy when it isn't goddess loving worshipper or priestess loving king, but woman loving man and praying that the miracle happens, that he loves her as she loves him.

'Oh yes,' groans Tamuz. My breasts are warm under the translucent white linen, my nipples hard and dark, and he cups them first and then lifts me to mouth fervently at them. His tongue feels hot and when he plucks at my stiff points my whole body vibrates. I clasp his face and whimper, feeling his throat and jaw working under his beard. Around us in the water our white clothes swirl like smoke. He pulls my skirts aside to bare my thighs before he eases me back on to his lap. The water takes much of my weight and I rest lightly upon him. 'Now these,' he murmurs, slipping the curved wires of my earrings one at a time from my flesh.

'Don't,' I moan, shy as a virgin.

He's amused. He lays the jewellery aside and tickles the naked lobes of my ears with his fingertips. 'Kiss me.'

I obey, leaning in to lay my lips on his. It's tentative and questioning and totally unlike any of the thousands of kisses I've known before: it's like I am learning to speak a new language. He cups my face in his hand and my pulse beats against his wrist as the kiss melts into liquid bliss. His other hand strokes my thigh and climbs to clasp my bare rump. When we break we are both breathing shallowly. His eyes are dark with desire.

'One more.' He lifts the gold crown from my head and traces the planes of my face. 'There. All gone. No priestess any more; just Ishara.'

I shiver and bite at his thumb. He's voicing my worst fears.

'Will you dare love me now?'

I picture the ribbon of stone spanning the abyss. 'I feel like you are holding me over a deep drop.'

He smiles. His words are slow and deliberate: 'So long as I live, Ishara, I will never let you fall.'

Tentatively I smile, and as our lips meet he slips his hand between my thighs and first one and then two fingers deep into me, catching my gasp in his mouth. I am cupped on his palm, nestling down on him as he flexes within me and presses up in circular motions against my mound. His other arm circles my waist, holding me tight.

'The Queens' apartments will be empty when Nergal's women leave,' he murmurs.

I struggle to grasp what he's saying; it seems strange to be talking of domestic arrangements while he's squeezing my most intimate flesh and my thighs are writhing upon his, but my discomposure is the very thing that delights him. I whimper and Tamuz catches the questioning flash of my eyes and chuckles.

'You may take as many chambers as you wish.' He nuzzles my throat, planting teasing kisses.

'I . . . ah . . . I can't live away from the temple,' I manage to stammer – then: 'Oh. Yes. Just there.'

'Like that?' The reaction he gets seems to satisfy him.

'Um. You've no idea of the work involved: the estates, the accounts . . . Ah!'

Tamuz licks my throat. 'I'm not asking you to leave the temple. Just . . . to give me the nights you can spare. I want you to be where I can reach you.'

His reach right at this moment is going deeper and deeper; I open up around his hand, sliding upon him, heat blossoming through my body and rising up my spine. I gasp, open-mouthed and wide-eyed, sliding my hands over his face. He sets his jaw with the effort of his work, the strain making his arm and shoulder like rock.

'Yes. That's what I want. I want you coming on me. I want

to know that any time I want I can reach out and find you. I want to be able to fuck you. Every night. Every day. Just like this. Whenever. I. Want.'

Sobbing, I lose control and he nearly crushes me in his efforts to hold me as I buck and thrash and score his shoulders with my nails. I end up pressed tight to him, my hot face scrunched into his neck.

He laughs softly to himself. 'Oh, I like *that*.'

'What?' I whisper.

'To see you blush at my touch.' He touches my temple gently. 'To see the sweat here when you come. Have you any clue how difficult women are to read? That paint is like a mask. I like to see the effect I have on you. That . . . excites me.' He takes my hand and pushes it down between us to show me just how his member has responded. Despite the cool water he's thick and hard and stirring impatiently. 'Now *that's* easy to read,' he groans as I take his girth in hand through the floating layers of cloth.

His hand slips from within me to make room for his cock and I feel like I'm dissolving into the pool. We fumble for a moment with our clothes, then he pulls me up against his erect length, almost bruisingly eager. His kisses are rapacious now. But all my slickness has washed away and there's too much friction underwater.

'Out of the pool,' I suggest, gulping my words, almost as frantic as he is.

Tamuz blinks and nods. Yet when I dismount from his thighs and start to climb from the pool he rises to his feet behind me with a great rush of water and grabs me, pinning me by the hips.

'Oh no,' he says. 'You can't get away with that.' His cock grinds into my buttocks; his hand grabs my round cheek. 'You ought to know not to turn your back on the King, Ishara.

That's not safe. Don't you know what will happen if you do that?'

Pulling me up against him, he fondles my breasts and bites my neck until I squirm, writhing my rear against that stiff intruder. My dress clings like a second skin. My nipples are erect with chill but his body feels red-hot against my back. He pulls up my skirt to expose my cleft and nearly stabs me then and there.

'Not getting away with that,' he repeats appreciatively, moulding my cheeks with his hard hands. Then he pushes me forwards on to the bank and down on to hands and knees, holding me in place with one hand. I tilt my hips and arch my spine, presenting him with the best possible view, my thighs splayed to display the invitation of my slash. I can feel my cream welling. Where he stands behind me at the stepped margin of the pool, knee-deep in the water, he's at just the right height to slide his cock straight into my open sex. I squeal with unmeditated shock and delight.

'Gods, yes,' he says with proper piety.

Both hands clap down to make my arse bounce, then he grips me by the hips and rocks into me, pushing deep and true. Bracing myself on one arm, I reach down between my own thighs to touch him; that thick unyielding shaft that slips in and out between my taut lips. He brings my wetness out into the open and I take that slickness and anoint my clit, rolling with the waves of sensation. His thighs pump like a stallion's. His loins slap into my rear. He's holding me in place and working me upon his cock. His arms are bars of muscle.

'Good?' he growls.

'Harder,' I groan, knowing that he's holding back for my sake. He's a big man; he has to be careful when he ruts.

'Can you take it?'

'I can take it.' I want to feel his scrotum bouncing off my sex.

Breath hisses between his clenched teeth. His rhythm changes; his thrusts become deeper and crueller, his weight heavier. He starts to grunt a little with each thrust. His breath is tight with concentration. He's forgotten to talk, forgotten his royal dignity, forgotten the trials we have been through. He knows only my beautiful arse which he's fucking. His fingers dig into my skin. He's going to leave bruises. I want his bruises. I want his cock splitting me. I want his helpless, desperate groans as he pounds into my sex and I want his seed spurting into me and I want his strength forcing me to the dizzy edge of pleasure and then I want to fall over that edge into the stormy darkness beyond.

I fall. And he catches me. He grabs me and holds me, holds me as we slide gently down that long glide into peace, cradling me in his arms even though he is above me. It's as if he's spread those feathered dust-coloured wings and is bearing my weight. We touch earth so lightly, and then he folds himself around me and holds me close, his lips on my shoulder, his arm under my head, his hand between my breasts upon my pounding heart.

He carries me through to the King's bedchamber to sleep out the remnant of the night, and drifts off with his head cushioned on my breasts, my hand twined in his black hair. Beneath a ceiling painted with lions I look down and whisper to myself words from the Great Marriage:

When he enters her holy temple, filling the Queen with joy,
When he enters her holy sanctuary, filling Inanna with rejoicing,
Inanna holds him to her and murmurs,
'Oh, Tamuz, you are truly my love.'

Ill Met by Moonlight

by

Portia Da Costa

1

It was a dream. She knew it was a dream. But somehow that didn't seem to matter.

She was in a warm place, and she was deliciously, tropically warm. And, even though she didn't recognise her surroundings, she felt as safe and enclosed as if someone she loved and trusted was holding her tight.

Sniffing the air, she caught the scents of pine and balsam. Woodsy odours that were both clean and earthy at the same time.

She was waiting for a man. She'd been waiting for him quite a while, but somehow that didn't seem to matter either. Just to be here, relaxed and ready, was a pleasure.

Who are you? Do I know you?

Lois wondered if it might be Oliver, her ex. But why would she be waiting for him, even in this floating unreality? They'd parted ages ago, in an easy break, and, when she was awake, she barely ever thought of him ... so why suddenly dream about him now?

In their heyday, though, the sex had been good. So maybe that was the reason? She was horny, so her body had fixed on its last source of satisfaction – other than her by own efforts. She remembered some of Ollie's finer moments with a twinge of hot nostalgia.

The room was dark and full of deep shadows, lit only by a nightlight and the flickering of a low burning fire. There was a womblike quality to the walls, something natural and organic, and she still couldn't work out where she was. She only knew it was somewhere new to her that felt irrationally like home too.

Maybe I was here in a former life?

Now there was a peculiar notion, if ever there was one . . . but, then, everything about the situation was strange and otherworldly.

Maybe I'm remembering something I dreamt once before? Now that's complicated . . . a dream within a dream. Whatever next?

Whatever it was, she couldn't deny that she felt mellow and loose and sexy.

Touching her hands to her body, she was surprised. What the devil was she wearing?

Instead of her habitual shabby T-shirt and overwashed knickers, she found the voluminous and enveloping folds of an old-fashioned brushed-cotton nightdress. Nestling into it like a small furry animal, she sighed. Who'd have thought that something so prim could also be so sexy? The long full nightgown was both cosy and erotic at the same time, and the contrast between being all chastely covered up on top, and bare and devoid of panties beneath was sinfully naughty. As her naked thighs slid against each other, her nipples stiffened and puckered, their tips chafed by the virginal white fabric in a subtle autonomic caress.

I'd rather have a man do that, but where is he? Where is he?

Someone was coming though, she knew that. He just wasn't here yet. And, in the meantime, she would make her own amusement.

Picturing a pair of hands that were long and elegant, but full of suppressed strength, she clasped her breasts through the soft cotton of the gown and teased them with light squeezes. The mind image was almost supernaturally clear.

Strong hands, sleek golden skin . . .

Graceful fingers that were gentle but strangely cool . . .

Curiouser and curiouser . . . but also mmm mmm mmm . . .

When she flicked her thumbs across the hardened peaks of her nipples, the slight contact sent streaks of sensation flashing along her nerves. She could almost see that too, like little pathways glittering and silvery beneath the white nightdress and her own skin. She watched them zip and twinkle until they popped tiny starbursts in her clitoris. Of their own accord, her hips lifted and she moaned.

Ohmigod, all I've done is touch my breasts and I'm almost there! What's going happen when I really get down to business? Or he does?

Suddenly, she couldn't wait . . . she could hardly breathe.

Wriggling against the crisply laundered sheets, she hitched up her nightgown. Up and up until it was just a scrunched-up crumpled bunch under her armpits.

She was a goddess of sex. An odalisque exhibiting herself for a hundred watching eyes. She'd kicked off the sheets as she'd pulled up her nightgown and now she was on display from her chest down to her toes, her skin lapped by the warm scented air.

Breasts. Belly. Thighs. Pubis. The Full Monty.

She could smell herself too. A new perfume had blended itself into the pine, the earth and the juniper wood smoke. Her arousal, salty and pungent and also of the earth.

She stared down at her body, pale as alabaster against the luminous white sheets, the curls of her pussy a wild sandy shock between her thighs. She could see a glint of juiciness sparkling through the hair there and, shimmying against the mattress, she clenched herself, tensing up her strong inner muscles, and felt the slow honeyed roll of her arousal.

I'm very wet, secret lover . . . very wet. I'm ready . . . where the hell are you?

Should she touch herself? Or should she save herself for *him*? For a moment, she fantasised that he'd tied her hands to the bed-rails behind her head, punishing her, preventing her from stealing that special privilege.

Then, suddenly, because it was a dream . . . her hands *were* tied!

She was lashed to the brass rails with what looked like the cords from a couple of old-fashioned dressing gowns. How bizarre was that?

Instantly, of course, the need to touch her sex ramped up to an almost agonising pitch. Unable to suppress it or ignore it, she threw herself around on the mattress, hips circling and weaving while she tried desperately *not* to imagine her legs being fastened too.

Uh oh, too late!

No sooner had she thought it than the deed was done and she was bound hand and foot with more dressing-gown cords. Had she ever had a dressing gown like that? Did she know anyone else who had one? Where the hell was all this stuff coming from? She only knew that her ankles were spread wide apart and there was no longer any way whatsoever to get ease from the ravening itch of desire.

And it was now, when somehow she'd managed to make herself totally vulnerable, that the unknown dream lover finally put in an appearance.

The door swung back just like in an old Dracula movie and a figure appeared in the doorway.

And she didn't have the slightest idea who he was.

Who the hell are you, Dream Lover? And, boy, do you know how to make a big entrance!

Dream Lover was a cliché as well as a total stranger. Your

actual tall, dark and handsome, but with a twist, and dressed all in black – a long coat, close-fitting T-shirt, jeans and boots.

And he had the most amazing hair!

It was almost black, yet also blond. Like ebony frosted with gold, and cut short, but not too short. A touch of wild, natural curl set off its startling pale tipping and made it appear to glow in the dim room like a halo, its brilliance second only to the fire in its owner's gleaming, flashing eyes.

Lois blinked. There was something weird about those eyes, but their very brightness made it impossible to work out what it was. She could only stare into them, like a willing patsy totally hooked by a hypnotist's spinning coin.

Talk about a fantasy man.

This is a dream, you fool! Of course *he's a fantasy man . . .*

But still, why the hair? And the eyes that she wished she could see better.

She must have conjured him up from the very depths of memory, from some long-lost book she'd read, or image she'd once seen. A world of faeries or earth spirits, of beings of supernatural power and alchemical attraction that she'd loved in more innocent times before she'd become a techno-geek.

But, however she'd cooked him up, God, how she wanted him! Between her thighs, she grew wetter, wetter, wetter . . .

The apparition didn't speak, and Lois couldn't. But still those amazing eyes pinned her to the spot, widening with an unmistakeable hunger. He immediately zeroed in on her cunt, and his fine-cut nostrils flared as if he'd smelt her. Which wasn't surprising, because she could certainly smell herself.

And the more she stared at him, the more she thought he was a dish fit for a queen.

He really was quite something. Face broad and intelligent, and vaguely familiar somehow now. Cheekbones high, jaw firm and a mouth that was strong and manly yet ever so slightly pouty in a way that made her long to nibble his plump lower lip. Even as she hungered for him and his eyes told her he was hungering for her in return, his tongue flicked out and moistened those succulent lips. It was pointed and very pink, darting lasciviously.

Almost expiring with lust, Lois hauled in a deep breath, and began to smell Dream Lover as much as he could smell her, getting yet another surprise into the bargain.

Not for him the smells of leather and sweat. Not for him the cool blue smells of male cologne.

No, as he approached her across the cabin, soft-footed on the wooden floor, he brought with him the sweet smell of flowers.

Violets, wild roses, delicate woodland blooms . . . and, most piercingly and headily, the scent of lavender.

It was like swigging down a triple belt of some perfumed liqueur made by monks in the wilds of rural France.

Lois squirmed around against the mattress, the very quick of her body aching like the devil as if the sweet odour was stimulating it directly. She throbbed and throbbed, her simmering flesh begging for contact. Just the tiniest little touch would do it. The stranger's mouth twisted in a slow knowing smile as he drew nearer. It seemed to light his every feature like a candle.

And still they hadn't exchanged a single word.

While Lois watched like a starving beast eyeing up a prime rib, Dream Lover flung off his long dark coat and then knelt on the bed. Having braced herself for the bounce of substantially muscled body hitting the mattress, she got a shock that made her gasp. He was big – tall and broad and solid – but the sheet on which she lay barely seemed dented. It was the oddest phenomenon, and Lois knew she should be frightened . . . but in a dream, she supposed, weird stuff like this was normal.

That was, if it *was* a dream? Some of it was far too vivid to be imaginary.

Free of his coat, Dream Lover's body was shown off to perfection. His arms gleamed in the firelight as if they were fashioned from polished wood and strength shone around him like an aura. The golden glitter that dusted his thick dark hair was even more breathtaking in close proximity, and his close-fitting black T-shirt embraced the ripped contours of his torso. Beneath the tough dark fabric of his jeans, his thighs were as sturdy as oak branches, and at his crotch there was a fine chunky bulge.

Lois's fingers itched to explore him, but her bonds were disturbingly real in an imaginary situation. She simply could not move, and Dream Lover's velvety, tantalising lips curved at the sight of her struggles. His hand, so conveniently *unfettered*, reached out towards her body, hovering for several seconds over her breast, before dropping to the full curve and cupping it. Lois hissed through her teeth, as his long thumb settled against her nipple as if it belonged there. His skin was as cool as she'd imagined it to be . . .

Her hiss turned to an outright groan as he flicked and tickled her; her mystery man smiled, his passionate mouth widening in a smile that was impish and knowing. With slow calculation, he strummed her again and again, and the compulsion to thrash about and rub the skin of her bare buttocks against the sheet beneath her grew stronger and stronger by the second. She tried to stay still, because for some bizarre reason it seemed important to show a little decorum, but it was hopeless. Wriggling like a strumpet, she knew she'd never looked sluttier in her life.

Why can't I just ask you who you are?

She opened her mouth to speak, but Dream Lover put paid to all questions by tweaking the nipple quite hard now, rolling it between finger and thumb, plucking at it and pulling at it, making it stiffer and pinker than ever. He cocked his gilded head on one side as she bucked against the mattress, attempting to widen her thighs and entice him with her sticky melting sex. She'd never behaved like this before, even in her wildest moments, and her own wantonness both appalled and excited her, goading her aroused body to even greater heights of shamelessness.

Please ... please ... she begged him silently, still unable to speak. *Touch my cunt. Stroke me with your fingers ... Fuck me! Please, please, fuck me now!*

The golden-frosted head cocked again, and he grinned like the sun.

You heard that, didn't you, you bastard? You read my mind!

Maybe mind-reading was standard operational procedure in dreams? Anything was possible. Watching her face, Dream Lover continued to play idly with her breast for a while, all the time watching her face with the intensity of a scientist.

I can't take much more of this.

Lois watched his face for an acknowledgement, but Dream Lover just regarded her benignly as he went on with his fondling.

But Lois didn't feel benign. She wanted to kill him, or fuck him, or even both. Between her legs tension gathered and gathered and her head seemed to be floating it felt so light. Her brain was emptying of thought. She was about to come.

Just from having her breast touched? Surely not? But anything seemed achievable in this wonderful warm place.

But just when it seemed almost about to happen, Dream Lover withdrew his hand.

'You bastard!'

So near, yet suddenly so far, Lois found her tongue at last, and Dream Lover's brow puckered. What was he thinking? Planning some devilish new sexual torture for her, no doubt. He snagged his sinful lower lip with his Colgate-white teeth, and his brilliant eyes sparkled with mischief.

Lois blinked. Surely not? It had suddenly dawned on her what was peculiar about those eyes – they were two different colours. The right one was a sharp, electrical sky blue and the left one was as warm and brown as Armagnac.

She was just about to remark on this unexpected phenomenon, or just simply beg him to fuck her now she'd finally got her voice back, when, without warning, Dream Lover scooted back to the edge of the bed, and then reached down to unbuckle his heavy boots. After kicking them vigorously away across the room, he plucked at the hem of his T-shirt and pulled it out of his waistband with equal impatience. A second later it flew away on the same trajectory as the boots, and she was gifted with the sight of the most awesome male pulchritude. Muscles rippled across his chest and abdomen as he moved, bunching and relaxing beneath skin the colour of honeyed sandstone, almost too beautiful and magnificently male to be real.

Well, I've never wanted to worship a guy before, but I do now, she thought hazily. *What are you, some kind of magical deity? A prince of the world of dreams . . . a perfect lover?*

Coming to her again, he lay over her, his chest hard and smooth against her nipples, while the coarse workaday cloth of his jeans was equally rough against the bare skin of her belly. Lois blushed furiously as he pressed his hard crotch against her mons. She was soaking wet down there and it would surely seep through his jeans and he'd be able to feel it.

But then she forgot about qualms and wetness and jeans

and everything. His mouth came down on hers, and she almost drowned in his sweet floral odour.

The contact of his lips on hers was soft at first, almost ethereal, like chilled velvet. Then, after a few seconds, the kiss grew wild and his tongue pushed inside her mouth, bringing with it a taste that was as heady as his smell. Lois gasped. His lips were candy sweet, and his tongue was cool and wicked, darting like a benevolent serpent inside her mouth, tasting and probing, then powerfully devouring. The pressure of the kiss became so intense that her jaw ached a little from the effort of giving back as good as she was getting.

Big hands settled over her smaller ones where they were fastened to the bedhead. He laced his fingers between hers as he used his entire body to caress and excite her, rubbing her with silky skin and with the denim and with the hardness of his muscles and his cock. His strong hips rocked and rocked, and the bulge of his erection somehow worked its way between her thighs, spreading her sex-lips so it could stimulate her clitoris.

And suddenly it was all too much . . . and yet not enough.

Muffled by his tongue, Lois growled a garbled sound of protest, her pelvis jerking against his, commanding him to give her more, more, more.

In return, Dream Lover laughed, his glee as sweet in her mouth as his taste was. Then he slid one hand down her body, visiting her breasts and her belly. His cool skin was a satin kiss against her heat.

Touch me! Touch me down there! Masturbate my clit and make me come and make me come before I die!

But, even if he'd heard her, he was determined to do what *he* wanted.

Working blind, still kissing, he worked deftly at the button and zip of his jeans and uncovered himself. Lois couldn't see his size, but, hot damn, she could feel it. He was huge and breath-taking against her thighs, hard and determined as he sought his target. With just a little help from his hand, he navigated himself inside her. His sex was as strong and sturdy as the rest of him and just its presence, cool inside her, was a thrill.

Aroused beyond anything she'd ever known before, she was stretched around him, and the bulk of his penis almost made her come without him moving. She lay beneath him, trembling on the brink, gasping and dreaming.

But he was a man – even in the dream – and he wanted action. With barely a stroke or two he had her in rhapsodies. Her body clutched and clutched at him, clenching and contracting, the sensations twice as spicy because she was help-less and couldn't wrap her limbs around him. When he freed her lips, she peaked again, howling and whimpering. When he thrust again, her soul soared, swooping and flying.

Higher, higher, higher she arced, and then descended, barrel-ling back down into her body like the little shooting star she suddenly and distinctly remembered watching earlier.

And with that, she achieved oblivion.

All went dark.

'Shit!'

Lois Hillyard jerked upright, her heart lurching with the sudden disorientation of waking up far too fast and not quite knowing where she was. She stared around wildly, her eyes skittering from object to object in the unfamiliar room.

What the hell am I doing in a log cabin and why is it so bloody cold?

She scrabbled for the quilt, which was on the floor beside her bed and, as she swaddled it around herself, she started to remember things. Things like why she was here in a log cabin in the wilds of nowhere beside the sea, which she could hear rolling outside instead of traffic noises to which she was more accustomed.

And things like stray hot fragments of the dream from which she'd just woken.

'Shit,' she muttered again, burrowing even deeper into the quilt and puffing out her cheeks, still in shock.

What the hell was all that about?

She'd had sex dreams before, but never one so vivid, so strange . . . or so kinky.

Bondage with an unknown man who had gold in his hair and smelt of lavender . . . Where had that madness come from?

Dreams were weird. You usually forgot most of them within moments of waking. But not this one.

Her Dream Lover sprang into her mind instantaneously, every detail like crystal.

He'd been tall, muscular, and graceful with the most astonishing hair and eyes. What possessed someone's subconscious to cook up details like that? Still in her duvet, gripped by the shakes, she tried to analyse him.

Well, the height might have come from a TV actor she was keen on, and the long black coat and funereal garb in general was *de rigueur* for vaguely threatening men of mystery.

But the hair? The eyes? The strangely cool skin? She hadn't the faintest . . .

Face? Well, funny as it seemed, she could pin that. The basic features were her actor again, but there was a touch, just a touch, of the man sharing the beach with her as well.

But why the hell dream about *him* though? It wasn't as if there was any chance, she'd quickly discovered, of getting off with him. No holiday romance there, no way.

Neighbour Guy, as she called him, seemed to have been going out of his way to avoid her, and when they had run into each other he'd been surly at best. He was worthy of fancying, in a purely physical sense, but, in terms of conversation, he seemed to begrudge every monosyllable.

Well, sod you, she'd thought, catching sight of him once or twice, stalking the beach or the rough gravelled track to the local shop, but, somehow, she couldn't help feeling sorry for him too. Somehow, without knowing why, she'd formed a distinct impression that he was a man with a load of sorrow hanging over him. And for that she could almost forgive his chilly grumpiness.

Yes, her fantasy guy of the gilded hair and other magnificent accoutrements had resembled her unhappy neighbour ever so slightly, but otherwise they couldn't have been more different.

Dream Lover had been full of the joys of life. And rambunctiously overflowing with the joys of vigorous pervy sex!

Her body was still tingling with the aftermath, and between her legs she was humid and sticky.

Ohmigod, I must have come in my sleep!

Well, all this sea air and the woodland ambience must be good for something. It had put her in touch with her earth goddess self, or something like that. Being out here in the wild beyonds of unconnected nowhere was going to be a blast if she had a dream like that every night, and with any luck she'd not miss the internet at all. With no television, and a mobile connection that kept dropping out every two minutes, all she had for entertainment otherwise were a couple of uninspiring novels.

You knew this, didn't you, Sand!

Sandy, her friend and partner in their small web-development business, had been moaning at her for long enough to take a well-earned holiday and get away from it all for a while, and had more or less strong-armed her into accepting this offer of a seaside-cabin break from one of their grateful clients.

Unbeknown to Sandy, Lois had brought her laptop, and had planned to work anyway . . . until, of course, it had dawned on her that she was miles and miles from the nearest wi-fi hotspot!

'Twit!'

That would teach her to take the digital, technological world so completely for granted. It served her right for trying to wriggle out of the rest that Sandy had so kindly levered upon her.

It was still frustrating though. Especially when the weather was unseasonably grim and icy for the end of May and the best place to be was inside the cabin, tucked up with a steaming-hot laptop. But her mobile connection was too erratic and slow and, even if she did work, she had no way to upload anything to the testing server without tearing her hair out waiting for minute after minute after minute.

Better just concentrate on erotic fantasies then . . . They seem to be downloading just fine!

Either that or do some cleaning.

Why the hell is this stupid place suddenly covered in dust? It wasn't here earlier . . . Where is it all coming from?

The cabin had been impressively spick and span when she'd arrived but now a delicate veil of dust lay over most of the surfaces and drifted across the floor. There were even whorls of dust scattered over the bed and on the pillows, with several strange heaps against the head and the foot rails.

What the f–?

She shivered. She sniffed the air. And then tentatively, almost reluctantly, she slipped a hand down into her knickers and touched her wetness. Of which there was a lot. Far more than there ought to have been from simply playing with herself.

But it wasn't the quantity that bothered her, it was the way it smelt.

As she withdrew her fingers, a familiar odour made her head spin.

Lavender . . . It was lavender . . . Why does my crotch smell of lavender?

Pulling the quilt over her head, she tried hard not to think.

2

In human form, Robin crouched on the woodshed roof and tasted the flutters of fear in Lois's mind.

No, this was not what he wanted. Not at all. He'd wanted to give her pleasure, not scare the living daylights out of her. Savouring the physical sensations of sighing, he sent out his mind, and touched hers again, filling it with soothing waves of peace that granted sleep.

There, that was better. Unable to resist the temptation, he disassociated and floated through the roof of the cabin so he could be close to his new object of curiosity.

Touching down, he reassociated, and stood by the bed, just looking at her. Not that there was much to see with human eyes. She was curled up beneath the thick quilt like a hibernating dormouse, and only a few tufts of her tousled blonde hair were protruding from the top of it.

There was much to be said for being what he was though. If she woke up now, and emerged from her hiding place, she would see a man . . . but what she couldn't perceive were the powers he still retained.

He could see through the quilt to the pretty face, and even prettier body that lay beneath.

She was delightful and complex and Robin liked that. Connecting with her gave him everything that was delicious about assuming human form. Every year in the month of May, when the transformation was possible, he tasted and interacted with humans, feasting indulgently on their complicated and sometimes turbulent feelings. His own kind had emotions, true, but they were mild, bland and somewhat basic. Contentment. Satisfaction. A kind of wistful regret, occasionally. The only emotion that really stirred him while discarnate was curiosity. And, in that, he knew he was unusual among his breed.

And one of the very few to pursue the ancient privileges of merry May.

But look where it had got him!

He was addicted now, perhaps polluted somehow. Even while discarnate, he was gripped by powerful yearnings. Feelings had filtered through by osmosis into the whole of his existence and he only felt truly alive when he was 'human' . . . or as near as to that condition as he could approximate.

And tonight, with beautiful Lois, he'd almost believed for a moment that he was a man.

Dipping lightly into her mind, he relived the delicious episode, smiling at the way her own subconscious had provided all the elements of the scenario.

You didn't realise you were so kinky, did you? he told her sub-vocally, relishing the words he'd picked up from her vocabulary and from others, over the years.

Binding her to the bed and tormenting her with pleasure had stirred him mightily. And it stiffened his temporary flesh now in a way that made his spirit swirl with emotion and heady pleasure.

Now this, he thought, placing his large hand over his swelling groin and giving it a gentle squeeze, was something his own kind were really missing. Yes, they had a melding of sorts, and it was exceptionally pleasant, but it was a pale shadow in comparison to the hot, wild, sweaty, pumping chaos of human sex with its pungent fluids, its loss of control and ecstatic release.

For that alone, with a special woman like Lois, he might be prepared to lose the many powers humans lacked.

As Lois stirred, probably sensing him, he stepped back from the bed, ready to disassociate and disappear instantaneously. Her head emerged from under the coverlet, and he was struck again by the sweet appeal of her human face.

It was elegant and oval, but with a soft rounding to the cheeks and a rather snub nose that he knew she sometimes fretted about. He'd modelled his own nose a little on it, to reassure her of the attractiveness of the shape. He'd noted too that, despite her qualms, she'd also found the very same feature subconsciously attractive in the man next door, so he'd taken elements of that face too, when creating the image of his own.

His thoughts balked for a moment, troubled as the consciousness of Lois's neighbour briefly touched his own.

Now there was a human emotion he *didn't* want too much of. Grief. Intense sadness. Inconsolable loss. The man in the next cabin had lost a lover, and lost her here, in this place, to the force of the sea. Robin knew what was in the thoughts of Lois's neighbour and, though he felt he understood them, the course of action that the man was planning was anathema to him. Did he not know how precious a thing the human condition was? Even in its darkest, direst hours . . .

Shaking his head as if that might dispel the received sorrow, Robin returned his attention to the warm sleeping woman who lay before him.

Her hair, he considered, was delightful; the shimmering golden colour of sunlight. He knew, of course, that it had been tampered with to make it look that way, but who was he, an entirely artificial human form, inspired by elements from many sources, to disapprove of a bit of creative enhancement? He'd taken his cue from her in acquiring his own sunlit streaks.

She was deeply asleep again now, without dreams, but the temptation to intervene once more was vivid. His penis was hard, stiff and aching, although the sensation was deliciously pleasant, despite the discomfort. Her body was smooth and warm beneath her untidy T-shirt and panties, and the odour of her sex teased his senses and reinforced them.

How delightful it would be to ensorcell her again and plunge his borrowed stiffness into her.

He experienced a momentary qualm ... guilt, he recognised. Guilt at exploiting the slumbering woman, and using her for his own satisfaction – even though he had given her pleasure and her subconscious had gladly welcomed him.

No, next time they joined – fucked, had sex, made love, as the humans so whimsically called it, even when they didn't love each other – next time, exquisite Lois would be an active conscious participant. That was a promise he silently made, and swore to keep.

Yet still his acquired flesh ached and ached.

Of course, the answer was to disassociate again. No body. No arousal. No physical ache. But he didn't want to do that. The month of May was precious and there were only a couple of days remaining. He wanted to remain human for as much time as he could.

Settling into his chair, he unzipped his jeans and drew out his cock.

How fine and delightful it felt to caress himself. To fuck the beautiful girl curled up on the bed was obviously the ideal satisfaction, but handling himself had its own particular charm. Curling his large fist around himself, he pumped greedily at his penis, working and working it. There was no need to take his time. No need to delay in order to increase his partner's sensations. He could rush, snatch his release quickly, come fast and hard.

But, when relief came, her name was noiseless on his lips.

For a while afterwards, he just sat there, letting his consciousness roam around the room, examining her possessions and her clothing, learning about her.

Eventually his attention settled on the device set on the rustic table, the one she called her laptop.

Robin had come to understand what the laptop was, and he applauded it as an excellent mode of communication. Humankind might be sorely limited in the way they interacted with one another, but they were ingenious in creating mechanisms to allow themselves to do the best they could, and this small computer was a prime example of what they could achieve.

He touched it and, energised by *his* energy, it sprang to life. Quickly, he rode its patterns of force and deduced the way to mute its operating noises. He didn't want to wake Lois yet. It would be better to 'meet' her for the first time in more acceptable circumstances. Finding an intruder in her bedroom wouldn't get their relationship off to a very good start!

As he played with the device, he sifted through thoughts and notions that he'd gleaned from Lois. She was vexed with her little computer, and vexed with herself over it. Out here, far from so-called civilisation, there was no way for her to connect it to the great web of energy lines she called 'the internet'. It needed something called 'wi-fi' to become a part of that matrix.

Robin smiled. It was simply a node that was required, a nexus that would focus yet another pattern of force. Swooping down, he caught up a big handful of dust and compressed it tightly in his palm.

A moment later, he looked down at a small gleaming lozenge shape that pulsed softly in the dim light of the cabin.

His kind weren't called magical for nothing, he thought

wryly, as he attached the little 'hotspot' to the underside of the desk, well out of sight.

A gift, my Lois, he thought fondly. In return for the pleasure you gifted to me.

With one last longing glance at her, he disassociated and floated away.

'What the fuck?'

Staring at the screen, Lois forgot the shivering chill of the cabin. She forgot the fact that her feet were blocks of ice and she could only keep marginally warm by wrapping the entire duvet and a couple of extra blankets around her. She even, for the moment, forgot the raving hot erotic dream she'd had, that seemed to have burnt itself into her brain in lurid Technicolor detail.

She had a wi-fi connection where one was impossible.

'This is mad!' She refreshed the list again.

But there it was. She was logged into a connection designated 'oooooo' and the signal strength was excellent and the speed frankly phenomenal!

Absently rubbing her chilled toes together to increase their circulation, she went through all the settings, and everywhere, where there should have been strings of figures, she got 'oooooo'.

'This is mad,' she repeated, and then clicked on the icon for Google, which brought up the search engine instantaneously.

The inexplicable connection bugged her, but after a few fruitless minutes of diagnostics, she gave up.

What the hell, at least the IP address wasn't 666.666.666.6.

By the time she'd checked all her favourite pages, and even uploaded a bit of work to her testing server, the sun was high in the sky and its soft yellow rays were cascading in through the windows to warm up the cabin.

Thank heavens for an oil-fired heating system!

Lois was grateful for that small mercy as she took a shower in the tiny cubicle. It might be absolute rubbish at warming the rooms of the cabin, but at least it provided plenty of hot water.

She needed to be clean after last night. She'd felt icky and sticky and foxy after that dream. Masturbating in her sleep? Nothing wrong with it, really, nothing at all, but still sort of disturbing that she should be so horny, and not actually all that consciously aware of it.

Touching herself before she stepped beneath the spray, she'd been almost afraid she'd smell the odour of lavender on her fingers, and she'd been relieved – but irrationally disappointed – when all she'd smelt was plain old Lois-smell.

The bay was bright and blue when she stepped out on to the shared porch connecting the two cabins. Despite its convenience, the phantom wi-fi connection troubled her more than she cared to think about and, contrary to her every usual instinct and inclination, she'd turned off her laptop and decided to get out into the fresh air and do some 'nature'.

But why is it so bloody cold?

Despite the late-May sun, she was glad of her fleece and her boots as she trudged down the short packed-earth track and on to the beach. With just the two holiday cabins sharing it, the tiny bay was deserted. Lois had no idea where her neighbour was. She'd thought she'd heard him tramping about on the porch earlier, but now there was no sign of him. It would have been nice to make friends because, when she had managed to encounter him briefly once or twice, she'd rather fancied him. He was good-looking in a slightly heavy-set sort of way. But there was nothing doing. His responses had been barely monosyllabic, and a dark pall of 'touch me not' sadness seemed to envelop him.

'Poor bugger,' Lois observed as she stepped out on to the sand and made for the firmer stuff, closer to the water's edge, 'but you can't be happy if you don't give anyone a chance to cheer you up, can you?'

Yes, it would have been nice to forge a little holiday romance with her bay-mate if he'd been amenable, but maybe she didn't really need one. Not with the hyper-real sex dreams she was having! She was having plenty of erotic kink without any of the effort of the courtship dance. It was perfect. She could be as lazy as she liked, and still get satisfaction. Result!

Away from the pull of her computer, and the puzzle of the mysterious wi-fi connection, her experience of last night rushed in again to claim her.

Boy, had it been hot!

Dream Lover might have been chilly-skinned, but everything else about him was nothing short of incendiary. Just thinking about it all warmed her up inside her fleece and jeans, despite the spiteful bite of the nippy wind.

Dream Lover rose up before her in her imagination.

The tall dark powerful man out of nowhere was a classic romantic archetype, but where the hell had the image of odd eyes and gold-frosted hair come from? She had no explanation for those.

Not to mention the funky smell of lavender.

She seemed to smell it now, that rich sweet scent. And her body was growing warmer and warmer and warmer, surging and rousing with a rush of reborn lust.

The mysterious stranger advanced through her mind towards her and she felt so weak at the knees that she was forced to stagger to a scrappy outcrop of sand grass that had created a small dune at the edge of the beach.

Cowering on the little hump, she hugged her arms around her, shaken by the intensity of returned lust.

This is mad! Just mad! I'm going crazy!

For the second time in a morning, it was impossible to focus on reality. She was right back in her sweet, dangerous, nocturnal fantasy even while she scanned the bright clear sky above the bay.

A solitary bird was wheeling in the brisk salty air. It was dark, and appeared tiny so far aloft, but, as she watched it, there suddenly seemed a new purpose to its circling. It swooped, and seemed to be flying right at her, inducing a wild rush of Hitchcock-related panic.

Don't be crazy! How can it have seen you? And, if it has, why would it fly at you?

Yet still the bird, a gull of some kind, was closing, diving on dark wings, but revealing a strange mottling to its plumage as it neared. There were lighter speckles among the feathers around its head and its eyes, possibly white, possibly yellow . . . possibly gold.

Lois wanted to spring to her feet, and run back to her cabin, pack up her gear and just get the hell out of Dodge . . . but all she could do was sit and watch, locked in place as the bird began to circle again, slowly, maintaining its distance in the air over the water.

The leisurely repeated sweeps were hypnotic. Her fear ebbed, and the strange warmth in her body grew almost tropical.

And so, to her astonishment, did the low, deep, sweet welling of desire. Night and day coexisted somehow; she was in her dream, but also awake, in the sunshine.

Half her mind watched a bird. Half of it was back in the cabin, in the soft lamplight, watching Dream Lover approach, anticipating his touch.

'Oh please,' she whimpered, repeating her plea from last night.

She yearned for him, desire flickering deep in her groin for this vivid, but imaginary man. Her nipples tingled, her sex clenched on emptiness, the hunger to be filled so intense it brought tears to her eyes.

No real man had ever satisfied her like him.

Without thinking, she clasped her hand to her crotch, squeezing, trying to ease the ache. Pressing and massaging, she stared up at the strange dark gull, watching it execute a graceful diving spiral, almost in response to her action. Then she looked down again, observing her own pale hand against the stonewashed cloth of her jeans, and wishing it were another hand. One that was bigger and stronger and totally male.

Imagining him behind her, she moaned, longing for it to be his great body on which she leant while she took her pleasure, longing for his arms to enfold her and gentle her through the spasms.

'Oh! Oh, God!' Crying out, she came in a sudden rush, out of the blue, dimly hearing the gull shriek too, as if applauding her or even sharing her crisis.

Still clutching herself, she wrapped her other arm around her torso, hugging and rocking.

She didn't hear the heavy trudging footsteps until it was too late, and, when they did penetrate her haze, she looked straight up into the frowning face of her next-door neighbour.

'Are you all right?'

Hot blood flooded her cheeks. Oh, God, it must be obvious what she'd been doing, and his dour frown seemed to confirm her worst suspicions. His grim set expression spoilt what was really a very personable countenance. Any normal man would have been smirking at her, turned on by what she'd been up to ... but not him. He appeared unutterably depressed and disapproving.

'Yes, I'm fine.' Even though it was a lost cause, Lois snatched her hand from her crotch and stuffed it surreptitiously into her pocket. 'Thanks. Just got a bit of a stitch. It's going now. Thanks.'

'Sure?' His brow was still crumpled.

She had no idea whether he believed her but, if he didn't, her little exhibition obviously left him cold. His eyes were bleak and bitter, as if he were already weary of talking to her.

'Yes, thanks, I'm fine,' she parroted, her face flaming.

'I'll be getting along then. Be seeing you,' he concluded gruffly, and, as he turned and stomped away, Lois didn't know whether to be angry or relieved.

He thinks I'm some kind of sex maniac. He thinks I'm disgusting!

'Well, screw you!' she muttered, hurling the suppressed insult at the broad retreating back that had already reached the path and was rapidly receding from view. 'Any *normal* man would be all over me like a rash.'

Attracted by a flash of movement, she realised that the dark gull-like bird had landed only a couple of yards away from her and was regarding her solemnly, its peculiarly mottled head cocked on one side.

'Yeah, yeah, yeah, birdie! I know the guy's obviously got some serious problems and I should feel sorry for him . . .' She paused, her throat tight all of a sudden, and her eyes hot with unexpected tears. 'But I'm lonely. I'm used to being around people . . . but Sandy said I needed a break.' Bright avian eyes blinked and Lois blinked too. There was something very odd about this creature, and yet she couldn't stop herself rambling on to it. 'I don't know . . . when I saw him, I was sort of hopeful; it's a while since I, um, was with anybody, and I suppose I was hoping I'd get a bit of holiday nookie.'

The bird hopped sideways and flapped its wings making Lois jump.

'Oh fucking hell, I'm talking to birds now! I've had enough of this . . . I'm off to the shop to get some wine and I'm going to get drunk!'

She leapt to her feet and, as she did so, the bird took flight and seemed to hover for a moment, floating above her, before flapping vigorously and soaring away.

Lois shook her head. *I'm going nuts here . . . just another day or so, to keep Sandy quiet, and then I'm back to town, no messing.*

Wondering what kind of wine the small local shop stocked, and how much of it they had, she stomped off towards the path, her sandy footsteps blending with those of her neighbour.

3

'Why is it so bloody cold in here?'

Lois hugged the quilt around her, and took another swig of her wine. It was supposed to be spring but this accursed place felt like the depths of midwinter despite the underfloor heating. The cabin was far from a wretched hovel, with its electricity and plumbing and whatnot, but at the moment she might as well have been residing in a primitive mud hut for all the benefit the mod cons seemed to be providing.

Not the only thing around here that's primitive, she thought, scowling fiercely at her laptop, which sat on the small wooden table, dead as a doornail. The bloody thing had insisted on repeatedly crashing all day, which was doubly frustrating now she'd mysteriously gained a wireless broadband connection. She could probably fix it, but it would take some troubleshooting, and she didn't feel like tackling it in this perpetual depressing cold.

Casting one last fulminating glance at the recalcitrant computer, she set aside her drink but not her quilt, padded over to the wood-burning stove and, using an old potholder to open the front door panel, she peeped inside.

Goddamnit to hell!

The bloody thing was burning down and there were no more logs chopped. The stove was the only thing that seemed to be keeping the room above Antarctic temperatures.

The logical thing would be to turn in, just throw all her clothes and all the available blankets over the top of herself and sleep. But she was restless. Feverish inside, despite the cold. She wanted to stay awake because she had the strangest idea that she needed to.

Nothing in the log basket. Not a splinter.

Was it worth nipping out the back and chopping some wood? Normally she would have copped out and waited until morning, but that funky sense of expectation – and the glasses of wine she'd drunk – made her grit her teeth and pull on her jeans and fleece over her jersey shorts and top. After stuffing her feet into her slippers, she shuffled outside.

The second thoughts kicked in when she reached the hard standing at the back of the cabin, where the chopping block stood. The high full moon made the night brilliant, almost unearthly, but was it really a good idea to start chopping wood at this hour, especially when you'd been drinking and you were probably the world's worst survivalist to start with?

'Just one or two, Lois.' She opened the woodshed that contained the boiler, the wood ... and the axe.

Third thoughts halted her once she had a log on the block, but dragging in a deep breath she lifted the axe and aimed as best she could.

And missed, sending the lethal tool sliding erratically sideways across the chopping surface.

Another blow resulted in a quarter-inch sliver off the edge of the log.

The third missed again.

'Oh, bloody fucking hell!'

Her profanity assaulted the beautiful night, and echoed back at her from the surrounding woodlands that backed on to the rear of the cabin.

'Can I be of any help?' enquired a soft amused male voice that seemed to emanate unexpectedly from somewhere above her.

What the hell?

Flinging the axe across the hard standing, safely clear of her feet, Lois looked up towards the moonlight sky.

There was a man crouched on the roof of the woodshed.

Oh, God!

She staggered, not even knowing whether she'd spoken aloud or not, and as she tumbled backwards, then landed hard on her bottom, she observed the most astonishing phenomenon play out in slow motion.

The crouching man was big and clad all in black and, as he launched himself from the woodshed roof and jumped down, his long black coat billowed and flapped like the wings of a great dark bird. His descent seemed to take an age, although she knew it was only in her mind, and, when he touched down, he seemed to land as lightly as if he'd been fashioned from thistledown.

'Are you all right, my dear?' The stranger swooped down in a low crouch again, and reached out to touch her.

Lois scuttled away from him, terrified for any number of reasons.

Do I know you?

To her astonishment, and shivering excitement, she realised that she did.

The descending man was also Dream Lover!

The same broad intelligent face. The same dark clothing. Dear God, the same astonishing gold-tipped hair ... Dazzled, she hardly dared look too closely at him, but she would have put good money on the fact that his eyes were odd too.

In the flesh, so to speak, and in reality, he was quite, quite beautiful. Big, in the sense of very tall, and built like the proverbial, but glorious with it.

His great head tilted on one side; he was obviously waiting for her answer, but the sheer impossibility of his presence had struck her dumb.

Her mouth opened, but nothing came out.

How the hell can you be here?

The words were silent, and she blinked at him, expecting him to disappear and for her to be back in the cottage, huddled beneath the covers and dragging herself out of sleep with her hand in her knickers.

But a second later, his gentle but firm hold on her arm was real. And so was the way he effortlessly helped her to her feet.

'Are you all right?' he repeated softly, and, now that she managed to look into his eyes, her suspicions were confirmed.

One was the colour of fire-lit brandy, the other a brilliant aquamarine blue.

'Um ... yes, I'm fine,' she lied. 'Thank you.'

He was gorgeous, and seemed benign, but still her terror made her lash out.

'At least I would be if you hadn't given me such a shock. What the hell were you doing up there? And who are you for that matter? Skulking around here at the dead of night on people's roofs.'

His face split with a wide personable smile that exhibited a set of brilliant, immaculately even and possibly quite *sharp* teeth. In the moment before he spoke, notions of vampires and werewolves flitted disquietingly through Lois's mind. She loved a horror fantasy as much as the next person, but, until now, that was all they were ... just fantasies and stories.

Until now ...

'I'm sorry, that was rather bad of me, wasn't it?' He nodded in the general direction of the woodshed roof. 'But there's such a good view up there, and I was concerned for your safety. Who knows what might be lurking in the forest at this time of night?'

Did he just wink then?

'Well, it's very kind of you to be concerned, whoever you are, but I think I can manage to look after myself, thank you very much.'

'Well, you weren't doing too well at chopping your own wood, were you?' He cocked his head towards her pathetic splinters and the axe lying at the edge of the woods where she'd flung it. 'Would you like some help?'

With what? her stirring libido suddenly prompted. Dream Lover was even more of a dish standing in front of her, and she was reminded alarmingly of her confession to the bird that morning. She *was* lonely. And it *was* a long time since she'd had the pleasure of a man.

Dream Lover looked as if he was more than enough man for any woman, and if there were the slightest chance that he performed as well in reality as he had in her fantasy . . . Well, wouldn't it be worth taking a chance?

Even so, putting a sharp and heavy axe into the hand of someone who might be a pervert or a stalker, and who peeped at women from roofs was tantamount to booking a slot on *Crimewatch* in advance, wasn't it?

I should run into the cabin and lock the door. Now.

But, instead, she heard herself saying, 'Well, yes, I suppose so. A few logs would be great, if it's not too much trouble?'

Dream Lover beamed, which did weird things to her knee joints, and even weirder, hotter things between her legs. He really did have the most sumptuous white smile.

'Not at all.' Still smiling, he held out a large capable-looking hand. 'And my name is Robin. What's yours?'

'Er, Lois . . . and I'm – I'm pleased to meet you.'

She put her small hand in his big one and only just managed to keep herself from trembling.

His skin was cool and smooth. Just like in the dream. And his lips were cool too. Deliciously cool and firm and supple as he drew her fingers up to them and pressed a light kiss upon her trembling skin.

'And I'm very pleased to meet you, Lois,' he said crisply, releasing her hand, giving her a little nod, before striding away to retrieve the axe. 'Now how much chopped wood do you need?'

'Oh, just enough for tonight, really. That'd be great.'

He nodded again as if she'd said something very wise and sensible, then, after setting the axe on the block, he shed his voluminous black coat.

And then his T-shirt . . .

Dear heaven, what a bod!

Lois watched entranced as Robin hefted the first log on to the block and began to splice and dice it like an expert woodsman. His torso was like wood too, honeyed gold wood, polished and gleaming in the brilliant moonlight, every bit as ripped as that of his dream counterpart and just as toffee-golden.

His muscles flexed and bunched as he worked, like visual poetry.

This is crazy . . . I just dreamt him up . . . Why is he actually here ?

But there was no denying that Robin was here. The rate at which he was racking up the firewood proved that. Within a few minutes there was a stack big enough to heat twenty cabins.

'Thanks ever so much. That's fabulous!' That prime body was making her gush like a giddy teenager, and she could feel her face getting hot as he straightened up and smiled at her again, axe still in hand. 'I . . . er . . . would you like to come in for a glass of wine or something?'

His strange eyes twinkled at her, almost as if he'd known she was going to say that. Unease fluttered through her, but faced with his beautiful smile – and his beautiful body – she squashed it, embracing the risks.

'Why that would be splendid, Lois,' he said roundly, setting down the axe and pushing his fingers through his crisp gold-tipped hair, 'Thank you, I would be delighted to share a glass of wine with you.'

Oh, his eyes, his mouth, his whole body, even . . . They were all saying how much more than wine it was he hoped to share.

'Cool.' Muttering, Lois scooted for the cabin door, too dazzled to be able to look at him any more. She heard him scoop up his clothes and an armful of firewood and follow her, yet strangely it was the rustle of his leather coat against the wood that marked his progress, not his footsteps.

What is it with him? He barely seems to touch the ground and yet he's such a great big hunk.

Swinging open the door, she wondered just what kind of madwoman she was being. But it was too late. Robin was right behind her and already inside.

For a log cabin, Sandy's hideaway was spacious, and Lois had been favourably surprised on arrival, having expected a dismal shack. But now, however, it felt as if she were in a rustic doll's house, complete with miniature furniture. The kitchen area, the cosy fireside with two comfy armchairs, and the large bed and chest of drawers at the other end of the long room were all dwarfed by the massive man who strode forwards and flung his dark coat and T-shirt across the back of a chair.

Still stripped to the waist, Robin jammed a couple of decent-sized logs into the stove, and then stacked the rest of them in the wood basket. With the age-old seriousness of 'man who make fire', he plied the poker expertly and coaxed the flames. Within seconds the freezing room became a tropical paradise. In fact, far more so than it had a logical right to be.

Stop standing around like a lemon just staring at him! Say something, woman!

But all she could manage to do was stare ... at a set of splendid pecs, a narrow waist and a luscious and suggestively packed crotch.

Robin beamed back at her as if he knew that before the night was out they'd be sleeping together.

'Er, would you like a shower or something ... with all that chopping and flinging wood about?'

She half expected him to laugh, but he didn't.

'Of course, that's a wonderful idea. Thank you.' Before she could stop him, he'd taken off his boots and kicked them away across the room. The next moment, he was at his belt and the zip of his jeans and then stepped out of them.

Lois's jaw dropped. It was a cliché, but she almost had to pick it up off the floor.

Robin wasn't a wearer of socks or underwear, it seemed. He stood there unperturbed, displaying his majestic male equipment as if it were perfectly normal to fling off his clothes in front of a woman he'd met just minutes ago.

'Through there?' He gestured gracefully towards the door to the cabin's small shower room.

'Um ... yes.' Lois's tongue froze and she swallowed. Hard. Somehow she was incapable of raising her eyes above his waist level.

He was so big ... and he was actually getting bigger as she watched.

'Thank you, I won't be but a few moments.' Robin's smile was calm, but there was a cheeky confidence in his odd eyes. He was totally aware of the effect he was having on her and, as he strode fluidly towards the bathroom in long loping strides, he had the gall to lightly frisk himself and look back to make sure that she was watching.

'What am I doing? What am I doing?'

Lois ran for the wine bottle on the table and poured a large measure into her glass. 'What am I doing?' she repeated, cradling it in both her hands like a magical chalice, hoping that the Merlot would wash away the last of her doubts and her qualms about Robin.

He's just bloody glorious!

She drank a few mouthfuls of the rich red wine, trying to concentrate on the positives of having the best-looking and best-built man she'd met in years tucked away with her in this cabin miles from anywhere. At the same time, she tried to dismiss the fact that there were some things that were undeniably strange about him.

Not bad. Just weird . . . very weird.

As the water sluiced down in the room beyond, Lois had a feeling that her new friend had been neither dirty nor sweaty. She'd noticed no odour of work-induced perspiration as he'd passed her, and there was no hint of it now, as she picked up his clothing and couldn't resist sniffing it.

What she did smell set her trembling and grabbing for her wineglass again.

Flowers again, and predominantly lavender.

Lois looked at her bag, her scattered clothes. There were only a few toilet items in the shower room. She could be out of here, in her car and on the road before he had finished showering.

But, almost before she calculated her chances, the water stopped, and she knew she wouldn't have gone anyway. Instead, she wriggled out of her jeans and fleece, then dived across to the mirror over the chest of drawers and frowned into it. The image disheartened her. Her tufted hair, her grungy old sleep shorts and top, and the make-up-free ordinariness of her staring wide-eyed face were less than alluring. She pushed at a few curls, pinched her cheeks to give them some colour and bit her lips, but it was already too late.

The shower room door swung open and Robin walked into the room. He was still nude and casually towelling at his hair.

Lois gasped, aware that this was becoming a habit in this strange man's presence. His naked body was sublime, gleaming and fresh from the shower, and he had no qualms whatsoever about showing it to her. The only problem was that she was having trouble forming coherent thoughts, much less sophisticated adult conversation, with all that male comeliness on show.

'Perhaps I could have that glass of wine now?' Robin let his towel drop around his shoulders, but made no attempt to cover his mighty nether regions.

'Yes. Yes, of course.' Lois scooted for the wooden kitchen table, poured out a glass of red for Robin and surreptitiously topped up her own.

If I'm going to behave as if I'm too stupid to live, I might as well use the booze as my excuse.

Turning, she discovered that Robin had settled into one of the easy chairs by the fire, and the towel lay abandoned on the floor. Lois smiled and felt strangely reassured. He might be her literal Dream Lover right out of her fantasies, but in term of household sloppiness he was a very normal man. She handed him his glass, swept up the towel and placed it over the little drying rack that stood against the wall.

'Oops! Sorry.' Robin's grin said he wasn't sorry at all, cheeky sod.

Lois let herself down carefully into the other seat, still tongue-tied and increasingly aware that her shorts and her little buttoned top weren't a particularly substantial covering. Of course, if she'd been in her right mind, she would've put her robe back on, but she was in her entirely wrong mind. All she could do was sit, frozen in place, unable to do anything but gaze and goggle at the man sitting opposite her.

His long limbs were stretched out like those of a classical sculpture, and his superb body appeared entirely too big for the modest chair. He looked comfortable though, leaning back into the upholstery, his peculiar eyes closed as if he were dozing.

Great! Just come in, make yourself at home and flaunt your fabulous tackle at me . . . and then fall asleep.

Robin's eyes flicked open. 'Does my nakedness bother you? Shall I put my clothes back on again?'

Yes, put them on and go, because I'm scared shitless of you!

No, stay and never wear a stitch again . . . because it'll break my heart if you cover all that gorgeousness up!

'No, not all. If you're comfortable, that's fine by me.'

Robin nodded and lifted his glass in salute. 'To you, Lois, I'm glad I found you.'

Lois gulped at her own wine, alarmed. 'What on earth does that mean?' she demanded, a droplet of Merlot sneaking down her chin and requiring a swift swipe of the hand.

Lashes that were far too long and pretty for a man with such a large cock swept down, giving him an almost shame-faced look. 'I'm afraid I've been watching you, Lois.' He toyed with his glass, one moment watching the flames from the little stove through it, the next, looking at her. 'You might say I've become enchanted by you. You're very beautiful and I like beautiful things.'

Lois laughed out loud. Oh great, she'd got a stalker with a nice line in compliments now.

'I think you need your eyes testing, Robin. I look like a bag lady tonight, and I haven't been looking all that great since I got here. I'm on holiday, and as there's no talent around – or there didn't seem to be at first – I haven't been making an effort.'

'Talent?'

'Men. Crumpet. Male totty . . . you know?'

She wasn't sure at first whether he did know, but then he smiled and looked pleased with himself. Obviously he was supremely confident that *he* was totty.

And the way his penis was growing said the same too.

'But you have a neighbour. What about him? Do you not like the look of him?'

'Well, he's all right, but he seems a bit solitary. He doesn't seem to be interested in company.'

Robin looked serious for a moment, his face very pure and solemn. 'Indeed, he is a very unhappy man. A pall of great sadness hangs over him.'

Lois narrowed her eyes. Had he been watching the neighbour too?

Robin shrugged. 'But you said as much yourself.'

What? What the fuck? Can you read my mind?

Robin simply smiled and lounged even more languidly in his chair, one hand loosely cradling his wineglass, the other spread upon his thigh, close to his cock, almost as if he wanted to draw her attention to its gathering might as a diversion.

His beautiful lashes fluttered down again, and he appeared to be dozing.

What the hell was happening? Could he read her thoughts? Again and again the mantra circled in her head: *Who are you? Who are you? What are you?*

But she got no answer from the silent relaxed man.

'I dreamt about you last night.'

The words were out before she could stop herself, and Robin's peculiar bi-coloured eyes snapped open again, instantly flashing their two brilliant hues.

'Did you know that? I dreamt about you,' she rushed on, panicking. 'How can I have dreamt about you when I just met you not half an hour ago? It doesn't make sense!'

Without warning, Robin set his glass aside and slid out of his chair and on to his knees. His cock bounced from side to side as he shuffled across the patchwork rug until he was kneeling in front of her, his great head tilted to one side a little, his gaze questioning and hypnotic.

Compulsively, Lois drank some wine, almost on autopilot, but the second she took the glass from her lips Robin reached for it, gently prised it from her fingers and set it aside. Still kneeling in front of her, he took her small warm hands in his much larger cooler ones.

'The woods and the sea are magical places, Lois, and this cabin is right at the nexus of both their influences.' He squeezed her fingers very lightly, as if they were crystal and he didn't want to damage them. 'It's hardly surprising that unusual things happen here. What you dreamt last night might have been a part of the future seeping back into the present.'

'That's ridiculous!'

But she was shaking. Could she do that? Could she want that? It was all very well to imagine kinky things in fantasies, but for real? That was another story. Especially with a man she barely knew.

'The world is strange, Lois,' he murmured cryptically, his thumbs circling her palms in a light soothing caress that seemed to impact all over her body ... especially between her legs. She suppressed an intense urge to squirm, experiencing his innocent touch deep in her sex. But then the look in his peculiar eyes said that he knew exactly what she was feeling.

'Your dream ... was it pleasant?' With a slow smile, he lowered his head, looking up at her from beneath his sumptuous lashes, and then brought first one, then the other of her hands to his lips for a kiss.

'I . . . er, yes, sort of. But it was strange . . . not something that could really happen.'

The touch of his lips was cool fire. She was shaking hard now, and she couldn't tell whether it was fear, confusion or extreme lust. Or a combination of all three.

'Are you sure?'

'I don't know! I don't know!' she almost cried.

He shuffled closer, reached for her, and this time brought her mouth to his in a delicate gentling kiss.

'What happened in your dream?' His words were like a whisper of perfumed air against her cheek and her ear.

Furious blood flushed her face as she remembered the game, and her body bound and open and vulnerable to him, hungering for him as it did now.

She tried to turn away from him, but he held her firm, his mouth against her hair.

'I can't! I can't say . . .'

But *his* lips were moving, and she realised he was murmuring softly, describing the fantasy.

'How do you know these things? How do you know? It's impossible for you to know what I dreamt . . .'

'Hush, my dearest.' He kissed her jaw, and then her throat. 'Just call it instinct, intuition . . . My dream, maybe, just as much as yours.'

'But I'm scared! I don't know if I want to do those things,' she protested, her heart fluttering in her chest like a wild bird, the strange gull maybe, in her chest. 'I don't know if I'd ever really want to do something like that.'

Taking her face between his large smooth hands, he forced her to look at him, straight into the disorientating beauty of his eyes.

'Then we can do other things, Lois, anything you like. Just say the word.'

'I d-don't know what the word is.'

'Why it's "yes", of course, isn't it?'

And then he kissed the whispered answer right from her lips.

4

His mouth was tender and flexible, and his cool tongue naughty and daring as it delicately pressed for entrance. Her face was cradled in his long elegant hands and there was no way to escape the kiss even if she'd wanted to.

And oh, his taste was so sweet! She'd read of kisses being described as delicious, but Robin's really were. The flavour of wildflower honey seemed to fill her mouth along with his tongue, the taste and scent of it as intoxicating as the sensuous exploration. Her hands fluttered wildly, and then she threw her arms around his large muscular body, embracing his magnificent back as she surrendered to his kiss.

Dimly, a far way back in her mind, she recognised that she could probably be accused of being wilfully stupid, encouraging this strangest of strangers to kiss her, touch her and much, much more. But she was too ensorcelled to do anything but silence the voice of dissent and hold on to him.

The kiss went on a long, long time, their tongues flickering around one another, teasing, challenging and tasting. Other delightful sensations impinged on her consciousness too.

The warmth of the fire on her skin was a counterpoint to the strange living chill of Robin's body. The contrast was thrilling. He seemed to be able to sear her with skin and flesh that had the silky hardness of polished marble, and her hands couldn't seem to explore it fast enough. Her fingertips roved feverishly over his shoulders, his back and his torso.

Eventually, he freed her mouth and sat back on his heels,

just looking at her. His odd eyes glittered with hunger, with devilment, and the flickering light from the fire danced like magic dust over his fast-drying gold-tipped hair.

'You are beautiful,' he said, stealing the exact words she'd been going to utter away from her.

Rapt as she was, Lois found herself compelled to laugh. 'And you're crazy! Have you really looked at me? I'm a mess. I look like a complete fright. My hair's all over the place, my skin is all pale and pasty, and these are probably the nastiest old clothes in my possession.'

He smiled at her and shrugged his big shoulders and silently mimed the word 'Nonsense'.

'Well, I think you ought to get those weird eyes of yours tested then!'

'You're beautiful,' he repeated, a small mild smile playing around his sensual lips. 'You're beautiful and I want to give you pleasure.'

Oh, God, I want you to give it me too!

But she could no longer speak because he came forwards again, and began kissing her neck, then the crook of her shoulder, then her collarbone and chest where her granddad T-shirt was unbuttoned. His hands rested on her thighs as his lips nibbled and travelled.

She looked down at his magical hair, and the smooth planes of his back. Tentatively she touched his satiny skin. The delicate way he was mouthing her almost made her want to swoon, especially when he touched her with the tip of his tongue.

Immediately, her sex surged, as if imagining the sensation of that determined little serpent flickering against the sensitive bud of her clitoris. Unable to prevent herself, the very thought made her groan.

Robin's gilded head shot up and he grinned at her.

Oh, dear Lord, he can read my mind!

Big hands reached for her top, deftly opening it to reveal her breasts. Lois gasped. Her nipples were already puckered and tight. The air wasn't cold, but the contrast between concealment and exposure was a little shock.

Robin swooped in with hands and mouth, his lips settling on one breast, while he cradled his fingers around her curves, flexing them lightly to hold her.

His cool tongue moved as it had in her mouth, darting, swirling, tickle-tasting. Lois kicked with pleasure, her bare feet sliding against his thighs, his shins. Her hips started to weave. She was out of control, grabbing on to the arms of the chair for stability.

He gave her breast a long hard suck and she wailed, shooting almost to the point of orgasm. He'd done that in the dream, she remembered hazily, fondled her breast and brought her to pleasure when it shouldn't have been possible.

But suddenly she wanted more, more. She wanted what she'd had in her dream. His cock inside her as he thrust, his strong hips swinging to get in deeper than deep.

She tried to tell him. She tried to rise. But he quelled her, and kept her in her seat. His fingers plucked at the elastic of her shorts, his eyes locking on hers, as if asking permission to remove them.

Oh yes! Go on! Yes!

Efficiently he pulled off her shorts and flung them away, baring her crotch to his gaze in the firelight. A moment later, his spread fingers settled on her belly, pressing gently, thumb stroking. Making a frame for her navel, he dipped his pointed tongue into it.

A sharp, almost painful jolt of sensation shot through her, right to her core. Again, she moaned, even closer to the edge. Her bare feet scrabbled against him again, and her knuckles went white where she gouged at the chair arm. Her hips wafted upwards as if they were inviting him of their own accord to go further.

He placed a slow precise kiss on her lower belly, just at the edge of her pubic bush.

If only I'd waxed, she thought, even though subliminally she knew he didn't give a hoot whether she was jungle-hairy, trimmed or even shaven. Who was to know she'd literally meet the man of her dreams out here in this remote little hideaway. Even her neighbour had been a surprise when she'd encountered him.

'Oh yes, oh yes . . .' he murmured softly, lifting his face a moment, and flashing her a hot look, before diving down again. As his mouth moved ever closer to its target, his capable hands slid beneath her buttocks to cup and lift her.

Like one cat greeting another, he lightly rubbed his cheeks and his chin and his closed mouth against the soft hair between her legs, his nostrils flaring as he drew in her odour. Frustrated by the lightness of the contact, Lois shuffled and stirred, trying to press herself against his face, all the time wishing that she was the one who'd just taken a shower. And yet, and even more catlike, Robin seemed to purr with satisfaction at the smell of her sex and his lashes fluttered like fans as he breathed her in.

'Delicious,' he whispered, just touching his tongue against the soft flossiness and teasing it. Then his juicy mouth curved into a devilish grin and, supporting her bottom on one hand, he positioned her leg over his shoulder. Deftly swapping hands, he repeated the process with the other, and then took hold of her bottom again to bring her crotch right to his face.

With his lips just inches from her, he paused again, as if surveying the landscape of her sex in intimate detail. With her thighs stretched around his head, she was open to him, moist and revealed in a way that even surpassed her dream. The sensation of being studied was like a caress in itself. Stirring and moaning, she reached back and grasped the chair back behind her to create a base from which to push herself against him.

She wanted to writhe. She wanted to buck about. She didn't dare look down at him, crouched and naked, his face between her thighs.

But she did.

Robin was staring at her sex. His eyes were intent with knowing expectancy, and he was smiling like a demon. The fine gold tipping of his dark hair was almost shooting sparks and, as she watched, he ran his tongue lightly over his lips as if preparing them to savour her flesh.

And then he looked up. Right into her eyes. His own were flashing with a brilliant eldritch light that owed nothing to reflections from the fire or the lamps. Something moved and danced in those duo-coloured depths, something not of this world. Lois gasped, riding high on a silvery strand of terror that only increased her arousal.

But, before she could process it, he plunged in – and she forgot it.

5

The touch of his tongue brought a sharp cry to her lips. She was so ready for it, yet still he surprised her. With cool, delicate precision, he explored her, he caressed her. Flicking his tongue-tip lightly over her slippery folds, tasting and teasing and pleasuring as he went.

The first contact with her clitoris made her drum her heels on his bare back, and her torso arch, pressing her opened sex closer to his face. The second contact made her howl like a woodland animal as he furled his tongue to a silky point and batted it to and fro over the sensitive little button.

The third contact, a firm assertive press with no hesitation or mercy, made her come, shouting and kicking at once.

She couldn't keep still. She twisted like an electrified eel, her muscles taut and her nails gouging the upholstery of the chair back. But still he held her, feasting and lapping at her sex while she struggled, her bottom a foot off the chair and cradled in his hands.

When he sucked her clit, she came again, and his name, wrought by her lips, filled the cabin in a ringing shout of triumph.

And then, it was like being in the dream again. Well, almost . . . Her consciousness wavered, her mind knocked sideways by the intense pleasure, and she blinked and blinked again, as she peered down the length of her own trembling body.

Robin seemed to be clothed in gold, his skin dazzling, and his outline mutable, misty and shifting. She opened her mouth to exclaim in fear and wonder, but then her perceptions shifted again, dropping back into place, and all she saw was the most handsome piece of flesh-and-blood male gorgeousness she'd ever seen, looking up at her, grinning at her across the humid planes of her abdomen, his red mouth shimmering with the moisture from her sex.

Gently, he let her down into the seat again, and slid her thighs from off his shoulders, setting her feet on the floor again. Lois released her death-grip on the back of the armchair and slumped against the upholstery as if she'd had every molecule of air in her lungs knocked out of her.

Kneeling up, Robin loomed over her. He touched her face, stroking it with utmost tenderness, smoothing her sweaty hair away from her brow. He seemed to be soothing her as if she'd endured some stringent ordeal, or suffered something terrible and gruelling on his behalf, and his beautiful eyes were solicitous.

'All right now?' he whispered, taking her hand and bringing it to his lips.

Lois had to laugh, and Robin beamed at her, laughter in his face too.

'Bloody fantastic, thanks to you!' she exclaimed, sitting up, flinging her arm around his shoulder and pulling him close to her for a proper kiss.

He accepted it, still smiling and looking disgustingly pleased with himself.

'I don't know where you learnt to do that, but, man, you are a genius!'

'Sheer instinct, my dearest,' he murmured, dropping an outrageous wink, then stealing another kiss as he drew her by the arms on to the rug in front of the stove.

The wooden floorboards were hard beneath them, and the old-fashioned rag-rug was bumpy beneath her bottom, but what were minor discomforts like that when you were in the arms of a beautiful magical man who'd just given you the best head you'd had in your entire life? It seemed perfectly natural to coil her arms around Robin and continue the kiss where they'd left off.

Only this time he was lying half over her, his body imposing itself on hers, but not weighing her down. As their tongues duelled, she savoured the sweet taste of his mouth, blended with the salty contrast of her own lingering flavour. His skin was silky smooth as it moved against hers, and the sliding contact set strange thoughts circling and flitting around her mind.

He's not normal. He's so not normal . . .

The fact that he was able to drape himself across her and she barely felt his weight just didn't make sense. His body had great size and substance, but seemed to lack the commensurate pounds and ounces. As he scooped his hands beneath her and held her to him, pressing her hard against a truly mighty erection, she seemed to see and hear him leap down from the woodshed roof again. He'd almost floated to earth. How could that happen? It defied all logic.

And then there was the undoubted mind-reading.

Maybe he's just very empathetic, she thought, sliding her hands over his back and his tight male bottom, loving the feel of his skin and its peculiar lack of heat.

And that's another thing!

How could he feel cool, yet warm her up. It wasn't only the stove that was heating her. Her skin seemed to glow wherever Robin touched her – which was just about everywhere – and yet the temperature of his own skin seemed far lower than that of a normal person.

I should be afraid. I should be very afraid . . . And yet I'm not.

No, the only feelings she experienced as Robin worked his hips, and rubbed his glorious cock against her were wonder, delight and pure desire.

Oh, how I want you!

The thought echoed in her mind. Really echoed. She'd actually heard it twice, the two versions very closely overlaid, Robin's voice on hers.

Without too much effort, she placed her hand on his chest and compelled him to break the kiss and back up a little, so she could look up at him.

His unusual eyes were dark, yet brilliant with desire, and with unfathomable complexity. She sensed great emotion in him, a turbulent well of confused feelings. His eyes were full of a perplexed affection, and warmth, and a poignant yearning.

Oh baby!

Enormous tenderness roiled inside her. She didn't know how, but she knew he was seeking something. Searching . . . reaching out for more than just sex. He was magnificent. Competent. He knew just how to stir her and to pleasure her, but beneath that skill lay innocence and longing.

Whatever it is . . . take it! Take it from me!

Her thought seemed to galvanise him, and his body surged against her, pushing at her with more force. And this time the hardness of the floor did make an impact.

She placed her hand on his chest, halting him. 'Shall we get into bed for this? It'll be much more comfy. The floor's a bit hard.'

Robin stared down at her, and in his face she saw gratitude and a glow of something ineffably sweet. For a moment, she thought he might speak but, instead, he just kissed her forehead, then slid off her, came up on his knees and scooped her effortlessly up into his arms. She coiled her own arms around his neck as he strode lightly to the bed and set her down on it. A moment later, he'd whisked up the quilt from under her, slid his body next to hers, and then settled the quilt back down over them like a soft cocoon of intimacy.

This wasn't at all like her fantasy. It wasn't exotic or kinky, but in many ways it was much, much better. She felt closer to Robin than to any man, ever, in her life. For a moment he just stared at her again, his head next to hers on the pillow, and she read questions in his eyes. She didn't know what they were, but she sensed she held the answers.

Then they were kissing again, their mouths fused as he passively allowed her hands to travel and fondle.

His body was beautiful to her touch, and that much was still part of her fantasy. No common man could be this perfect, this muscled and smooth. She ran her fingertips over his back, his waist, his bottom – all as splendid and cool as living alabaster. When he adjusted the tilt of his hips, she slid her hand naturally to his cock.

Dear God Almighty, he was big! And he felt bigger now than ever. It was as if his very flesh had read her desires and reformed to comply with them. She'd always longed to be with a really big man.

He let out a soft huff of encouragement as she handled and explored him, tracing the veins of his shaft and the flared shape of his tip. From what she could tell, he was circumcised, and a thin slippery fluid was seeping silkily from his love-eye.

Why did it not surprise her that the feel of it was cool?

There was a lot of it too and, even if she'd not been running wet between her own legs, Robin's slipperiness would have been more than adequate lubrication for his entry . . .

As if that notion somehow shattered his passivity, Robin rolled towards her, then over her, pinning her effortlessly on her back. Between her thighs, his great penis nestled and then pushed.

Condom!

The word rang in her mind like a bell, and, still poised, Robin came up on his elbows and looked down at her. His gold-frosted hair glinted like a halo in the soft light from the lamps, and his eyes were steady, and almost curious.

'You have nothing to fear from me, dearest Lois,' he said, his voice ringing oddly, almost like a hypnotist's.

The cynical man-suspicious Lois of old would have replied, 'Is that a fact?' but the Lois of now, cuddled in the magic womb of the duvet and the heat that wasn't of Robin, and yet came from him, believed him utterly.

Some ancient, primal, unexplainable knowledge in the pit of her brain told her unequivocally that Robin hailed from somewhere that was outside the fear of disease. He had no connection with the world of pain and infection and, if he could make her pregnant, so be it. She suddenly even wanted that despite the fact she'd never ever wanted it before.

She stared back up at him, and thought, with all her power. *This is a dream again, isn't it?*

Robin's beautiful mouth curved in a teasing smile. 'Does this feel like a dream to you?'

He pressed harder, and she could feel the broad silky tip of his penis nudging its way imperiously between her sex-lips, then sliding with unerring accuracy right to her very entrance.

Lois shook violently, her body almost vibrating with a befuddling concoction of pure fear and a lust and desire to be filled so intense it made her push back against him and tilt her hips to aid his entrance.

He can read my mind! He really can!

But then fear, uncertainty and the ability to question were all subsumed in the wild overload of sensation. Robin slid into her, slowly, slowly, stretching her as he went, and the feeling of being full, right to the brim with solid male flesh, drove out all extraneous thoughts from her mind as if by main force.

Sublime penetration eradicated all doubt, and Robin settled in as if her body was his home.

As he rocked his hips, and sealed the fit, his voice was a soft zephyr in her ear. 'Are you all right, my love? Are you comfortable? I don't want to hurt you.'

'Don't worry,' she murmured back at him, hitching her own pelvis, trying to get closer and tighter with him, even though it probably wasn't possible. She smiled too, suddenly touched by his question. He was just trying to ease her mind, she knew that. Given what he could do, and what he could sense, there was no way he didn't know already that his cock felt incredible inside her.

And then he began to kiss her, his mouth like lavender honey as he thrust and thrust smoothly inside her. It was like being part of some divine, reciprocal engine, and each movement, each long, delicious plunge, seemed to make contact with a new pleasure receptor in her depths.

She moaned into his mouth with each smooth, deep shove, sipping at his sweetness as the interior stretching did insane things to her clit. His every movement created a divine tugging sensation in the tiny sensitive organ, and on the profound instroke his pubic bone seemed to knock against it. She wriggled to adjust the angle of their bodies for even greater perfection, but still Robin kept up his rhythm and momentum.

How can he do this? she questioned dimly, her entire body throbbing, pulsating, teetering on the brink of some great starburst of pleasure. *He barely weighs anything, yet he has this power, this force?*

A heartbeat later, there were no more questions, no more thoughts, no more conscious analysis of any kind.

Just pure sensation as her body sparked and heart and soul flew upwards, borne aloft on a giant wave of loving pleasure.

I love you . . . I love you . . . I love you . . .

She heard the words like bells as she soared among the stars, but for the life of her she couldn't have specified who'd said them.

6

Sitting up, letting the quilt slide from his shoulders, Robin gazed down at the sleeping woman at his side.

His human fingers tingled with the intense need to touch her again, and in his heart, also temporarily human, emotion surged.

How beautiful she was with her sex-tousled hair and her flushed cheeks. Her body was warm against his, radiating heat and life. He ached to be able to stay and sleep with her in his arms but, even during this special and almost finished month, he could only be the Robin she knew for a limited period. He could only touch, and feel, and experience this depth of passion for a couple of hours, or a little more, after which he was compelled to disassociate.

And he didn't want to do that in front of Lois.

But just how much would it faze her though?

She was brave, bold and curious. From her thoughts, he knew she was aware that he wasn't quite what he seemed. Yet still she embraced him and gave herself to him.

And, for that, I love you.

And he loved her even, he sensed, in his discarnate form, where emotions were fainter, rarefied and far less intense. When May was over, he might still feel the ache of loss.

She was compassionate too. His fingertips hovered a centimetre above her lips, her cheek and then her brow. He sensed the sympathy she felt for her surly neighbour, who had not been polite to her. She'd seen through the man's bluffness to the sad state of his heart.

Would you feel sorry for me?

His ersatz heart twisted with anguish, as he glanced towards her watch on the bedside cabinet, and heard its tick, tick, tick like a giant tolling bell. His sharp vision noted again the date function.

Tomorrow was the last day of May. The last day of his approximate humanity. How he wished that she'd arrived here on the first of the month.

As if affected by the proximity of the month's end, his form began to waver, so he rose from the bed and gathered his clothes. Not that they would remain if he disassociated. They were part of his illusion. But it seemed important to be as human as he could for as long as he could.

Dressed, he circled the room, wishing there was more he could do for her. When he touched the dark screen of her small computer, he sensed a fault in it and remembered her frustration with it. With a flick of his wrist, he scattered dust across the keyboard and watched as it glittered and sank into the guts of the device, healing the patterns of force as it went.

Well, at least that would bring her some satisfaction in the days to come, and distract her from the loss of her temporary playmate. He knew he could wipe her entire memory of him, just as he could have wiped the laptop's electronic memory if he'd so wished. But the humanity that gripped him made him selfish.

He didn't want to be forgotten. He wanted her to think of him. And at least remember a little of what they'd shared.

Lifting the curtain at the window, he looked outside. The moon and stars were beginning to fade in the sky across the bay, and already the pink intimations of dawn were slowly gathering.

His hand, where it held the cloth, was fading too, and a stir from the bed said that Lois was waking.

With an ache of regret, Robin abandoned his form and drifted upwards and away through the cabin's ceiling.

Lois woke early, and for a moment, before her faculties fully reconstituted themselves, she lay warm and huddled in the quilt, bathing in contentment. Never ever had her body felt so relaxed, so sated, so complete.

But as cold – really cold – reality set in, so did a profound and jumbled whirl of feelings.

You were *real this time! You* were *fucking real!*

Gathering the covers around her shoulders against the chill of the cabin, she ran her fingers over the sheet at her side.

No residual heat. No indentation of a large male body. But he *had* been here in the bed, she knew it. He really had.

There was other evidence.

Lowering her face to the sheet, she drew in a great breath of lavender and, as she sat up again, she studied her hand and saw on it that faint veil of glimmering dust she'd seen in the cabin the previous morning.

It was insubstantial. Not in the least bit gritty, it was smooth as silk and seemed to dissolve against her skin. But it was real, and it wasn't just confined to the bed.

Padding around the cabin, she found it dusted across the rag rug, on the floor, and even scattered thinly across her laptop.

'Great! Now I've got dust in the works as well as corrupted programs!'

But, when out of habit she fired the thing up, not only did the wi-fi connection spring into life, but also files she seemed to have lost yesterday were restored and full of data she'd believed gone forever.

She began to shake. Hard. So hard she had to sit down on the bed again.

'What the fuck are you, Robin?' she demanded of the empty air.

It was impossible to ignore now, the strangeness of him. He'd sprinkled her bloody computer with fairy dust or whatever . . . and mended it.

'Oh, God, help me, what's going on?'

The temptation to dive under the duvet and just hide again was enormous, but she resisted it. The temptation to pour herself a tot of brandy was enormous too, and that she succumbed to, thinking it was a pretty poor turn of affairs that she was driven to drink, boozing first thing in the morning because she was afraid she just might have fucked a supernatural being last night.

She prowled the cabin, stirring up the Robin-dust with the trailing duvet that swept the floor much in the style of a geisha's formal kimono.

'This is stupid! There are no spirits, ghosties, sprites and fairies and what-have-you! And I'm sure you're not a vampire because you've got such lovely teeth!'

But, if he was a real man, where the hell was he? Surely he would have stayed, especially if there was the prospect of a repeat performance?

'Now this is just fantastic! You're either a supernatural spook and you've turned into a pumpkin or something in the daylight . . . or you're just a normal bloke who also happens to be a fuck 'em and run bastard!' She swigged her brandy, then coughed at the bite of it. 'Bloody hell, I certainly know how to pick men!'

But she couldn't sit round getting drunk.

Still trying not to think too hard about anything, she showered and dressed and picked at some cereal for breakfast. She tidied the cabin and swept up, but that just swung her thoughts back to things incomprehensible.

The fairy dust or whatever it was seemed to disintegrate as fast as she brushed at it, and irrationally, seeing it go, she felt an aching wrench in the place where she knew her heart was.

He was magically beautiful and she was destroying his very essence.

She stopped cleaning up and tried to do some work. But it was hopeless. The code danced before her, and all she seemed to see were a pair of bi-coloured eyes, a glinting smile and gold-tipped hair ... All that, and the most perfect male body, either fantastic or real.

She could feel him too. Deep in the quick of her, it was like having an echo of his penis still there, displacing the tender flesh that had embraced his as he moved and thrust and loved her. As she clenched her inner muscles, caressing a ghost, a deep pleasure gripped her and made her catch her breath.

Staggering almost, she collapsed into one of the easy chairs, her body trembling finely, her nerves, her heart – yes – her sex on fire as if Robin were with her, touching her, fucking her. Ripples of sensation licked over her skin like flames and she couldn't tell if the feeling was real, in her imagination, or in her memory. The agitation in her flesh made her toss her head and writhe against the upholstery, the turn-on far more intense and visceral almost than those moments of displaced lust on the beach. She cupped her breast and her crotch, her heels kicking against the rug as her hands seemed to become Robin's to stir her.

Where are you? Where are you? I need you!

Opening eyes she didn't realise she'd closed, she looked down and seemed to see his glorious face looking up at her from between her legs, just like last night.

He smiled, he winked, and her body surged, the sudden sharp arousal capsizing in an instant, as she kneaded herself and the rough pressure made her come.

As she fell back into herself, the absurdity of her actions scared her. It was either that, or the fact that she wasn't entirely sure they'd been her actions. Her impetus . . .

Had that just been a visitation? What had happened?

Oh, God, I think I'm going mad!

'I can't go on like this! I've got to get out of here!'

The sound of her own voice snapped Lois mercifully from her fugue, and she grabbed her coat, threw it on and set out for a walk.

The day was grim and cold again, and the skies leaden. A brisk wind was whipping up high seas and making spray lash the beach. Gritting her teeth and huddling into her puffed jacket, Lois took the path into the woods, her walking shoes squishing as she tramped the packed earth that had partly turned to mud. She wasn't quite sure where she was going, but her feet just kept putting themselves one in front of the other.

Are you out here, Robin? Is this where you hang?

The silent trees mocked her, and there was no sign of life other than a few dubious-sounding rustles in the undergrowth. She wondered whether to turn back. What if there were foxes, or some other wild animals that might attack her?

Probably nothing more dangerous than the man-thing I fucked last night, she decided, shaking her head, and then strode on.

The woods were dark and dank, and were frankly starting to scare her. But, just on the point of turning back, she seemed to burst out into a little glade that was chocolate-box pretty and lifted straight from an illustrated Victorian fairytale. It was bright here too and, when she looked up, she was astonished to discover that the sun had finally come out and was peppering the little dell with golden light.

There had been nothing about this on the BBC Weather site, but, with her face still lifted towards the welcome sunshine fragmenting through the higher branches, Lois unzipped her jacket. With the light had come heat. She stepped forwards into the glade, and then laughed out loud. Not only was she in a circle of light and warmth, but she was also standing in a fairy ring of toadstools.

'I don't believe this! It's got to be a joke.'

Although she was half expecting Robin to pop out from behind a tree and answer her, nothing happened. She was still alone. Vaguely disappointed but also slightly relieved, she crossed the ring and sat down on a large fallen log, puffing out her cheeks.

'So where are you, Magic Man?'

Her words echoed strangely, almost as if she were in a church, ringing and rebounding.

Still nothing.

Well, not completely nothing. As she sat motionless on the log, there was a rustling in the low brush, and an animal hopped out into the circle, almost floating over the short cropped turf.

It was a hare, long-shanked and lop-eared, mottled in colour, cream and dark brown.

Laughter burst like a bubble from Lois's lips and she instantly expected the timid animal to bolt back the way it had come. Instead, it cocked its head on one side, studying her with bright intelligent eyes.

Bright intelligent eyes that had something really peculiar about them. Peculiar and familiar . . .

Lois opened her mouth to speak, but suddenly there was a loud crack in the underbrush behind her, like the breaking of a twig, and she almost leapt up from the log, swivelling around.

Nothing behind her this time, but, when she whipped back around to face the clearing and dappled light and the toad-stools, she was no longer alone.

Robin, standing tall and dark in his long black coat, his head cocked on one side, was studying her with bright intelligent eyes.

He was on the very same spot the hare had occupied.

She'd heard no sound of the animal's movement or his.

No rustle of grass or undergrowth. No displacement of air.

The hare had simply disappeared and left Robin in its place.

The broken sunlight faded, becoming splodged with black as the dell began to spin violently.

Lois fainted.

Struggling back to consciousness, she found herself firmly held and encircled. Fight or flight reflex made her jerk and wriggle and try to get free.

She knew whose strong arms were around her.

Or *what's* arms.

That idea made her fight hard. But to no avail. His hold was unbreakable.

'Let me go! Let me go! Get off me!'

The hold loosened, but bizarrely, now she was free, her limbs felt too heavy and lethargic to allow her to move. She stared at her booted toes and his much bigger ones beside them.

They were sitting on the short firm turf, their backs against the log, their legs stretched out in front of them. She could not, dared not, look at him. But his large cool hand gently stroked her face and, against all the odds, it seemed the simplest and most comfortable thing in the world to rest her head against the strength of his shoulder. The backs of his fingers moved slowly and soothingly against her cheek.

'Hush, don't be afraid,' he whispered. 'Nothing to be scared of.'

Lois huffed out a little breath. Easy for him to say that.

'That hare . . . it was you, wasn't it?'

There seemed to be no way she could get away from him, even if she'd wanted to, so it made best sense to meet the issue head on. She shifted around a little and, adjusting her position, she managed to screw up the courage to face him.

His luminous eyes – both blue and brown – were steady, clear and candid.

'Yes.' He gave a little shrug, and his splendid mouth quirked. 'And I was also the bird, down on the beach, yesterday.'

The little well of bravery she'd gathered around her faltered, and she dragged in a great breath, utterly shaken.

'H-how can that be? How is it possible?' She shook her head. 'I mean, I've watched *Buffy* and *Doctor Who* and all that . . . but they're just stories. Fiction, made-up stuff . . . You can't seriously be, um, I don't know . . . a shape-shifter or whatever they're called. That's just crazy! It's not possible!'

Robin blinked at her, his glorious face troubled, his brow crumpling. 'I am what I am, Lois, and I can change form, become other creatures . . . and be human sometimes.'

Suddenly, a real sadness glittered in his eyes, and Lois realised to her astonishment that the azure and the brandy brown both were shiny with the gloss of real tears.

Human tears?

Her fear vanished. What was wrong? Why so sad? A great need to comfort and nurture surged up in her. It was kind of maternal, and yet not motherly at all. She was too close to him, and he smelt too wonderful and felt too strong to deny more earthy feelings.

'What's wrong?' she whispered, turning her face into his palm, and kissing it impulsively to offer comfort . . . and more.

'I'd like to stay human longer, but, after tomorrow, when June arrives, I can't.'

She supposed there was some great mythology to explain this, and that it would probably be wiser to understand it if she could, but a sudden urgency compelled her to ignore it for the moment. And forget anything but the here and now of Robin, the most beautiful and extraordinary *man* she'd ever met. She was probably being ten dozen different types of brainless bimbo-fools, but, if he had less than 24 hours in the shape he currently wore, she couldn't waste a minute debating parapsychology!

And yet, as she took his soft mobile lips in a tender kiss, and breathed in his sigh of relief and happiness, she couldn't help but see how many things now made sense.

His lack of physical weight and the coolness of his skin had seemed downright bizarre, but she supposed a part of her mind had just not asked questions. Or maybe they had, but those questions had been squelched . . . because Robin could read her thoughts, and probably manipulate them.

Which accounted for the erotic dreams too, she supposed.

I should be angry . . . but I'm not.

Oh, and there'd been other clues too.

His hair and eyes could be explained rationally, but not the sudden uncanny manifestation of wireless broadband and the self-mending computer.

It's all magic! Robin's magic . . .

There was magic, too, in the feel of his mouth, although the delicious contact was far from imaginary. He felt real, completely real, and of the flesh.

He's a . . . a . . . something, and I still want to kiss him. He's not human, and I still want to fuck him. This is insane, but it makes perfect sense.

Of course it made sense! If Robin would be gone soon, she had to have him now.

Sliding her hands inside his coat, she pushed it off his shoulders, and then, impatiently, tugged at the hem of his black T-shirt and snuck her fingers under it to cruise his silky skin.

He was cool, of course, but not cold. The contours of his chest and torso were like marble that was just beginning to feel the kiss of the morning sun. Flawless to the touch, and almost as hard in its muscular perfection. That was what magic did, she supposed, caressing his abs, and then flickering up to circle his taut male nipples. Why settle for second best when you could recreate a girl's ultimate wet dream?

Suddenly, she had to see him. In the arboreal sunlight, and maybe for the last time.

'Coat off, whatever you are,' she commanded, sweetening the order with a pepper of kisses against his throat.

Robin obeyed, and his grin showed that he'd forgotten his momentary distress and was now into the spirit of things. He slid off his heavy coat, then whipped his black T-shirt off over the top of his head, ruffling his golden-tipped hair endearingly in the process.

What the devil are you? Lois demanded silently, admiring the sweetly ripped lines of his chest, arms and shoulders. *In fact, are you a devil?*

Robin shook his curly head and Lois felt a great rush of relief.

'What then? An angel? A ghost?'

Again, he shook his head.

'You must be something though . . . just tell me!'

Leaning forwards, he pressed his lips to her ear and whispered a few words into it, all very low and very quiet.

7

'Get away with you!' Lois laughed and reached out to stroke his cool face. 'You're too big and butch and macho. Whatever happened to gauzy wings and pointy hats and perching on bluebells and all that? And, anyway, I thought they were all girls?'

'Oh no.' Robin smiled slyly at her, his eyes naughty. 'I can be whatever I want, if necessary, but my natural inclination is towards the male.' His big hand settled on her cheek, then slid down her throat and her shoulder, before settling on her breast. 'Especially now ...'

His fingers cradled her flesh with perfect delicacy, and his lips were just as apposite as they pressed against hers. He seemed confident, but also a supplicant.

Be with me, I beg of you, he seemed to say in her mind. *Please be with me, there isn't much time.*

Lois responded, fighting the anguish that threatened to overwhelm her. She'd finally found her ideal man, but he wasn't actually a man. She wanted to be with him forever, but there were only a few hours before she'd lose him and not see him again for a year. If then.

She kissed him back hard, letting her own hands wander again over the firm muscular contours of his body. His need, and her own, made her bold. Pushing him by the shoulders, she urged him downwards, making him lie on the turf so she could surge over him and revel in the male splendour laid out for her pleasure.

And his too, really, she supposed. She couldn't imagine him making himself look ugly if he had the choice.

He tried to reach for her again, but she took him by the hands, and then pressed her lips to his palms, one after the other.

'Relax, Magic Man, let me explore you,' she murmured, pressing his arms back at his side, forcing him to lie inert, waiting, accepting. He seemed to be submitting, but the hot glint in his strange eyes told another tale. The King of the Grove was only *allowing* her to play with him. He looked more like a pasha accepting homage than a boy-toy at her bidding.

She touched her fingertips to his chest, flicking them over his nipples and then smiling when he wriggled and made a little sound of appreciation. She let her hand drift lower and the sound became closer to a growl.

His hips lifted when she traced his zipper with her fingernail.

'I think it's time we took a look at your wand, eh, don't you?'

Robin's strong arms came up, grabbing for her, but she pushed him back down again, tut-tutting and revelling in the way he allowed her to master his strength. For the time being at least.

As if accepting the status quo, he folded his arms behind his head, as a pillow. 'Help yourself,' he purred, a twinkle in his eyes.

Lois attacked his belt with gusto, unfastening the heavy buckle, then the button that lay beneath it. The black clothing, the archetypal garb for the dark predator ... where did it come from? Were the coat and the boots et al. magic too? A part of him? What would happen if he disappeared while he was out of them?

Toying with his zip, she looked into his face rather than at his crotch, knowing it was quite likely that he was reading her mind.

'All this – the way you look? Where does it come from? I mean, is it from your imagination, or do you have some sort of ... um ... template or something?'

'Inspiration comes from many sources, my sweet.' His gaze flicked from her hovering fingers to her face. 'Just as you garner images for your web designs from here and there and everywhere, I gathered them from around me ... and from your mind.'

Pausing in her explorations, Lois sat back a little, frowning. Peering at him through narrowed eyes. The face, yes, she could see it now ... Familiar elements ...

Looking at Robin, she suddenly recognised the likenesses.

One of her favourite actors, yes, there was a bit of him there. And the clothes, she suddenly realised, they came from a different character in a different show that she liked. His nose, faintly snub, she realised with astonishment, was not dissimilar to her own, only bigger of course and innately masculine ... and, by God, he even had a bit of a look of the neighbour about him too if you looked closely enough!

'Well, I've never seen anyone with hair like yours before or eyes that are different colours. Where the hell did those come from?'

Robin laughed softly and, defying her edict, he half sat up and reached out for her hands again, drawing them towards his groin area.

'Well, those touches are uniquely my own. I have to be allowed a little creativity, don't I?'

'It's pretty bizarre though, isn't it, to have one blue eye and one brown, especially when ...' She crumpled her brow, and peered more closely. 'Especially when the colours actually seem to swap places from one time I see you to the next!'

'But I *am* bizarre, Lois, aren't I?' His large but deft fingers stroked the back of her hands where they rested against his crotch. 'But a good fellow all the same, don't you think?'

The glint in his eyes shimmered like a spinning Christmas firework, and his words seemed to dance and shimmer just as teasingly. For a moment, just a tiny, tiny fraction of a second, her paramour seemed to ripple and glitter and become all the colours of the rainbow, then just as quickly, he was simply a man again.

A beautiful big, very male man, with an imposing hard-on swelling in his jeans.

Lois shook her head. Enough already! Enough of this fanciful madness. Robin was completely real, for the moment, and he wanted her. He wanted her, he was gorgeous . . . and she wanted him right back.

She resumed her attack on his jeans, undoing the button and whizzing down the zip. His erect cock sprang out in a way that was as comical as it was sudden, and before she could stop herself she'd giggled.

Immediately she felt a wash of remorse. Were supernatural male beings as sensitive about their equipment as their human counterparts? In which case, had she mortally offended his feelings and put him off?

'Whoops!' said Robin cheerfully, an inordinately proud grin on his face.

No insecurity problems there, obviously. Lois grinned back at him, and reached for the member in question. It was hard, as cool as the rest of him, and silkily textured.

'Well, I must say I like your magic wand!'

'So do I, and I . . . I like it even more when you're touching it!'

Robin stirred against the greensward, lifting his hips to meet her caresses as she handled him and traced the beautifully defined veins that adorned his cock.

He was thick and long, and the tip was flared and red and hungry looking with a stretched and open 'eye' that was already weeping copious pre-come. Taking a little of this satin fluid on her thumb, Lois slowly and meticulously massaged him.

'Mmm, oh, my dear ... that's wonderful, wonderful,' he burbled, his eyes closing and his hands clenching and relaxing, clenching and relaxing against the turf as she ministered to him.

Lois had never been a great one for giving hand-jobs. Oh, she'd done it often enough, and been praised for her touch sometimes, but mostly she'd always been keen to move on to more mutual pleasures.

But not with Robin.

To touch him was a joy in itself. His skin was so smooth, so fine to the touch, and holding him and stroking him seemed to impart a refined aesthetic experience that was quite unique. She'd also never touched a cock that seemed quite so very clean before. It was as if it was brand new, and expressly fashioned to please her senses.

Which she supposed, in a way, it was.

Of course, it was totally impossible to resist tasting him.

Inclining over his strong, jeans-clad hips, Lois settled her mouth over the crown of Robin's penis – which, despite being what she most wanted to do at that moment, she still found to be quite a job.

The head of his cock was as big as a shiny ripe plum and ten times as delicious, and she had a dainty and feminine mouth. Her lips stretched around him as she took him inside, and she was aware that she was probably drooling all over him.

I probably look an awful sight!

But when she snuck a peek at him, up the length of his

glorious torso, she discovered that Robin was smiling at her with such tenderness, such wonder and such gratitude that her heart turned over with love and a huge desire to pleasure him.

Washing and lapping at him with her tongue, she folded her fingers lightly and ripplingly around his shaft, co-ordinating the actions of her hands and her mouth. She sipped and tasted him, adoring the sweet perfumed, honeyed flavour of him that reminded her more of the old-fashioned confectionery of her childhood than any other man she'd ever given head to.

You're like the most delicious lollipop I ever tasted!

No sooner had the thought materialised than Robin laughed out loud with joy and cradled her head gently in his hands.

Working with fingers and tongue, and with suction and long sweeping licks, Lois went about her sacred duty with enthusiasm. It suddenly, almost, didn't seem as if she needed pleasure of her own. This attention to Robin was the sole focus of her being. He'd be gone soon, but, before he went, she'd make him come.

Magical fingers tightened around her cheeks and ears, and she felt him trying to encourage her to lift her mouth from him.

'Lois, my love, you must stop now. If you don't, I feel it'll be too late . . . and I'll be selfish.'

Lois held station and, still holding him lightly between her lips, she shook her head infinitesimally. Then went about her fellatial duties with new gusto and as much artistry as she could muster.

She swirled her tongue. She sucked as hard as she could. She flicked and flirted and played, stroking him all the time with fingertips that travelled the length and breadth of his shaft, and even ventured down into his jeans to stroke his balls and his perineum.

When she managed to crook her wrist enough to get a finger in and press against his anus, he wailed almost like the gullbird on the beach, and then jerked and filled her mouth with perfumed semen.

Pulse, pulse, pulse . . . it leapt from the tip of his cock, coated her tongue and then trickled down her throat. Lois swallowed eagerly savouring his pleasure as much as his taste, as the creamy fluid overflowed her lips and ran down her chin.

As if from a great distance she seemed to hear her lover sobbing. And then, as she released him, she realised he actually was in tears.

When his glittering, jewel-like eyes met hers, he sat up, reached for her and drew her up along his body and embraced her. Murmuring and muttering almost unintelligible thanks, he kissed her sticky lips and caressed her face with utmost reverence.

'You are a wonder, sweet Lois,' he whispered, his long pink tongue swooping around his own lips for a moment, cleaning his own transferred essence from their surface. 'A true miracle. If there's magic here, it's in you, my love, in you.'

My love? Did he really mean that?

For a moment, Robin put her away from him a little distance, so they could look into each other's eyes.

'Of course I love you,' he said simply. His face was beautiful with emotion, and yet, in the mismatched depths of his eyes, Lois could see pain.

'What's wrong? There's something . . . Is it because you have to – to go tomorrow?'

'Yes.' He bit his lip, hesitating, and Lois screamed silently for the whole truth.

'But it's more than that,' he went on, his expression serious. 'When I can't be human any more, I stop feeling as a human does . . . I might lose this emotion. I might forget what I feel for you, and that I love you.' He took her hand in his and squeezed it in a way that came closer to hurting than anything he'd done to her before. 'And, though I don't want that to happen now, in a while, it might not matter as much to me.'

'I don't understand.'

'Nor do I, completely, when it happens.' His broad intelligent brow puckered in a frown.

'But don't you feel emotions when you're – you're how you normally are?'

'Yes, sort of, but they're faint. Like tiny ripples on a pond. Whereas now, when I look at you, I feel like the sea out there, surging and crashing and full of wildness. I feel love. And I want to *be* loved.'

She could see it, the turbulence of feeling in his expressive features.

'But I'm afraid that, after tomorrow, in the space of a few weeks, all I might still feel is curiosity, and not much more.'

Lois tried to imagine it. But she couldn't. Her life had always been a tapestry of feelings, richly coloured, not always happy, but mostly. How would it feel not to feel? It was incomprehensible.

'I just can't imagine how that would be,' she said, touching her fingertips to his face. His skin was smooth and cool, and she realised that there was no stubble, as such, on his cheeks. 'I – I mean, what do you remember of other years? Have you, um, interacted with other women?'

'Not in this way.' He turned his face, kissing her palm. 'I remember observing mostly. Observing couples. You're the first woman to come here on her own.' Long, long eyelashes flicked down, as if he were bashful, and a little ashamed of himself. 'I fear I may have taken advantage of you because of that. Forgive me.'

Lois laughed. He looked like a naughty little boy who'd stolen some sweeties. 'If that's being taken advantage of, keep on taking, Magic Man, keep on taking.' She slid her hand down his strong jaw, his neck and across the hard muscular planes of his superbly formed chest.

'I serve your wishes, beautiful Lois –' his eyes darkened – 'for as long as I'm able.'

Silent communication passed between them. It wasn't his mental telepathy. It was deeper even than that somehow. It was as if they were having the same thought.

'Let's not waste any time then.'

8

Assertive in her hunger, Lois pushed hard on Robin's chest, compelling him to lie back so she could enjoy him and savour his astonishing male beauty.

First she pulled off his boots, then his jeans, rendering him naked in the enchanted little glade. Submitting to her, he lay back like some kind of strange amalgam of utterly masculine stud and compliant sex slave. He was like no man Lois had ever encountered . . . in more ways than one.

She touched his skin. She kissed his eyes, his throat and the inside of his elbows. She adored him, with her heart, with her eyes and fingertips. But, before long, just exploring and caressing was not enough.

'Why have I still got all these clothes on?' she demanded, then laughed when Robin gave a 'search me' shrug and it made his gloriously stiff erection dance and sway.

Ripping at her jacket and her shoes, her jeans and the rest of her clothing, Lois got naked faster than she could ever remember doing before. Buttons and zips, hooks and elastic all seemed to give way with supernatural ease. She laughed again as she realised that her things *were* coming off unnaturally fast. Robin might be lying there like a lounging gigolo, but he was helping her disrobe at the same time.

At last, she was as bare and untrammelled as he was . . . and she wasn't even cold. The chill of the coolest May for many years had disappeared completely, and they might have been basking in the gilded sunshine of midsummer.

She threw her leg across Robin's pelvis and hovered over him.

'I . . .' She paused, distracted by the slow slide of his silky tip against the inside of her thigh. 'I mean . . . Do I need protection? Do you know what I mean? Condoms and all that? I don't suppose I do, do I?'

Robin's face grew momentarily solemn. 'This body has never been with another. And it isn't human. There is no danger to you of any kind.'

Only to my heart . . .

Once again, Robin's remarkable face darkened with remorse. She felt his guilt, his regret that he'd made her fall for the most impossible of partners. One who might forget this tryst, and feel no pain of loss in the months to come the way she would.

'I'll *make* you remember, Robin! I swear I will!' she cried, flashing him a brilliant, imperious smile as she positioned him carefully at the snug entrance to her body, then began a slow, slow descent upon his cock.

She seemed to slide down, and down, and down, for what seemed like an eternity, her body flexing and expanding to accommodate his splendid, magical length and his impressive girth. He seemed to be moving not only into the quick of her sex, but also into her heart, her nerves, her cells.

Maybe he was even doing that literally? Somehow managing to infuse her flesh with his enchanted aura, stirring it to pleasure on a molecular level as well as simply entering her as a man?

Sliding, settling, Lois swayed. It was too much. Robin was too much, but somehow she seemed to open to him, accept him and take him all.

'Are you all right, my love?' He came up on his elbow, watching her face closely, his own face twitching a little with strain, as if fighting a huge rush of pleasure. 'I'm not hurting you, am I?'

'No! Not at all! You feel amazing!'

Big hands settled around her hips, holding her, securing her while he bucked upwards, plumbing her even deeper, possessing her utterly.

Lois groaned, overwhelmed, undulating slowly on the fulcrum of Robin's sex, loving the sensation of being stretched and being loved so hugely from within. Her clitoris leapt, and then leapt again when she saw his smile of hot delight when she reached down to touch herself. To stroke her own pleasure centre was to caress her lover's too.

She flicked her finger, and it was Robin's turn to toss his gold-frosted head, subsiding back against the turf, his hips lifting again and again. His long hands tightened, pressing his fingertips into the flesh of her buttocks, and Lois relished the desperation she felt in his grip.

'Lois! Lois!' he cried, writhing as she writhed, rising as she descended, grabbing at her to hold her on him, as she grabbed and caressed him from within.

'Lois! Oh my love, my love,' he exhorted her, his neck arching, his head tossing from side to side.

Then suddenly, his powerful hips came up and he remained still for moments, moments that seemed like frozen time, and then he was pushing again, his pelvis jerking convulsively in the rapid unmistakeable dance of orgasm.

Filled in heart and body, Lois joined him, almost fainting from the exquisite rolling ripples of sensation. But, even as the pleasure threatened to overwhelm her, she exerted a supreme effort – and kept her eyes open when they would normally have fluttered closed.

Remember this! she commanded silently, staring down at Robin's face, still so beautiful despite his tense orgasmic grimace. *Remember it! Remember everything about it!*

But, as she cascaded forwards, wilting over her lover's prone body like a lily whose stem could not bear the weight of its flower, she couldn't work out which of them the unspoken cry had been really aimed at.

They did not speak much as they gathered their clothes, dressed again and returned to the cabin. They did not speak much as they made love there, again and again, sometimes tenderly and sometimes ferocious in their passion.

But, all the while, Lois was acutely aware of Robin's total focus on what they were doing, and his concentration.

He is trying to remember it all, she thought in wonder as she looked up into his face when he entered her yet again, his eyes so dark and intense that for that moment they did appear to match each other. *He's trying to imprint it on his mind, his consciousness, or whatever he has . . . so he can retain it.*

Eventually they rested, though, because Lois was exhausted. She suspected that Robin could go on indefinitely, and his body would rouse again and again where a normal man's could not, but she was just human, and prone to fatigue no matter how fabulous the sex was.

Sleep claimed her for a while, and she drifted and skittered through strange dreams of loss where she was running through the woods and along the shore, chasing something intangible. Which, she realised, when she awoke again to find Robin watching her, might be an accurate reflection of the next eleven months without him.

'I'm going to keep coming here, you know.' Sitting up in bed, she grasped his large hand and squeezed it. 'I'm going to be around here, reminding you of all this. I'm not going to bloody well let you forget me because I'm going to be in your face, Magic Man, even when you haven't actually got one!'

For a moment, she thought she might have offended him, but Robin's guffaw of mirth immediately dispelled her worries.

'I'll watch you, beautiful Lois, I'll watch you, and, if there's a way to remember this feeling, I will.' Leaning over her, he kissed her again, at first tenderly and then with increasing purpose.

Again?

'Yes, again, my love, again,' he growled, pressing her back against the pillows.

A long time later, after night had fallen and the moon was in the sky, they tumbled from the bed, showered together and donned their clothes. Neither one of them spoke much, but, time and again, Lois found herself sneaking swift peeks at her little alarm clock.

Midnight was approaching. And with it the end of May.

'Let's go for a walk on the beach,' said Robin suddenly, reaching for his long dark coat.

'Um, yes, OK,' Lois agreed, her heart sinking. Even though they were no longer naked, she'd wanted there to be the option.

He held out her jacket, helped her into it, his fingers settling it on her shoulders almost lovingly, and then turned her around so he could zip it up and dress her like a daddy dressing his little girl.

'When the time comes, Lois, when the time comes, let me walk away as if I were a real man. Let me pretend to be a real man. Your real lover.'

'You *are* a real man to me, Robin.' She grabbed his arm, forcing him to look at her. 'And you're certainly the realest lover *I've* ever had!'

His eyes gleamed and, despite the angst of the moment, she could see he was pleased with himself. Lois grinned up at him.

Men! Even if they were magic imitations, they still liked to hear praise for their sexual prowess!

'Come on then, let's go for that walk.'

As she led the way to the door, though, something caught her eye. Her digital camera, on the table.

'One minute, Robin, let me take your picture! That way, I'll have something to remind me of you while you're ... well ... away.' She paused, thinking, thinking. 'And, when you come back, you'll have a template for when you take human form again.'

Robin looked impressed, but then he shrugged. 'We can try it, my love. It's a very good idea ... But my kind are extraordinarily difficult to photograph.'

Lois snatched up the camera and, directing Robin to pose, she reeled off a few shots of him sitting, standing, smiling and looking moody.

She took upwards of twenty fast shots, using a variety of settings, but, frustratingly, they all came out strangely fuzzy and lacking in definition.

'Why are they so blurred?' she railed, flicking through the shots.

'Maybe because I'm becoming blurred, losing my focus.'

Lois's eyes flicked to the clock. Not long to go. With a sigh, she set down the camera, and then reached for Robin's hand – which still felt substantial and wonderful to her touch.

'Shall we walk then?'

They headed for the beach by silent mutual consent. Again, no telepathy. Lois just seemed to know that was the right place to head for.

The full moon was high as they walked, and she found herself stealing glances, again and again, at her companion, and tightening her fingers around his.

He was so real. And that perplexed her utterly.

How could she love a man who didn't really exist? A man she'd known for barely more than a day? A man, but one who was nothing more than a magical construct, made up from fragments and images in her mind, an amalgam of many other men?

And yet she did. Mad as it seemed. She simply did.

The sand was firm beneath their feet and, in the brightness from the moon, they could see it stretching away ahead, along the shore, unnaturally white and scattered with driftwood and skeins of dark seaweed.

'What's that? Over there?'

By the edge of the lapping waves lay a small dark bundle. Clothing, what looked like a pair of boots and the glint of glass.

With Robin padding behind her, Lois ran to the bundle. She recognised her neighbour's warm coat, his beanie hat with a watch laid neatly on top of it, and an empty bottle that had once contained Glenfiddich whisky beside them.

'Where is he?' She scanned the water, and then turned to Robin. 'Surely he's not gone swimming at this time of night? In this cold and full of booze? The water must be freezing.'

Her companion was peering out into the bay, his eyes narrowed. 'He's out there.' He pointed to the waves. 'He's swimming now, but I don't think he will be for long.'

'What do you mean?'

'I believe he's trying to end his life. I sensed it in him before, but I thought that it was just a fleeting notion, not a real intention.'

Oh, God, she'd sensed the neighbour was unhappy, but not this bad.

'But we've got to try and help him! He's been drinking . . . He'll feel different when he's sober.'

She surged forwards, kicking off her shoes as she went, and flinging off her coat, but the water knocked the breath out of her before she reached waist depth it was so cold, so bitterly cold.

'Fucking hell!' she gasped, staggering and almost falling into the waves.

But, before she capsized, strong arms grasped her, and lifted her up on to her feet.

'Go back into the shallows! I'll get him,' Robin commanded her. He'd already flung off his long coat and his boots. His face was hard and determined in the moonlight. 'Go back to safety now.'

'But Robin, I can help . . . Help drag him in.'

The bitter irony of the moment suddenly crashed in on her with more power than the biggest of the waves.

It was almost midnight. These were their last moments before eleven months apart, and yet she knew the man out in the bay stood his best chance of being saved if she let her lover plunge into the water after him.

'Go back, my love, I'll get him.'

For one brief second he crushed his lips against hers, and then he put her from him and threw himself forwards into the dark and bitter water.

9

Robin had never swum in human form before, but like all natural skills it came to him effortlessly and he struck out hard in the direction of where they'd last seen Lois's neighbour, the man known as Edgar.

But was he too late?

Edgar had already slipped beneath the waves and was descending into the depths, his lungs waterlogged and his hold on life ebbing. Plunging down after him, Robin grabbed for his shoulders.

The reaction was predictably violent. Just as a normal man would have struggled for survival with every last fibre of his being, Edgar seemed bent on struggling to achieve his death and he thrashed and struggled, kicked out and punched with what remained of his strength, and even Robin found it difficult to hold on to him.

Let me help you! Please don't do this! It's not the way!

He spoke directly into the man's mind. It was the only way. It was too late now to worry about the niceties of explaining who he was ... and what.

A life was at stake. A precious life. A *human* life – something he would have cherished, at all costs, if he'd had it himself.

And, in this strange, unnatural hinterland between life and death, Edgar seemed to accept the fact of unspoken communication.

Leave me alone! Let me go! She's here ... I want to be with her ...

His thoughts were weak, yet Robin understood. He didn't know what to do, and his grip on the rapidly ebbing Edgar faltered.

The dying man wriggled feebly and slid away.

Robin grabbed for him again.

No! Please! Let me be with her!

Such desperation. Such love.

Robin felt the keen pain of it. He felt it himself. Wouldn't he undertake the most drastic and most extreme act in order to be with Lois? And it could well be true. Edgar's lover might be here in spirit, somewhere close.

Disassociating momentarily, Robin sent out his consciousness.

Yes, indeed, he sensed a hovering presence, watching, waiting.

The weight of human sadness, passion and love descended on him. This was how they lived, and it was terrifying, yet still it seemed worth all the tumult if it meant a life with the one you adored. A woman like Lois.

Robin hesitated.

Life was sacred. He couldn't just let Edgar die.

He attempted to reach for the fading man, and found he couldn't.

No!

Midnight, the perennial witching hour, had just this moment passed.

It was June, and he could no longer assume the form of a human man.

But could he still persuade Edgar to live? He reached out again, this time in intangible form, searching for Edgar's mind.

Too late. He was gone. Robin felt a rising, rushing surge in the ether as the human's spirit swept up, flying to meet the one who waited, and, at the same time, his mortal shell began to descend.

Robin watched the body dropping in the water.

Until moments ago, it had been hale, hearty, strong and alive. A perfect vessel.

Could he? Dare he? Would it work? His people spoke of such things, passed down tales, stories . . . but had such a phenomenon ever really been achieved?

The vision of Lois seemed to shimmer before him, and he sensed her back there on the beach, distraught with worry and fear, readying herself to wade into the water again.

He had to try it. He had to try. Even at the risk of his own extinction in the process.

'Robin! Robin! Are you all right?'

Lois had never shouted louder in her life, and it was making her throat sore and her lungs hurt, bellowing out into the bay again and again. But she couldn't see anything. There was no sign of her lover or her neighbour at all now, just the waves and the glitter of moonlight glancing on their crests. She waded out into the water, thrashing and struggling, then realised it was pointless. Not the strongest of swimmers, she'd never had any lifesaving training, and she wasn't even sure what direction to go in.

'Oh, Robin! Please!' she howled, staggering backwards and falling in a heap on the sand beside her neighbour's abandoned clothes.

What about rescue? Was there a lifeboat she could summon or something? Struggling into a sitting position, she felt in her pocket for her mobile, and discovered she'd left it in the cabin.

'Fuck!'

What about her neighbour? Did he have one? Plunging into

the pile of clothing, she rummaged in all his pockets, but found nothing.

'No! No!'

Tears streaming down her face, she sprang to her feet again, staring out into the empty bay and the waves.

The cabin. There was a landline there. She could phone from there.

But, just as she was about to set out, something caught her eye. Or, more correctly, the *lack* of something.

Where was Robin's coat? His boots? They'd been flung out on the sand, next to her neighbour's stuff . . . and now they were gone.

'Oh noooo!' she keened again. 'Robin! Robin!'

He was gone. Turned back, along with his clothes, into whatever he'd been before.

What if it'd happened under water? What if he'd drowned too?

Could he drown? Maybe he was still around here somewhere?

'Robin! Robin! Robin!' she yelled, shouting now to the intangible presence, not the man.

As she stared out over the surface of the waves, shielding her eyes against the almost unnatural brilliance of the moonlight, she suddenly saw a shape breach the surface of the water.

A head!

Someone was coming. Wading towards her.

'Robin!' she screamed, plunging back into the cold sea, floundering towards the human figure that was labouring in her direction, staggering to his feet when he hit the shallows, then falling into the surf again.

'Robin,' she sobbed in a small broken voice when she reached the naked retching figure, who knelt on all fours, coughing up seawater and gasping for breath.

Not Robin, she thought, her heart bereft as she slid her arms around her neighbour's bare shoulders and helped him half crawl and half stagger towards the safety of dry land.

Robin, where are you?

Lois sat in the armchair by the stove, cradling a cup of tea in her hands as she tried to warm up. It had a hefty slug of brandy in it, in an attempt to fire her up from within, but, so far, it wasn't making much in the way of an inroad into her inner chilliness.

It was over an hour since she'd half dragged and half carried her neighbour into her cabin and helped him on to the bed then rubbed him dry with towels and spare blankets. He'd seemed virtually comatose on his feet, and unable to speak, and had lapsed into what could be unconsciousness or maybe just sleep almost as soon as he was horizontal.

When she'd decided it was safe to a leave him for a moment, Lois had run back down to the sand, calling for Robin – in vain, she knew – and scouring the moonlit ocean for any sign of him. She'd even peered up into the sky, hoping to see him in the gull-like form he'd assumed before.

But there was nothing. No trace of him either physically . . . or intangibly.

With a heavy heart, she'd scooped up her neighbour's clothing, and, on returning to the cabin, had discovered from a postcard in his jacket pocket that he was called Edgar.

She stared at Edgar now, sleeping the sleep of a baby, in her bed.

I wish you were Robin!

Immediately, she felt guilty. She wished that *both* of them had come back out of the water, improbable or impossible as that might have been. She padded over to the side of the bed and sat down on the hard chair bedside it, staring down at the slumbering man, something keen twisting painfully inside her as she observed certain aspects of his appearance that reminded her of her supernatural lover.

'Well, he did say he took some "bits" from you,' she muttered, recognising a certain line to the jaw, and perhaps the shape of an eyebrow, the tilt of a cheekbone.

Edgar was older than her beautiful Robin, though, and stockier, and his drying hair was frosted with grey rather than highlights of gold. Under other circumstances, she might have found him attractive, especially now the colour was coming back to his cheeks and he was starting to look healthy and normal again. But it was all she could do, at the moment, to battle with the resentment she felt against him, and her own guilt at thinking ill of him.

God, the man had been unhappy enough to want to take his own life, and here she was near to hating him because he'd snatched away her last few minutes with Robin. The fact that it'd been the final precious fragment of time they'd share for eleven months was bad enough . . . but the possibility that something had gone wrong, and that was it for good, for all time, forever, she couldn't bear to think about.

Even thinking about it made her groan with pain and, as tears filled her eyes, she just gave in and slumped slowly forwards, across the sleeping man, weeping.

The sobs wrenched at her. It felt as if someone was pulling at her soul and mangling it up. The idea of never seeing, or even sensing, Robin again was agonising. She clutched at the inert body and arms of Edgar for blind consolation.

Moments passed, or maybe hours, but suddenly, as her tears were beginning to subside out of pure weariness, the man beneath her moved, and sighed, and she felt the very lightest touch of fingers on her head, slowly stroking.

'Oh, you're awake,' she said awkwardly, straightening up,

unable to look at the rousing Edgar, not quite knowing how to greet him. 'Are you all right?' She fussed with a blanket, tweaking it a bit further up his chest. 'Er, would you like a hot drink or something?'

'Lois?'

The voice was soft and strained, as if speaking was still an almost insurmountable effort, but the single word seemed to twinkle like a silvery bell, ringing beautifully through her consciousness. There was deep exhaustion there, but also – familiarity?

Slowly, fearfully, she turned and looked down into Edgar's waking face . . .

And saw a miracle.

Yes, it was the face of her taciturn fellow holidaymaker, who'd barely spoken to her . . . and yet it wasn't him. A subtle metamorphosis seemed to be under way, perceptible perhaps only to someone who knew what to look for, but the features of Edgar were beginning to change into those of her beloved Robin.

The exhausted eyes were still a little dull and weary, but, already, they were no longer the nondescript hazel they had been.

The left one was blue, and the right one was brown.

'Robin?'

Joy, confusion, fear, relief, a jumble of belief and disbelief suddenly rushed through her like a tidal wave.

She flung herself forwards to kiss his strangely mutable physiognomy and threw her arms around him. His body was warm, deliciously warm, and, when his arms came around her, the sensation was so sweetly that of one coming home after a long and dangerous journey that she burst into more tears, sobs of wrenching relief, and could not speak.

They hugged for quite a while, and as Robin – she supposed

she must call him that now, despite the lingering resemblance to Edgar – gained strength, he sat up and drew her on to the bed beside him.

Lois simply couldn't stop smiling, despite the strangeness and incomprehensibility of their situation.

'How is this possible?' She touched his new face, trickled her fingers over his hair, which looked less grey now and bore a growing hint of gold. A thought occurred, and she reared back a little, not knowing how to feel about it. Everything was so confused. 'You didn't snatch his body, did you?'

She was half laughing as she spoke, but felt a thrill of fear that was as dark as it was delicious.

'No, Lois, I didn't snatch his body,' replied Robin amiably, 'although I can see why you have to ask the question.'

'I'm sorry . . . I didn't mean it that way.' She searched his face, wondering if she'd hurt his feelings.

'It's all right, it was a fair conclusion.' He took her hands in his big warm ones. 'I didn't snatch Edgar's body. I simply slipped into it when he left it to go elsewhere.'

'Elsewhere?'

'Oh, he's around here somewhere, I think. Not too far . . . But he's not alone now. He's with somebody he loves.'

Lois blinked, and Robin lifted a long finger to wipe away a stray tear from her face.

'And I'm with somebody I love, so now everyone's happy.'

Lois smiled, still filled with wonder. 'So you . . . you're completely Robin in there . . . Not Edgar at all then?'

Robin shrugged, rolled his eyes and seemed suddenly to go inwards somehow. 'There're memories, knowledge, information that are available to me.' He looked at her and smiled. 'Which will no doubt be useful now that I'm going to have to live my life as a human being, don't you think?'

'Best of both worlds then?'

'Most definitely,' he declared roundly, his eyes twinkling now, looking brilliant and far more colourful. Cradling her jaw, he brought her face to his to steal a kiss.

The healthy human warmth in his lips might be new, but the way he kissed her was completely and utterly Robin. She sighed with pleasure beneath his mouth at the sweet familiarity, and low in her belly she felt another sweetness stir.

She wanted to ask him if he could still read her mind, but it seemed his body was certainly interpreting all the signals.

'Shouldn't you be resting?' she purred as he drew her further on to the bed, and moved over her, unfastening the cord of her dressing gown before plucking it open to reveal her bare skin underneath it. She'd not bothered to dress after the hot shower she'd taken to warm herself. 'I mean, you did just drown about an hour ago.'

'Ah, but it seems our dear friend Edgar was in prime physical condition, with superb powers of recuperation,' murmured Robin, beginning to kiss his way down her throat, towards her breasts, in a way that was unmistakeably and utterly and completely 'him'.

'Yes, he's not in bad nick at all,' concurred Lois, running her hands down the firm and muscular form of her lover's torso.

And reaching his loins she got a deliciously welcome surprise . . . Not quite Robin's fantasy dick, but still a magnificent specimen.

'Not bad at all,' she purred, beginning to slowly fondle it.

'And the best bit is . . . I still know how to use it.'

For a while, they touched and caressed, Lois entranced by the warm human feel of Robin's skin and his sex.

Until a thought occurred to her . . .

She looked up at him, gnawing her lip. She was almost certain that he couldn't accurately read her mind any more, but she knew he could sense her emotion, her quandary.

'What is it, my love?' he asked. His expression was kind and far more tolerant of her hesitation at this crucial moment than any of her previous lovers would have been.

'Um, well, you're human now ... we need ...'

'Protection?' His eyes twinkled.

'Well, yes. I'm sorry, I mean, I don't ...'

Robin drew her back into his arms, close and sweet. 'Don't worry, sweet Lois.' His breath was a whisper against her ear, and, as she nuzzled him, she realised that, very faintly, he still smelt of lavender. 'If you don't have condoms, there are plenty of *other* ways to give each other pleasure. I have the imagination of *two* men now, remember?'

'Well, actually,' she began bashfully, 'I was sort of half hoping for a holiday romance when I packed for this trip.' She pursed her lips. 'There are some condoms in the bedside drawer.' She pulled back a little and looked up at him, with a little smirk. 'Although we can still do some of that other stuff first, can't we?'

'With pleasure, my love.' His lips began the process that his hands and his body would soon complete, beginning the journey down her body, tasting lightly and sampling her skin with his tongue. 'With the greatest of pleasure,' he murmured, looking up at her, his odd eyes twinkling as he kissed the gentle curve of her belly.

Epilogue

The sky was bright, the sun was high and the air was warm. It was summer already, a gorgeous June day, when just a week ago it had felt like deepest winter.

Lois squeezed Robin's hand as they strolled contentedly on the beach. They were barefoot in the surf but the rolling water held no fear for them. A short while earlier they'd taken a swim, frolicking happily.

'Look!' Robin gestured elegantly to a large chunk of driftwood a few yards away and, following his eye-line, Lois saw a pair of birds perched together on its highest branch.

They were billing and cooing, preening each other, a perfect picture of mutual devotion and affection. Lois squinted, in the sun, and wondered if her eyes were deceiving her. The two birds looked vaguely familiar, and very much like the gull-like form her Robin had taken before he'd found this new body, lately vacated by the unfortunate Edgar.

'They could be us,' she observed, as the birds continued to canoodle, despite the presence of two humans so close by.

'Not *us*,' replied Robin, turning to her, an odd expression on his broad handsome face. His hair was gold-tipped now, and it shone in the morning sun. 'But perhaps someone we know . . . and the one he longed to be with.'

'Really?'

Lois's astonished exclamation finally disturbed the two lovebirds, and they took to the skies above the bay, whirling and wheeling, their glossy wings seeming to entwine as they soared in an aerial ballet of sheer exuberance.

'Looks like they're making love, doesn't it?' observed Robin, smiling as he watched their play. 'Shall we go back indoors and do the same?'

Lois looked up into his eyes, smiling back at him. The blue one was bluer and the brown one browner now that, more and more, he became the natural resident of his brand-new body.

'I'd love to, Magic Man, I'd really love to!'

Tugging on his big warm hand, she led the way towards the path.

The Dragon Lord

by

Olivia Knight

'I'm dying, Lord Drake.'

He nodded, expressionless. It was clear. Her bright sheen had dulled. She was discolouring and flakes fell as she shifted in the golden bed, suddenly harder to see as his eyes swam. Through the archways, the wind came keen and chill, but his front was warm. Heat radiated from her, even now. His trousers tightened around his groin as he swelled. Greying, withered and decaying on her deathbed, the Queen still blazed. She inflamed them all. He closed his eyes, waiting for the tears and the surge of lust to pass.

'Is there a new egg?' he asked, his voice strained.

'Yes.' She watched him wrestling with himself and added, 'It won't be for some time yet, but the riders must begin the search.'

He opened his eyes again and inclined in a deep bow.

'Thank you.' He was dismissed.

He went from her bedside to Lady Tanya. She'd been out riding; her hair was tousled and her leather breeches were still hot beneath his palms from the animal's flanks. They unpeeled each other's clothes and her hard limbs pulled him in. When he lay sunk inside her, he pressed his forehead against her neck and said thickly, 'The Queen is dying.'

Her quake of shock gripped his cock hard and, almost involuntarily, he thrust.

'We must ride then,' she said through her moans.

'Yes.' He drove harder into her, then both were silent and intent until strangled screams slid from their throats like the smell of burnt silk.

Part one

Princess Nina of Navarone sat resplendent in lace and gold brocade at the centre of the head table. The layers of fabric draped around her, hiding the warm lively body beneath. She was sure she looked like a pile of curtains. Even her fiery hair was hidden by a close-fitting lace cap, with dangling pearls that tickled her forehead. At least her face was free – until tomorrow, then that too would be veiled or masked for the next twelve days. She was stifling beneath the engagement gown and envied the shivering guests.

Marsh damp crept up through the flagstones of the castle's great hall. When the door opened, the wetland stink mixed with the smell of guests' perfume, wax and fatty meat. Dignitaries from all twelve countries jostled politely for elbow-room as they worked their way through the stodgy fare. When the meal ended and the Navarone musicians stopped sawing their instruments, a collective sigh of relief was hastily disguised with clapping. Two servants wheeled a harp forwards and the Sirattan minstrel's hands ran across the strings as he said, 'Perhaps the Princess would like to choose a personal favourite?'

She raised her eyebrows and glanced at her parents, who nodded, then at her groom-to-be, who smiled encouragingly.

'Yes,' she said, strong and deep. 'Would you play the Song of Kâo?'

'Nina!' hissed her mother.

'What? He said I could choose.'

'It's a nursery tale! Are you trying to embarrass us?'

Nina's face set angrily and the King scowled. 'Won't you choose something more fitting?' he asked loudly.

'I want the Song of Kâo.' Nina's voice carried too.

'It'll be *The Three Riddles* next,' muttered the Queen, 'Or *The Snow-Swan!*'

The Duke Mahli wrapped Nina's hand tightly in his. He beamed at her and raised his chin defiantly to the gathering. 'What could be more fitting? My wife-to-be retains a childlike simplicity of spirit, and I hope she may always keep her youthful innocence. A pure soul is the finest flower a maiden can offer her husband.' He kissed her hand to a smattering of applause.

The King nodded curtly. The musician's arms flowed around the harp and he sang.

> *Karitta go karew karew*
> *In the land of Kâo, the words were true.*
> *The Lords and Ladies flew by night*
> *In the land of Kâo, the moon was bright.*
>
> *Karitta go karew karack*
> *In the land of Kâo, the moon went black.*
> *The Lords and Ladies fell today*
> *And all the people ran away.*

The harp was clear as a bell and he whisked up fancy variations, but it was still a nursery rhyme. The guests looked rigidly ahead. The delighted children raced to the centre to dance. Nina's chin rested on her hand, her eyes staring unfocused and dreamy across the bobbing little heads. As it ended, all the children scattered, shrieking and giggling, then pelted back as the musician took up a reprise. Mahli followed Nina's gaze and smiled to himself. She had all the makings of a fine wife: gentle, simple and motherly.

'I can't think what the wretched girl was playing at!' snapped Queen Yonta.

She and King Daurio moved swiftly around the freezing room, preparing for bed. Daurio shifted the warming pans so their toes wouldn't meet icy sheets.

'Knowing Nina, she just wanted to cause trouble, or make fun of the proceedings,' he said.

'I've never known anything like her!'

'No one has.'

Yonta twisted her hair into its nightcap. 'And what did you make of Mahli tonight?'

'His sententious little speech, do you mean? Very diplomatic. I can only hope he didn't believe a word of it.'

Yonta looked at him sharply. 'Nina didn't react, so I imagine he did.'

The King grimaced and the Queen sighed, her hands falling into her lap.

'Are we doing the right thing, Daurio?'

He pulled the warmers out from the bed and tucked himself hastily in. 'What else can we do? The priest said only marriage will cure her, so she must marry.'

Yonta still sat forlornly. 'But Mahli? Is he really the best man for her?'

'He's solid and sensible, his farming estates are well run, he's a noble, and he's learning the business of kingship fast. He's a good man. He's even decent-looking. And besides – he's the only potential husband she hasn't actually tried to set fire to.' He shrugged. 'What more can we ask?' He patted the empty space next to him and she clambered in.

'How much have you told him?'

'Almost everything,' admitted Daurio. 'Which spies we have in Ysk, the secret trade agreements with Crewer, the Sirattan conspiracy . . .'

'No – about Nina.'

The King shook his head slowly.

'He doesn't know? Nothing at all?'

'No.'

'But I thought we agreed –'

'What was I supposed to say?' he exclaimed. 'Anyway, if all goes as the priest says, the problem will be fixed and Mahli need never know.'

'I just don't think I can bear it any more.' Tired, heartsick tears made the candlelight spangle.

Her husband gripped her hand tightly. 'Twelve more days, Yonta. That's all. We've borne it for nineteen years, we can last another twelve days. Then she'll be married and all this trouble will be over at last.'

At the prospect of relief, her tears spilt over and she snuggled into the curve of Daurio's arm as he blew out the candle.

As the engagement ceremony dragged on, Nina's eyes wandered behind her veils. The morning was thick with cloud and the candles fought unsuccessfully against the gloom. Her mother had anxiously pointed out the beauties of a winter wedding – the magic of candlelight, the mystery of early dark – but no one in their right mind visited Navarone at this time of year. Her parents just couldn't bear to wait another six months. Nor could she – everything would ease. She wanted to do right, but her nature betrayed her every time. This man, apparently, would end it all.

King Daurio was echoing the words that pledged his daughter to the Duke. Through the blurred embroidered flowers on her veil, her eyes settled speculatively on Mahli's face – large-boned and handsome, with fleshy lips and the first hint of jowls which disappeared as he jutted his chin. She was just beginning to imagine his sturdy build without his clothes, when the vows came to an end and she extended her covered hand. A gust of freezing air swept up the aisle. Her eyes shot to the church door, which had creaked open. A figure darkened the narrow rectangle of grey light and shut the door again behind him. He leant against a pillar, beneath a brazier. The congregation craned their necks and the priest raised his voice for their attention. He was winding a ball of wool around the couple's joined hands, but eyes kept straying to the latecomer. Nina faced her betrothed but her green eyes fixed on the stranger. He was dressed in armour she'd never seen before, with a breastplate that spiked into a sharp metal ruff at the nape of his neck. The brazier's orange light fell over a haughty wistful face. He stood, patient but distracted, as if the ceremony were a conversation that he was waiting to interrupt.

'And so,' pronounced the priest, making half the congregation jump in fright, 'this couple are betrothed, before the eyes of God and of you all, and in twelve days they will make good their promise and be wed, for God has said so.'

'God has said so,' mumbled the congregation automatically.

Their hands still tied together, Nina and Mahli walked up the aisle. The stranger studied her keenly – at the sense of eye-contact, even through her veils, she rushed with heat. His expression intensified, the blood rose in her cheeks, then she was outside in the cold.

In state at the head table, the royal couple received their guests and their gifts one by one, the names shouted by the doorman. The King and Queen of neighbouring Siratta bowed and curtseyed, but not too deeply – their kingdom was richer. They'd already provided the Princess's trousseau and now presented the two with a wooden 'secrets box'. The carved patterns and inlaid ivory were linked to mechanisms inside and opened only to those who mastered its secret. Every one was different. The envoys from the frozen wastelands of Ysk gave them each a cloak made from the soft white fur of the katak. From the equally barren but hotter land of Jarth, men in spiked black armour brought a lump of crystal the size of the Princess's fist. It was éolith, supposed to have magical properties, and extremely rare. Clumps of dirt still clung to it – only the owner should handle it. Mahli reached out his hand, but Nina's was still tied to it. The envoy fumbled; a clot of earth broke off and the crystal touched her skin first. It was hers, then. Two huntsmen from Crewer gave a bow and arrow to the new King-in-waiting and a coil of silvery rope to the Princess. They were famous for their rope – they lived in the mountains and were great climbers, as happy dangling over a cliff-edge as strolling down a mountain path. They were less happy in this clammy air and both had streaming colds.

The stranger lingered by the door, Nina's view blocked by the stream of well-wishers. When he stepped into the doorway, the doorman hesitated over how to announce him. The stranger murmured; the doorman pulled back, sneering in disbelief. Everyone watched the quick argument, then the stranger shrugged, turned to the hall, and said, 'I am Lord Drake of Kâo.'

He may as well have said he was from the moon. Ignoring the snorts, stares and babble breaking out, he strode down the length of the room and swept into a bow. Under her veil, Nina stared open-mouthed.

'Forgive me that I have no gift.' He spoke low and musically. 'I beg you will accept my congratulations.'

He was led to a place setting crammed on to the end of a table. Nina watched his dinner companions avoid and stare at him by turns, before curiosity triumphed and they leant over, their mouths phrasing questions that the hubbub of the hall drowned out. The stranger simply nodded or shrugged to each one.

'Do you think he's a spy?' said Mahli.

King Daurio huffed through his nose and shook his head. 'A spy would have a better story, draw less attention to himself.'

'He must be a madman,' said the Queen darkly.

'He seems quite calm.'

'That's the worst kind. We won't be safe in our beds! We should have him locked up –'

'And break the laws of hospitality?' Nina's voice cut in from beneath her veils.

Mahli considered her words then squeezed her hand. 'The bride is a model of propriety.'

Behind him, Queen Yonta rolled her eyes at King Daurio, whose mouth twitched.

The parties were dull. Navarone was hospitable, but its chill crept into the marrow of one's bones. Everyone complained under their breath about the draughty rooms and heavy food, except Lord Drake. No one knew where he was staying, and they joked that he flew back to Kâo each night, or turned into a bat and hung upside down in the rafters, or had a magical castle in the clouds. He kept himself apart, always with the same air of waiting. His remote eyes followed the Princess's tall figure as she wound through the crowds like a flame, her face hidden. When people teased him about coming from 'Kâo', he looked through them and smiled distantly. After a few days their inventiveness failed, the novelty wore off, and they left him alone. He didn't seem to notice.

The eighth night was a masked ball. Flocks of birds were sacrificed for the masks, which were feathered, gilded and embroidered in precarious designs. Drake obediently accepted a falcon mask and wandered from room to room, wishing the ball over. Tomorrow – perhaps even tonight – he could return to Kâo from this wild goose chase, rest and begin the next search. Musing, he opened a door and found a candlelit room, blessedly free of musicians.

The open curtains let in the dank fog, and he leant on the windowsill to look out over the dark wetlands. Occasionally, a distant marsh fire flared green. For a long time he stared, then, with a deep sigh, bowed his head and saw shoes peeping out beneath the curtain. He watched fascinated as one of them shifted. He chuckled. 'You can come out if you like.'

The curtain unwrapped to show a woman, the top half of her face masked in red with gold filigree curling around her eyes, her lips painted blue. Her hair was bright as fire.

'I'm sorry,' she said, confused. 'I didn't expect you to stay – I couldn't bear another polite conversation!'

'The very reason I stayed here myself,' he said smiling.

'I feel so silly – I was watching the marsh fires when I heard the door. I didn't think at all, I just hid.'

'We can watch them together, if you like.' He offered his arm to escort her out the alcove and she laughed, taking it. Side by side, they leant on the sill.

'So, if we don't have a polite conversation, what shall we discuss?' he said.

'Well,' she said thoughtfully, 'we can't admire the climate or the musicians – or, I suspect, the food.'

'Or the bride's beauty, considering she's always covered in veils.'

The girl started. 'Of course – you arrived late, before the engagement, it was all display and parade.'

'Is she really thought beautiful, then?'

'It's hard to say what is genuine in Navarone,' the girl said cautiously. In a rush, she added, 'The custom here is to lie continuously – to mouth platitudes – to say whatever is expected, to conceal truths, to scheme and plot – all of diplomacy is just a mass of lies – everything is a pretence, not just the words people say but how they live, who they are.' She stopped her tirade abruptly, embarrassed.

He lifted her hand to the spiky letters engraved on his breast-plate. She traced the metal grooves. 'What does that say?'

'*Karayeethra ga Karayu* – Honesty and Honour, in your language. It's the motto of Kâo.'

'Are you really from Kâo, then?'

He sighed. 'Yes. Though I realise that everyone here has difficulty believing me.'

'I believe you,' she said quickly. 'At least – I believe that *you* believe it.'

'And perhaps that's the best I can hope for.'

'I love that song. It's always been my favourite.'

His eyes turned sadly out to the windows, but his hand held hers tighter. His quest might be a failure, but the party was brighter for containing this girl.

'And now I'm holding hands with a man from a story,' she mused.

His fingers released hers abruptly. 'I'm not from a story,' he growled. 'I'm real.'

She stared. 'You said honesty. I'm only being honest; that's truly what I believe.'

He smiled thinly. '"What the heart believes to be true is never untruthful" – that's a saying of ours. But there's always the polite option of silence. You could do me the courtesy of not saying you think I'm made up.'

'But even silence misleads – not telling a truth can help someone believe a lie.'

He laughed, delighted. 'You're passionate about truth. In Kâo, that's important. And, of course, you're right, it's a delicate line to tread.'

Whether the silence lied or not, they let it settle over them, except for murmuring 'Look' or 'Over there' as the pale lights flared and vanished. Like another quiet language, her drooping sleeve brushed his wrist, his upper arm returned from a gesture to lie closer to hers. Both seemed not to notice the furtive touches; both were hypersensitive to every hair-tip's contact. His fingertips ran across the inside of her wrist, breaking the pretence. Neither breathed as he traced lightly. They kept their eyes averted, hypnotised by his invisible drawing. His hand slipped higher, under her loose sleeve. In feathery increments, his fingertips crept to the crease of her arm and when they found it she moaned.

'Look at me,' he murmured.

Her dilated green eyes lifted. His were dark grey, searching. He glanced at her lips, back up, then at the swell of her breasts. He knew she could see where he was looking, and she knew that was deliberate. Under his eyes' caress, her lips parted, as her breasts got goosebumps. Her breath came faster and made her cleavage rise and fall. Her eyes flickered to his lips and shyly away.

'No,' he said. 'Be honest.'

So she studied them, thinking about kissing them, and with the thought clear on her face met his eyes again. He put a hand on her waist and guided her closer. Their lips touched and their bodies brushed. His groin swelled as their tongues twisted wetly.

'Now am I made up?' he asked.

She shuddered in his arms. 'I don't think so.'

The heat from her skin came like waves and he closed his eyes, the lust rolling. He burnt for her and a terrible thought occurred to him: it could be her, that could be why, and, if so, he was compromising his honour. She nudged her hips from side to side until his bulge rested in white-hot longing at the apex of her thighs. His mind was drowned out by sensation, and he thrust the thought aside. She was lovely, sexy, and she was sliding against him; that was enough to explain the roaring lust.

His hand clutched the hem of her bodice, his fingers against the bare slope of her breast beneath. They lapped each other's tongues and she whimpered as his nail caught her nipple. Their hips rubbed harder, trying to complete what their clothes made impossible, and with one hand each they tugged her skirt upwards.

The door creaked. The girl sprang away, twirling to the window.

'Look at that flare!' she exclaimed. Facing away from the door, she rubbed the back of her hand over her mouth, wiping away the smeared blue lipstick. Surprised, Drake surreptitiously copied her example.

'Princess Nina,' said a servant. 'Your parents and the Consort have been looking for you – it's time for the speeches.'

Only the marshes saw the horror that crossed Drake's face.

Deep in the marshlands, in the top room of an abandoned stone fort, Drake sat alone. The weathered table knocked from side to side as his arm rested to write then lifted again. The dirty greens and greys of the countryside through the arrow-slot were thick with mist. In the hearth, his fire blazed, the only brightness in this melancholy land – that, and the Princess's flaming hair. He sighed, abandoning his parchment, and climbed the ladder to the parapets. On the rooftop, a vast creature lay. Only his head showed through the trap door, as Drake eyed it warily. A massive green eye stared back, unblinking. He stepped up another rung and it swung its jaw, a gust of hot air running over him like a furnace. A flame darted out, just missing him. It was a warning. Drake retreated to his stone room and his attempts at a letter.

'Forgive me,' he had written and crossed out. Asking for forgiveness was dishonest: he hadn't committed a deliberate wrong. 'If I'd known, I would never have kissed you' was also false: 'never' was a powerful word. He watched the fire for a long time, his face remote with thought, and finally he wrote the careful deliberate words: 'I didn't know who you were, though I briefly suspected. You are engaged and so I believe our deeds were wrong . . .' His pen hovered for a long time while he thought about the words *and I regret them*, but instead he simply added a full stop and his name. With a piercing whistle, he summoned his hawk as he rolled the parchment.

'Take this to the flame-haired human, when no other humans can see,' he said in birdcall as he tied the message to its leg with twine. His hawk cocked its head, beady-eyed. 'Go.'

For the rest of the evening, he watched the fire burn down, banishing thoughts of kissing and grinding into Nina. He went to bed, only to have his head swarm with what might have come next. His fantasies raced to her nakedness, were suppressed, made their way more slowly through undressing her, were sternly halted, and drifted into kneeling in front of her. He turned over restlessly on his thin straw pallet, refusing to think what she might taste like. He fell at last into a restless sleep: his honour slept and his passion raged. He had just sunk himself into her heat with a bellow of joy, when a flutter of wings woke him.

In the dark, he could barely see the hawk and smelt no trace of blood – it hadn't eaten, then. He held his wrist out, wondering why, and as it leapt on he felt the circular stamp of a parchment roll on its leg. By candlelight, back at the wobbly table, he read the graceful script.

'Do you truly believe it was wrong? Every law and principle says so, but I have always trusted my feelings and it didn't feel wrong. I don't know what to think – except that I wish we hadn't been interrupted.'

He swallowed hard. That, too, was his wish.

The next evening, he sat again in silence at the bottom table furthest from the royals. His eyes were drawn to the Princess, but he couldn't see hers, under the gauzy purple. Heart hammering, he ate even less than usual. She could still be the one – or he could be besotted by the only girl to show him warmth in this miserable place. When the dancing began, he lingered, wanting to take her in his arms – if only on the dance floor and for the length of a song. He watched her sitting, unmoving, until disappointment sickened him and he left the hall.

In a quiet dim passage, he laid his forehead on the wall, grateful for once that the stone was ice-cold. He should have left Navarone – except now he couldn't leave. He had deceit in his heart, but where it lay was a mystery, except that somehow he was deceiving himself so well he didn't know how.

Something rustled beside him. His stomach somersaulted as he turned.

'Lord Drake,' she said softly, stepping closer.

Her hands touched his, her body near. Desire dizzied him. That was the key – it could be the proof of what he longed to believe, or it could be the very thing that blinded him to the truth. He backed away, the stone cold and hard behind him. 'Your Majesty – no,' he said hoarsely.

His shaft was making a tent of his trousers, and she moved against it. As the fabric rubbed, he groaned.

'Honesty and honour, you said.' She was breathless. 'So which is greater?'

'Honesty.' That was one of the tenets of Kâo and part of the catechism – so it could still be her, in which case ... His cock twitched against her and she shivered. 'But this is not honest,' he said through gritted teeth. 'This is ... furtive, and wrong ... and, and, and ...' The effort of not seizing her, not ramming her against the wall, and not tearing her clothes off made it difficult to speak.

'Then we shouldn't be furtive.'

He was silent.

'You didn't answer the question in my letter.' Her breath was humid on his ear through her veil. His hips rocked up against hers and he felt her sigh.

'I can't think,' he gasped. He managed to hold her away, at arm's length, and studied the gauze that hid her face. 'I will write – I promise – but, when you're next to me, I can't think. I must go.' He bolted abruptly and she watched him stride away. He didn't look back.

In heavy Yskian fur, Nina paced through the lily gardens. Wooden walkways criss-crossed above the sodden ground. The water-table was highest in winter, only the grass-tips breaking the surface. Mist clung to the ground, making it hard to see where the air ended and the water began. She tried not to reread Drake's letter, repeated it to herself in her head, unrolled it again to check a word, then put it in her pocket with new resolve.

'For once, I no longer know what is right or wrong, and until I can be honest in my own heart I'm trapped here. I want you intensely. You must know that. You must have felt that. What I feel is pure as fire but I no longer know whether to act on what I feel. I am striving for honesty, Nina, to clear my slate, and I'm afraid I'm only making it worse by saying: honestly, my strongest feelings are that I should, we should – but you have pledged yourself to be married, so all this is an impossible nonsense. I would leave if I could. I don't even know what I achieve by sending this, except for keeping my promise.'

He'd cut short the very thought she most wanted to know

by reminding her of what she most wanted to forget: her marriage. She thought in circles as she walked, trying to come at the problem from every angle, but always returning to the same two warring facts: she was engaged; she felt no guilt. She was engaged and she'd kissed another man, and worse, and lusted after him even now, and everyone would be shocked and disgusted if they knew; her parents would be so angry; she should feel like the most wretched of sinners – but it still felt right.

Staring at the white sky, she tried to think of her wedding and instead pictured Drake's hands on her breasts, reaching under her skirt . . . She remembered a third term in the argument: her problem. Perhaps, if marriage were the cure, and marriage was about bodies and touching like that, then these powerful feelings for Drake were just another symptom and tomorrow evening it would all be cured. Her eyes narrowed. *I will do right*, she told herself sternly. Those words rang true with the centre of her being. She didn't need to fret over what was right: the church and the law were clear. *I will do right*, she thought again resolutely, but this time it rang hollow.

Once more, Nina faced Mahli in church, heavily veiled. Her eyes had already found the dark corner where Drake leant against the wall. Her insides burnt as her father made the vows, and she reasoned that, like a fever, the problem must get worse before it got better. Familiar rage gripped her as she stood, determined and still. When the congregation prayed, Drake closed his eyes and spoke to his own gods.

'Spirits of Kâo,' he said, 'purge me of dishonesty and restore my honour. Let me be guided by what I know to be true.' He shut out the priest's drone and prayed more fervently. 'Let the truth be revealed to me.'

When Nina made her vows, that would be the end of it and

he would know for certain that it wasn't her, it never had been, and he was nothing but a fool of passion. The scene he was really waiting for, however, was the moment that Nina opened her mouth to make her vows and howled, ripping her veil off.

'I can't do this,' she'd scream. The long wedding dress would billow as she spun and leapt away from the altar, before racing towards the doors where he'd be standing already, holding them wide open. He'd grab her in his arms and kiss her hungrily, in front of everyone – no, he'd fall to one knee, head bowed – no, they would snatch each other's hands and run together into the marshes, not stopping for hours until they reached the fort, and there he would sink to his knees and swear his loyalty.

'For God has said so,' intoned the priest.

'God has said so,' repeated the congregation. The dreadful Navarone violins struck up and the couple walked down the aisle.

Drake's eyes widened. Could these people be so stupid, so far from the ancient ways of Kâo, that the bride herself didn't even speak? He stared at the clouds of white that hid her face, then at the faces of the guests who were filing out after them. He'd prepared his heart to wait until now – but it was as if they'd all come to church and forgotten to hold the wedding.

There was another way to find out but it meant waiting till morning. His heart sank at the thought of another lonely night in the fort, tormented by thoughts of her, clinging to his stupid fantasy and trying to persuade himself of the truth. His face rigid, he headed out into the marshes. Perhaps, as he waded through mud and skidded on ice, he could finally make himself accept the glaring, obvious fact: *it wasn't her*.

The monstrous bulk of the fort was swathed in mist. One moment the horizon was white; the next its stone walls blotted out the sky. Hundreds of years ago, when the Twelve had been squabbling and fighting among themselves, this had held three hundred soldiers and the stones had clattered with armour. Now it held only one man, climbing slowly to a room at the top, repeating with every step, 'It isn't her.' When he reached the top, he walked through the room to the stepladder and climbed the rungs. In the terrace at the top, bigger than the castle's great hall, the coiled dragon lay tightly squeezed. On the upper rungs, half out, Drake willed his heart to be as clear as his mind. The dragon's scales rasped as it turned his head and an eye bigger than he was studied him. He met its gaze. A jet of flame scorched him; he leapt back, spinning through the air, and smashed on to the hard floor of the room. He lay winded. One hand cautiously explored his face and hair – he was only singed. The dragon had given its second and final warning: there was still deceit in his heart. If he'd spoken, the dragon wouldn't have been so kind. He crawled to the pallet and wrapped his arms around his knees.

'You're a fool, Drake,' he said aloud. No one fooled the dragons and no Lord of Kâo should fool himself. He'd told himself he believed, at last, it wasn't her, but even while he sat here his mind saw her stepping into the room. She'd made no vows; she could still come to him, instead of going to her wedding bed. Any moment, she would appear. Right now, she'd be walking through the marshes, following his tracks through the mud . . .

The newly married Princess was in her room, opposite the new Prince. Mahli stepped forwards with a loving smile to lift back her veil, but she tore off the headdress and tossed it on the ground. Her hands tugged her hair free and she shook it out, long and brilliant.

'What now?' she asked.

He blinked, hunting for words. 'It's perhaps – uh – better if

I show you, than explain. I don't know if it's suitable for me to explain, to a woman.'

She stared at him. 'I'm supposed to *do* something that it's not suitable for me to hear *described*?'

The cure wasn't working yet. The rage had worsened and burnt inside. She needed to do something to release it – break a glass, smash the writing table, set fire to the curtains, anything except this infuriating quiet. She bit her lip, hard.

Mahli poured mead into two goblets. She was afraid, he reminded himself. If she seemed less maidenly than he'd hoped, that was just false bravado. He handed her a goblet and stroked her hair gently.

'It's normal for a bride to be scared,' he said.

She frowned. 'I don't think I am.' She sipped, looking for something she could surreptitiously set fire to. Unfortunately the wood in the fireplace was already crackling merrily. Sending the furnishings up in flames would cause comment. Wasn't the marriage supposed to have cured this? 'When will it work?' she muttered.

He moved to stand very close to her and chuckled softly. 'There are a few more steps, first.' His palm found her waist.

'Oh!' Realisation dawned on her face. The cure wasn't the ceremony – it was this bit. 'Right. OK.'

His arm slid further around her. She thought of the sparkle Drake had lit up in her – this was as comfortable as being hugged by a chair. His large face loomed towards hers and she pulled back.

'Don't be afraid,' he said. His other hand cradled her head, holding it still, as he moved in again.

'I'm not.' She twitched her lips away and he laid his heavy cheek against hers. She thought of his fat lips on hers with distaste. Her instincts told her to fight free, but she forced herself to stay stiffly still as his mouth found hers. His tongue hunted for an entrance and settled instead for licking along her cheek – like a snail crawling, she thought, disgusted. He drew her against the lump in his trousers. With Drake, she'd wanted to rub against that; with Mahli, she wanted to recoil.

Take your medicine, she told herself. The cure couldn't be worse than her problem, and after this she would be pure and proper again – normal. He was beginning to pant, his hands clutching at her waist and buttocks.

'Open your mouth,' he whispered.

She did and his tongue intruded, sluglike. She recoiled.

'It's OK, trust me,' he soothed, gripping her tighter, and in it went again.

She wasn't sure if she was supposed to suck it or just let it explore the roof of her mouth. Either was disgusting. She shoved it back out with her own tongue and he groaned her name, his hips digging into her. As he rubbed harder, she was forced backwards against the wall. Each time his tongue slid into her mouth, she ejected it but, instead of stopping, it returned more eagerly.

'You see?' he gasped. 'Oh, Nina, you're like fire!'

He was writhing against her, his swollen groin bucking up against her skirts, his chest squashing her breasts this way and that. He'd ripped off his heavy coat and belt and his hands were tugging her bodice open, scrabbling to unravel the ribbon. The strange thing, she thought, was she'd wanted exactly this, with Drake, but with Mahli it was nasty – yet Mahli was her husband, while Drake was surely a deluded nobody who thought he came from a fairytale.

He sucked at her tongue fiercely; it felt odd, keeping it stuck out like that, but it was better than having his shoved into her mouth. Her bodice's ribbon snapped and he grabbed a breast in each hand. He kneaded them like dough, sighing and moaning. He left her tongue alone, at last, to snuffle at her breasts.

He hauled himself upright again, lifting her skirts too and they frothed around his waist like a cloud. Her eyes were wide with tension, her mouth set, as he gazed in raptures at her face.

'Don't be afraid,' he said again, his voice strangled as he rooted under the puffing layers of petticoats. One hand tugged at her bare bottom and she started in shock. 'Yes!' he cried. His face buried itself in her neck. His hand had withdrawn, and he was fiddling with his trousers. Against her hair, he kept up a stream of mumbled words, that he hoped he wasn't going fast, that she was more passionate than he'd ever dreamt, that he couldn't wait to have her, and so on. She felt horribly exposed with her skirts held up and him so close to her nakedness. With one hand, she tried to lower them. Misunderstanding, he seized her wrist and guided it through the layers to his shaft, which throbbed hot. She snatched her hand away, appalled, trying to shift away from him along the wall.

'Sorry,' he said, shrinking at the shock in her face. 'Too much, too soon – I know.'

She slid further away, shaking her skirts back down.

'Nina, it's OK.' He followed her so she couldn't shuffle to the side without fighting him. She didn't want to fight; she knew this was what she was supposed to do, but it felt invasive. He kissed her more and she submitted patiently, wishing they could get it all over with. Soon her skirts were rising again. She stared over his shoulder. She knew the basics of how this worked. His hand touched between her legs and she shoved him violently. He staggered backwards.

'I'm sorry,' she said, covering herself. 'I just can't.'

'I know you're afraid . . .'

'By God, Mahli!' she snapped. 'I'm *not* afraid! Will you stop saying that?' The tension and burning in her were dreadful, fuelling her anger. 'I just don't want to.'

He stared at her, bewildered. His cock still swayed, fat and hopeful, as he kicked his trousers off his ankles.

'I don't want to and I can't and that's it,' she said firmly.

'But you're my wife.'

'So?' She folded her arms.

He approached her again, his hands moving to her hips. 'I know it's hard at first,' he said. His eyes glazed as he lodged himself like an arrow through her petticoats. Only the fabric's constraint kept him from forcing his way in as his hips jolted. His breath was rising, his cheeks flushed.

'Soon,' he urged breathlessly, 'very soon – we're husband and wife, Nina, this is what happens. God, you inflame me, I must have you!'

Their hands fought over her skirts, and as she broke free a long strip tore.

'You're not going to!' she yelled. 'I don't want to!'

'But we're married!'

'So what? Are you going to force me?'

He lunged at her and she side-stepped swiftly, one ankle darting out to trip him. He fell headlong and scrabbled back to his feet.

'If I must,' he said grimly. 'If this is how you treat your husband.'

She laughed scornfully. 'Don't fight me, Mahli, you won't win.'

'I don't want to fight you, but you are my wife and you will act like one, in the way that is proper and right, and, however you feel about it now, you'll get over that.'

The marvellous thing was that he believed everything he said; she'd know if he didn't.

He went on. 'Now I don't want to force you, but one way or another we're going to have to do this for the first time, and it'll be easier if you just accept that.'

'What do you mean, you don't *want* to force me? You can't!'

'Oh yes, I can ...' He advanced towards her.

'Have my parents told you nothing? Don't make me do this, Mahli! I know you're an honest man ...'

'Don't make *me* do this,' he retorted, grabbing her wrists and forcing her backwards on to the bed.

Her eyes met his, perfectly calm. 'You don't want to force me, Mahli.'

He stopped as suddenly as if a bucket of water had been thrown over him and looked down at his bride's torn dress, his own half-naked body, his fingers digging into her arms.

'No,' he said, slow and wretched. 'I don't.'

The next morning, as was customary, the bloodied sheet was flown like a flag from their bedroom window and the locals hooted and applauded. The guests belatedly joined in. With this proof that the Prince had indeed pushed himself into the Princess's virginal flesh, the marriage was complete and they could all go home. Lord Drake stood at the back of the crowd, inscrutable, watching how the folds billowed around the tell-tale red stain. He disappeared into the mist. It was time to return to Kâo.

In the castle, Nina heard the shouting and raced up flights of stairs and down corridors until she burst into her room, breathless. She took in her parents and Mahli standing by the window, then the knots of the sheet tied to the pole.

'What is this?' she screeched.

The three spun around. Her face was wide and twisted with fury. The King and Queen, to Mahli's amazement, shrank back from their daughter in terror as she stalked forwards, her hips sinuous as a snake.

'What have you *done*?' she yelled in their faces.

'Nina, don't be angry, darling, keep calm,' babbled Yonta, while Daurio was saying, 'We had to, what would people think, we have to show proof . . .'

'It's a lie!' Her voice rang in their ears as her eyes narrowed on the sheet, her lips parting.

'Don't, stop it, I can't bear it!' Yonta had covered her face with her hands, sobbing. 'Please, Nina, no, it's supposed to be over now . . .'

Daurio wrapped his wife in his arms as the sheet went up in flames. Mahli's nostrils flared. He backed away, revolted, his eyes huge. Nina was watching the sheet burn with grim satisfaction, the fires reflecting in her eyes.

That night, Prince Mahli, gibbering with terror, was given a different room, so Nina woke alone to the fluttering of hawk wings. She opened her eyes to the bird's silhouette perched on her bedpost. As she lit the candle, it extended one leg stiffly.

> *Princess Nina,*
>
> *You said in a note that our acts didn't feel wrong to you, and that you didn't know what to think. I don't know what to think either, but it seems it must have been wrong. I wouldn't write, but I'm also implicated. If I've been dishonest in any way, I can't leave – and it seems I have. I must clear my slate. I hope this note to you will be enough and a public confession won't be necessary. Honesty also dictates that I say I would do almost anything rather than bring you pain.*
>
> *Lord Drake*

Tears sprang to her eyes at his implied judgement. 'Wait,' she whispered to the hawk, 'Oh please, wait . . .' Barefoot on the stone, she bent over the writing table to scribble her reply.

Lord Drake
There are things I can't explain in writing, that are still
true. You have only my word for this. If I look in your eyes,
I can tell you, I think. Like this, I don't dare. Please, let me
visit you.
Nina.

Drake's heart shook as he read her words. He looked around the desolate room and saw Nina sinking on to the straw pallet under him, her breasts bare, her dress hitching up. He convulsed with longing and began to write.

Only visit me if you can greet me with a passionate kiss
and not run away afterwards – or else, hide your face in
shame before my eyes can ever touch you again. You've
left my nights unquiet – leave my days in peace, unless
you're free to never leave. But oh – I want to say – come
to me anyway, and let me burn your skin with kisses! Let
me free your body, let your breasts tumble loose into my
hands . . . These are the thoughts you've left me with. This
is all you've left me. I should hate you as a deceiver, spurn
you as faithless. But I can't refuse even the brief proximity
of these words. To know, where my hand has passed, your
bright-green eyes will fall.

He stared at the parchment until the shining ink had dried to matt, then cut off everything but the first sentence, which he rolled into a tube and tied to his hawk's leg. In the fire, the rest of the letter shrivelled black beneath the marching lines of blue, gold and purple flames. He would have done better to write nothing. She deserved nothing – but he had to hold out that tiny offering of his hope. He thought of the fragment, high above the ground beneath the hawk's flapping wings. Now, it would reach her chamber window. Now, her hands would touch the bird, release the scrap of paper, read his words. Perhaps he should have defied honour and said: come; meet me at this hour, at this place. Would she? Could he turn his fevered imaginings into reality against her skin? If he tried to mount his dragon, it would incinerate him with a single breath. He had come to Navarone hoping to find the finest of them all. His heart and loins still insisted it was her, glorious her, but cold fact said otherwise. He sank his head into his hands.

Lord Drake,

You cut your message, but what you left was harsh. Was what you cut harsher still, or did your pen confess what you don't dare? Was it more, or less, the truth, than what you sent? Here is my truth. I live in two worlds, now. From the outside, I go about my days the same as ever. Behind the screen of my eyes, other scenes play out, endlessly. I imagine the servant hadn't come in, that we'd finished lifting my skirt (your hand and mine, acting in unison) and your hard heat was pressed closer, as I longed. I imagine coming to you – I don't know where you are, so I give us different settings every time. At the same pace as daily life, these scenes take place inside me: we talk, sometimes argue, see the truth in each other's eyes, we touch. Nothing will prevent this ceaseless inner reality. I scan the skies and catch my breath at every bird that passes. I dread your ill opinion and I know, if only we could speak, I could make everything clear – but explaining that muddle, here, is impossible. Now I have given you my truth. Will you give me yours?

Nina

Princess Nina

My heart tears. My loins ache. Your words worsen my own wild thoughts and make me feverish, but seem to be the medicine I long for. You guessed correctly: I cut away the truth I was ashamed of. I can't leave – so, if I'm blackened already, why not be blackened entirely? But my honour is my life: without betraying the secrets of Kâo, I can't say why. I pace this small room and the rest of me is elsewhere, in that secret world of imaginings, with you. Yes: I imagine. Each day, we succumb to each other a dozen different ways inside my head. I have undressed you for the first time a hundred times by now. You ask for truth, but what if the truth is dishonourable? I was taught it never can be. There isn't enough parchment in the world for the whole truth, but here is a fragment: last night, you found my hiding place, and while I lay restless by the dying coals you walked in. Without a word, you undressed and lay against me. Our movements were sweetness and truth itself, and all night we loved, heralding the dawn with your cries of bliss – all night, I dreamt sleeplessly of this, and met the dawn with a groan of shame. Now, I am wretched, confused, and long to be

Your lover,
Drake

Lord Drake,

Only you understand me when I speak about truth and what you say is right. It's always been something I've instinctively known. Felt, would be more accurate. I've never needed to think about it. And this longing for you that muffles every other sound, drowns out every other thought, feels true. My thoughts grow mad and frenzied. What you described, I then imagined. I think of how you

201

touched me, before, and in my dream we don't hurry. You
explore every part of me as lightly and patiently as you
did my wrist, my arm. If you can't leave, let me come to
you. Our thoughts, our letters, are only a shadow of our
skin. I sound mad and cheap. You must think me the lowest
kind of slut. When will you let me see you? Forget this mad
desire – I must speak to you.

    Nina

Drake paced the fort, tugging his hair. The way she wrote made it so easy to believe, still, against all reason, that she could be . . .

'It's impossible!' he yelled, slamming his hand into the stone. A deep growl from the dragon overhead shook the fort's masonry and loose plaster pattered on to the floor. As long as the dragon refused to take him home, he was stuck here. The longer he stayed, the more likely he would make an adulteress of her. He squeezed his palms into his eyes. What could he write honourably? Her low breathless voice echoed in his ears – *Honesty and honour – which is greater?* He sat and picked up his pen.

Princess Nina,

    To me you're neither cheap nor a slut – I don't care any
more what the facts say. My heart tells me you're perfect.
My body tells me you'll fulfil me. And still I hesitate. I wasn't
exaggerating when I said my honour is my life: I'll die if
I'm dishonest. How do I wrest honesty, now, from this situ-
ation? To take you in my arms, bring you absolute joy, would
be the most honest to myself – and to you. But it would
deceive your husband and, in the case of a child, your whole
kingdom. So I can't offer you the pleasure that my body
promises every hour. In my dreams, we are always entwined.

The emptiness around my hard shaft is unbearable. I remember your kisses like a drowning man remembers air. And still I vacillate between begging you to come and trying to salvage some semblance of honour. Oh, Nina, truthfully, I've been your lover since we first touched.

Drake

Lord Drake,

When you say 'honour', do you mean truth or custom? You say you value the former, but you follow the latter. I criticise you because I'm raging. I'm burning. I feel as if I've heard the opening bars of a Sirattan ballad and the tune hovers indefinitely out of reach of my ears. You said truth was precious in Kâo and you'll write the truth but you won't let it be. Is it just something to be mouthed, then, is it a matter of form and ceremony as false as any courtly rite, or is it something that beats in your blood, defines your existence and dictates your steps? I'm married to a man for whom I feel only distaste, and dream of a man whose mere memory gives me fevers. Is this what you call honour? Then honour be damned, if it only sanctifies a lie!

Nina

Her pen slammed down as she reread her words. *Married,* she'd written, and she supposed she still was, but Mahli wouldn't be troubling her to do her wifely duty any time soon. Since the scene over the sheet, he blanched and hurried away whenever he saw her. Occasionally, her mother tried to have a little talk with Nina about 'physical things' – these usually ended with Yonta patting her daughter's hand nervously and saying, 'You and Mahli will sort it out soon, I'm sure,' as if it were a little squabble.

03

The hawk leapt off the windowsill and she watched its black speck disappear then turned back to the table. Her fingers worked deftly, depressing and twisting the fastenings of the secrets box. She slid Drake's last note in with others, then clicked it all shut.

'Nina.'

She spun around. Mahli hovered at the doorway, as if poised for flight, his face white.

'You learnt how to work it then,' he said nervously, nodding at the box.

'Yes.'

'Will you show me?'

Her heart jumped into her throat. 'No.'

He nodded. 'Can I . . . come in?'

'If you like,' she said with raised eyebrows. 'I didn't think you wanted to see me.'

He sat on a chair, twisting his hands, not looking at her. 'I've been talking to the priest,' he said. 'About your – your problem. He's explained. I didn't know. And he also said some things about the – the sanctity of marriage. You're my wife.' He didn't look pleased at the prospect, but she couldn't blame him. 'He also said about the cure. I – Nina, I won't pretend I'm not disgusted by you, but you are my wife, and I can't turn my back on that.'

'Why not?'

He gaped. 'What do you mean?'

'I mean – so what, we had a ceremony, we haven't even shared a bed. What does it matter?'

'Nina, be reasonable,' he said, sounding more like himself. 'One doesn't just walk away from a marriage.'

'Why not? It's hardly started.'

'Because that's not how things are done!' he snapped. He breathed in, regaining his control. 'I know a lot of what you say and do is only . . . it's part of your problem. And the priest says it can be cured. So I've come to say I won't turn my back on you. And to say I realise, the first night, was partly my fault.'

He really thought it was.

'So I will be more patient with you, now that I understand. And I'll come back to our bed. And we'll be slow, until you are ready.'

Which will be never, she thought to herself. He thought he was making a huge concession and she'd be grateful. 'Even though I disgust you?' she asked pointedly.

With a determined air, he nodded.

From that night, Mahli shared his wife's bed again. She lay stiff as a plank next to him. When he reached a hand out to touch her, she flinched and he rolled on to his back, sighing. Her 'problem', as he was being taught to think of it, sickened him to the stomach, but he still wanted her. His cock waved hopelessly under the sheets. *It's a good thing to want your wife*, he reminded himself, but it felt dirty. He'd been so excited the day of the wedding; the strange, lovely Nina would be his alone, his completely, his to hold, his to bury himself in . . . Lying next to her like this, sleepless and hot for her, night after night, was torture. When it was too much, he got up and prayed for relief. When prayer didn't work, his hand did. On his knees by the bed, he watched her sleep and tugged desperately. She was a restless sleeper, mumbling, flinging her arms, scissoring her legs, discarding the covers. Once, memorably, she pulled her nightgown down and exposed her breast. The nipple puckered in the cold and his fist suddenly dripped with cream. *One day*, he told himself miserably, trying to mop up the mess with his nightshirt.

At mealtimes, King Daurio nodded approvingly and Queen Yonta beamed at them. She searched her daughter's cheeks for a new flush, a glow of satisfaction, but Nina was implacable. Again, she tried speaking to her in private.

'You and Mahli, is it . . .'

Nina turned away to the window, staring up as if the clouds would reveal something.

'Have you . . . ?'

'No.' Her eyes still scoured the sky.

'Oh, Nina . . .'

'What do you *want*?' snapped Nina. 'I married him like you said – I'm sharing his bed like you said. *I'm trying to do right.* I'm trying!' Her eyes filled as she looked back at her mother. 'I want to be good, I want to be cured. But I can't do what I just can't do. OK? I physically *can't*. Not yet. I don't know when.' She looked out and up again as the tears escaped.

For more nights, Mahli lay awake watching his wife toss and turn. Whenever she talked in her sleep, he raised his head from the pillow, ears straining. If he could hear the secrets of her dreams, perhaps he could unlock her heart – and, in turn, her body. *Lust is a sin*, he thought wretchedly, and then, *But she's my wife.*

'Write to me,' she said distinctly one night. His heart pounded. Her eyes fluttered. 'Please, write to me, I'll come, I'll . . .' She rolled on her side, mumbling, and murmured, 'Drake.' His blood turned to ice. Her sleeping face curved in a dreamy smile; a soft moan slipped from her lips. He shook, mind racing, until exhaustion tugged him into sleep. He didn't hear the fluttering wings.

Princess Nina

You are angry with me. Rightly so. And yes, truth is action as well as words. I call myself a Lord of Kâo, but you put me to shame me with your bravery. All these long days

and nights I've stormed in confusion, unable to decide.
Sweetest Nina, blinding woman of truth, I am lost. You're
my only beacon. Be my guide. Ten miles to the north-west
of the castle is an abandoned fort. There I pace and dream
of you, growing stiff and weak in turns at the thought of
you, rereading your words, honouring your soul, craving
your body. Now, with blood beating like drums in my ears,
I'll wait for you. Come to me – I beg you.
      Your lover,
      Drake

Dawn haze hung over the landscape as Nina picked her way
across the muddy ground. It diffused the rocky shards of distant
outcrops to ethereal turrets. In the stagnant pools, drowned
lilypads made a green carpet with flashes of crimson from the
underwater flowers or a dart of silver from a fish. She buried
her hands deep in the pockets of her fur coat, rubbing the éolith
stone. With the moment so near, she didn't dare imagine Drake
moving against hers or even the light caress of his lips. Her
insides lurched when she saw the dim outline of the fort. Even
while she stood there, he might be watching from the window,
waiting. She closed her eyes and took a deep breath, thinking
of his words: *honouring your soul, craving your body . . . I will*
wait for you. Come to me – I beg you. With resolute steps, she
walked forwards.

In the castle, the Queen wrung her hands while the servants
ran back and forth.
   'Your Majesty, she is nowhere to be found.'
   'What about the lily-gardens? She walks there often.'
   'We've checked there, Your Majesty. She's not in the church,
either, or any of the state rooms, or anywhere in the grounds.'
   'She said his name,' repeated Mahli, his face like iron. 'In

her sleep. When I woke, she was gone. Does *no one* know where the man was staying?'

'It might have been just a dream,' pleaded the Queen.

'Then where is she?' He gestured at the empty room and his eyes fell on the secrets box. 'Of course,' he said slowly. 'Yes. Now how does this thing open?' He poked at the carvings.

Drake turned from the table where he sat. She stood in the doorway, motionless, as if she had sprung into flesh and blood from his imagination. Her dress was hemmed with a foot of mudstains, her lips open, her bright-green eyes wide and wild. For the first time, he saw her face. Some truth still remained in the courts of Navarone: she was lovely – imperfect and painfully beautiful. His throat constricted as he stood.

'I've come,' she said simply.

'Yes.'

He stretched his hand out and she stepped forwards. He touched her fingertips then traced her jaw with his thumb.

'You're frightened,' he said.

'Yes.' She laughed. 'This time.'

'We don't have to . . . we can just talk . . .' His warm hand rested on the inward curve of her waist.

Her hands explored his face as if she were blind: his high forehead, long straight nose and thick dark eyebrows. His face was strained, his eyes suffering, with longing kept rigidly in check. When her fingertips found his taut lips, they parted in a despairing moan. Terrified of scaring her but unable to resist, he gathered her closer in his arm and touched the slope of her neck, down along her collarbone, stroking towards her breast.

'Your hands are like feathers,' she said with a shiver.

He lowered his head and spoke against her lips. 'If you want to stop – at any moment – you have only to say the word.'

In answer, she parted her lips a fraction and the touch of

his tongue on them sent sparks through her. His errant hand kept running back and forth above her bodice, steadily lower, and undid her buttons as his kisses probed deeper. The bodice loosened and her breasts swayed free. She whimpered. He stepped back, struggling to keep his eyes from drifting.

'Must I stop?' he whispered, as if the reeds might overhear them.

She shook her head mutely.

With both hands on her shoulders, he eased the open bodice down. It fell from her arms and hung about her waist, so that her bare torso emerged from the skirt in golden curves. His eyes roamed; his palm touched the side of her breast. She swayed. Every gesture he made was caught between wild lust for her and fearful caution. He pulled her hips close to his, but his lips were light on her neck. She was shuddering and leaning backwards as his wet tongue trailed downwards. His lips closed over her nipple and sucked steadily. She groaned and her hips shifted in time with his clasping mouth.

When he broke away, her eyes were unfocused and dazed; his were knowing and confident.

'I'm going to kiss every part of you,' he said, sliding her dress down her hips.

The box clattered off the stone at the far end of the room and bounced across the floor. Mahli breathed heavily. He looked at the maid who hovered, frightened, in the doorway.

'Get me an axe.'

'But it's so valuable,' said Queen Yonta.

'It's not more valuable than my wife's purity!' he yelled.

The axe was brought. Mahli set the box on the stone, in front of the fireplace, and with three rapid strokes he shattered the delicate mechanisms, splintering the layers of wood. At the centre of the mangled gift lay seven small rolls of parchment, one sliced in two by the axe. He unrolled the two pieces and read. Wordlessly, he threw them aside and reached for the next. The Queen crouched down to grab them; her eyes ran over the words, and her face whitened.

When they finished, the two stayed kneeling by the box, stilled with shock.

'I would never have dreamt –' began the Queen.

Mahli lifted the biggest chunk of broken wood and dashed it into the fire. 'I will rip her faithless hide apart,' he said quietly, as the Queen cried.

'You will do no such thing!' The King walked through the doorway, his face white with fury and red blazing spots in his cheeks.

In answer, Mahli scooped up the letters and dumped them on the bed. 'Would you like to see what my wife has been up to?'

The King looked from the small pile on the soft down of the mattress to his tearful wife, who nodded. His jaw set. 'If *our daughter* has committed adultery, she will be dealt with – but *you* will not harm a hair on her head.'

In the fort, on a mattress stuffed with straw instead of goose down, the Princess floated naked. Bare-chested, with a knight's hard muscles, Drake bent over her. His trousers bulged as his mouth dipped between her legs. Her timidity was forgotten. Long wails poured from her mouth as his tongue played. With wet strokes, he outlined her folds and lapped her cream, then nuzzled and nipped at her little bead. She clutched handfuls of his hair, rubbing against his face. When a finger slid into her drenched opening, she flailed.

'I've never . . .' she screamed. 'How can it – is this . . . ?'

His cock juddered painfully against the trouser cloth. The stricture around his fingers warned him to go slowly, still; her bewildered cries confirmed she'd never been given bliss before.

How much her husband must have hurt this narrow passage, forcing her with cruelty! This time, she would discover how sweet the strain of being filled could be. His fingers moved faster as her cries rose in pitch, feeling the telltale clenches. When she was writhing at the brink, he withdrew. She sobbed, begged him, shook, but he only sat smiling at her, his eyes clouded with hunger.

'Why?' she wailed, meeting his gaze at last.

'Because I want this to last forever,' he said huskily. 'Because now you're kindling and every touch is flame. Because I want you to see me, as well as this bliss, so that when we make love it's to the whole of each other.' He guided her hand to the burning rod between his thighs. His breath came in pants as her hand explored its thickness through the fabric; he could barely speak. 'Because all that will be inside you and I want you to be ready.' He ran his nails down her skin, making her lurch as she reached for the drawstring at his waist.

The King, the Queen and Prince Mahli rode with two young guards. Daurio didn't like his son-in-law's new ferocity, but he *was* the girl's husband: he had the right to confront the pair. The Queen was still blind with tears, but she refused to leave her daughter's fate in the hands of men and kept up a flow of excuses.

'It's our fault – it must be her problem; she's mad; she doesn't know what she's doing . . .'

'From the tone of Drake's letters, she knew exactly what and was begging for it,' the King said roughly.

'It's not her fault, it's her problem! We should have smothered her in her cradle!'

'If you can't control your hysteria, I'll send you back to the castle with one of the guards!' snapped the King.

She spoke no more for a few miles, tears rolling down her face, then blurted out, 'What will we *do* with her?'

'The punishment for adultery is death,' said Mahli grimly.

The Queen screamed and the King's blow nearly knocked the Prince from his horse. 'You presume, Princeling!' he spat. 'She's the Crown Princess! And we lack evidence that this is yet *adultery.*'

Mahli snarled, but shrank from speaking again.

Nina's hands were all over him and Drake was close to tears with agony. She knelt, her mouth round his swollen head, and he yelped with ecstasy, rocking back and forth between her lips. He guided her knees over his head and she sank on to his face, his tongue gulping her cream, his lips tugging hard at the sensitive swollen nub. She was breathless, approaching ecstasy again, and once more he stopped. Kneeling opposite her, he stared greedily at her transformation. Her thighs were parted, her pink slit inflamed. Her fire-coloured hair was tousled, sticking to her shoulders and forehead with sweat. Her breath came fast, heaving her hard-tipped breasts. All of him was rigid, his muscles standing out, his shaft rock-hard.

'You teach me the truth of myself,' she panted.

'Are you ready?' he said tensely, his voice shaking.

'Yes. Oh, please, Drake, yes . . .'

He laid her back, lifting her hips with his hands to help her accept him. Two fingers glided in and out; she was still tight, but slippery as butter. His eyes fixed on hers as he bowed over her, pushing slowly in. Her whole body had become a rippling orgasm as he slowly penetrated – and stuck fast, a few inches in. He pressed again, gently, and felt the barrier. He stared at her in disbelief.

'You –' he began, flummoxed. 'You're still . . .'

'Yes,' she whimpered, her eyes huge and tense with expectation.

'But . . . the sheet . . .'

She shook her head. 'They lied – I wouldn't let him near me, I couldn't. They took blood from the slaughterhouse.' Tears formed. 'Don't you want me, if –?'

'*Yes*,' he cried, his heart flooding with elation. 'But it might hurt you.'

'Please . . .' She contracted around his partial penetration.

'It *is* you,' he wept. 'The one I've been looking for – it *must* be! – you're the one.'

And, with a firm shove, he launched hard into her, the flimsy membrane giving way and her depth clasping him as she yelped and bucked against him. He withdrew and sank into her again, bellowing with joy as the door of the fort flung open and the King roared in fury.

'Kill him!' he shouted to the guards behind him, though he still stood blocking the doorway. 'No one is to lay a hand on the Princess! But kill that fornicating traitorous son of a bitch!'

Belatedly, he stood aside to let his men through. Drake had already leapt away from Nina who was screaming at him to run. He raced up the ladder to the top of the fort, yelling frantically behind him, 'Yes, I love the Princess! Yes, I've been held inside her! Yes, I believe she's the one!'

The guards bolted after him, the King following, while the Queen crumpled at the sight of her naked flushed daughter. At the top of the fort, the guards froze. Lord Drake was poised in front of a scaly beast whose jagged wings extended into the sky as high as the fort again.

'I love her and she loves me!' he exclaimed, as if he were hastily reciting a liturgy. 'We've exchanged letters, dreamt of each other, and now we've made love! Nina . . .' His voice rose and changed to a heartfelt call. 'Be true to yourself!'

With a leap, he ran up the dragon's back. The sweep of its wings sent a rush of wind that knocked the guards to their backs as it took off, circled and flew into the distance.

The King clambered to his feet uncertainly, looking around. The guards were staggering up, staring madly at the vanishing speck. He heard the Queen scream downstairs and wondered dully what had happened. On unsteady legs, he climbed down and saw Mahli approaching the Princess, his dagger drawn and aimed at her throat. That revived his senses. With the flat of his sword, he lashed out at the Prince, sending him sprawling.

'She's an adulterous!' yelled Mahli.

The King stared at his still bare daughter, cowering on the red-stained mattress. 'No, she isn't,' he said vaguely, gesturing with his drawn sword at the blood soaking through the cloth into the straw. 'She's a fornicating slut, but it seems you still hadn't consummated your marriage.'

'It's a lie,' wailed Mahli desperately. 'It must be her period. I've had her, I have, she's mine!'

At that blatant untruth, the Princess turned her head and tongues of flame burst from her mouth, singeing his eyebrows and shrivelling his locks. The sudden silence was full of the smell of burnt hair.

'The Princess says otherwise,' the King noted dryly. 'Whatever else, her problem is at least reliable.' He unclasped his cloak and threw it at his daughter. 'Cover your shame, you whore,' he said bitterly, and to the guards, 'Get out – one more glance at her and I'll put your eyes out. Speak of it and I'll have your tongue as well. You too, Mahli.' He dropped the 'Prince' pointedly. 'Get out of my sight.'

Part two

The trapdoor, the room and the entrance to the fort were sealed with stone and mortar. An iron rod was inserted below the sill of the thin arrow-slot window with a pulley for food and water to be hauled up and the empty copper basket to be let down. The Princess wasn't going to be starved, just deprived of fuel. It was the priest's original advice which, the King reflected, he should have followed years ago. Fire without fuel burnt itself out, eventually. The two young guards were left at the base of the fort and his instructions were unequivocal: 'She dies and your life is forfeit. She escapes, your life is forfeit. You touch her and you'll live long enough to watch me tear your balls off and feed them to the dogs. Make no mistake: she is still the Crown Princess. Send her up food and water, but not a stick of wood or anything combustible. Shoot down any bird that approaches the fort. If that flying beast returns, blow your horn. Guard her with your life – if I find her gone, I want to find your bleeding bodies.' That seemed to cover everything and he rode back to the castle to resume governing his kingdom.

The Princess's awakened passion and betrayal was left to flame in the stone room. She raged like an animal. From their tent, the guards heard her guttural howls and saw the flames flicker in the distant high window. The warped desk burnt first, the scraps of parchment crackling and the quill pen shrivelling. When it was sticks of charcoal, she set fire to the mattress, whose straw combusted instantly with a brief unsatisfying flare. The stained embroidered gown and the fur in which she had walked to the fort were next. The room stood empty, then: just ashes, charred wood, the naked Princess, and the chunk of éolith, impervious to her fire. She screamed and splintered her nails against the mortar. She begged for wood and the guards stuffed their ears with wool. She drew her hands down her face as she rocked and moaned, leaving trails of blood from her fingers. At last she curled up on the cold stone and slept, the night mist dampening her skin.

The dull clank of metal against stone woke her. The basket dangled on the pulley outside the window. Stiff and sore, she could barely walk across the room, but she grabbed the food with grateful tears: meat, bread and fruit. The guards, standing bored at the base of the fort, sniffed the wind with surprise when they smelt toast, then glanced up to strands of grey smoke gusting through the narrow window.

'No more bread, then,' said Hugo.

Vario pulled a piece of wool from his ears and the words were repeated. He shrugged.

'And the fruit?'

'Too much water. She can't burn that.' He frowned. 'I don't think,' he added, as the smell of roasting apples drifted across his nostrils.

The initial rage died down. Nina was left with nothing to do but clean the éolith on her hair and contemplate her sins. Her father had vindicated her of adultery and granted her her life. Still, she'd betrayed her husband. If she'd let him take her, none of this would have happened. He'd been gentle and patient, even though he had a right to her body, and she had refused him repeatedly. She had fornicated with another man and let her virginity be stripped outside of matrimony. Locked in the fort, she saw through the eyes of her mother, her father and her husband. She was disobedient and loose, a shameless slut. She'd let herself be used by another man, who'd fled and left her ruined. As her shoulders heaved in remorse, the terrible burning grew worse. She gulped sobs, thinking of every crime against purity she had ever committed, and her insides stung with fire. Staggering to the window, she begged through streaming tears for wood – she was burning! The fire would kill her! She would die if she did not get *fuel*!

If she hadn't chosen that word, the guards might have given in. With hunted eyes and tight lips, they shook their heads, then looked down and feigned deafness while her wails echoed over the landscape. When she'd worn herself out, she slept restlessly on the hard floor, tossing and turning in dreams and waking to bruises, aches, tears and burning. On the seventh day, she broke and howled her confession from the windows.

'Tell my father I'm sorry! I'm sorry! I promise I'll be good. I'll let Mahli have me, I'll be pure, I'll never look at another man. I'm *sorry!*' Her words broke off in a scream of agony as the fire sizzled inside her like a red-hot brand and she fell back, tearing at the blazing heat inside her. Nothing eased the hideous pain. When she couldn't bear it any more, she climbed on to the window sill and threw herself on to the floor. Her arms kept instinctively breaking her fall; only on the fifth try, with them tightly clamped over her breasts and jumping backwards, did the stone floor knock her blissfully unconscious.

She must have come round but continued sleeping, because she went from blankness to dreams: midnight in a forest, lusher than Siratta with huge black leaves and warmer than Jarth. The sky burnt and her body was fire, not hurting any more but running up and down her veins. In the shadows were people, lurking in silence, hidden by the dark and the foliage. Their bodies tugged and their ripples of lust ran over her – then Drake was with her on the hot muddy ground, his torso blotting out the glowing sky, and all her wild fire was centred where he rammed into her; she was heaving, the world blackening, the skin of his shaft deep inside her, and, as he rubbed in and out, she rose up screaming – her hands slamming on to the cold stone, her bare legs stretched wide apart, the dawn breaking, and the sound of her scream still reverberating in the fort room. Her forehead dripped with sweat.

'No!' she howled, that it was snatched away so close to ecstasy. She curled her knees inside her arms and rocked, willing the hot lust to subside. 'No, she said again, whimpering this time, and starting to cry. She'd vowed to be good and her dreams betrayed her. Even in the secret places of her mind, she was a black-hearted slut. 'I'll be good!' she screamed at the silent walls. 'I don't care how I feel, I'll be good!'

The burning inside rekindled so fast that she couldn't even cry out in pain; she just arched back, croaking.

'Stop it, I'll be good,' she wheezed, but it only intensified. On her hands and knees she dragged herself to the wall. Halfway there, the pain capsized her and she crumpled, clawing at the stone for its coolness. She scrabbled onwards, forcing herself to climb on to the sill again. Unconsciousness beckoned like a black sea and she threw herself on to the floor. This time, she only had to leap twice before her forehead smacked on to the flagstones, and she sprawled senseless and still.

Drake's dragon swooped down through the moonless starlit sky, arching its neck to release a ball of fire, which billowed red and gold through the blackness. A cheer went up from the ground, rippling into the corridors and halls of Kâo where it was taken up into stamping and shouting. Lady Tanya, on a rocky outcrop, stood up to watch the massive beast descend, Lord Drake a speck on its back. Her skin prickled with excitement as she slid down tree stems and darted through the forest towards the entrance. She ran up, breathless and glowing, as he disappeared into the dark mouth of the halls' entrance. His metal boots rang out against the gold mosaics, echoing downwards into the distance. Her smile faded. Of course – he would see the Queen first, to report. Drake, more than any of them, followed the laws of honour to the last degree. She turned instead to his dragon and bowed low to greet it. Its eyes regarded her coldly for a long minute, then it inclined its snout gracefully. Two of the other lords hovered on either side of it and to them she said, 'I'll tend to Zenerith.'

The dragon slouched down into the halls, Tanya following behind it.

Drake knelt at the Queen's bedside. She smiled weakly and her hand brushed over his hair, sending shivers of longing through him.

'Your heart is pounding,' she said.

He raised his head. 'I've found her, Your Majesty – it must be her, it must. She's everything, she's . . .'

'Calm yourself, Lord. Tell me everything, from the beginning.'

He stood to recount his time in Navarone. Soon, he was striding up and down as he spoke. His hands waved in the air, he clutched at his hair, he spun around to implore her, emphasising everything that supported his case. The Queen watched him impassively. When he'd finished, instead of stopping, he returned again to his main points, labouring them till the Queen held up a hand.

'Enough. From what you say – never mind the manner of your saying it – you're very taken with this young woman.'

Drake nodded.

'Many people in the twelve tribes still have the true blood in their veins,' mused the Queen 'None of them knows what it is, their inheritance mixes this way and that, and sometimes a particular combination will yield a child that's almost true to the original line. These children show many of the qualities of a queen, but not all of them. She had no brothers, no sisters?'

Drake shook his head.

'That would have helped us tell.'

'Your Majesty, I'm sure –' he burst out.

'Of course you are,' she interrupted, 'or you wouldn't have come. But consider this, Lord Drake. You're very passionate about this girl. Now it could be that she truly inflames you, as a queen does. It could also be that you're so enraptured your judgement is blurred.'

'I wrestled with that point,' he said quietly. 'But the dragon wouldn't accept me until I admitted it was her!'

'If I understood your story correctly, you also confessed your affair with the Princess, to all the relevant people, at the same time.'

Drake's head sank. The Queen stretched out her hand. She was weaker than when he'd last seen her, and it shook in the air as his own clasped it.

'I understand you didn't want to expose her, if you could help it,' she said gently. 'That is your honour speaking. But beware your honour doesn't make you dishonest, my Drake. The affair itself was a deceit, you realise that?'

'Yes,' he whispered.

'And, when you confessed it, the dragon let you mount.'

'Yes.'

'So.' The Queen sighed and her head lolled back on to the pillows tiredly. 'Tell me, from everything you know, is she the new queen?'

No one lied to a queen. Drake swallowed, his muscles trembling, and he answered, 'I don't know.' He looked down at her withered hand, still lying in his, on the bedspread. His lips compressed. 'I swooped back at nightfall. They've locked her up in the fort. She screams.' A tear slid down his cheek and splashed on to the Queen's hand, where it evaporated in steam.

'Did you break the law? Did you speak to her?'

He shook his head mutely.

'If it is her – and it might be, still – then you've done your part, and she must free herself from the Twelve. We can't help there. A chick that doesn't have the strength to hatch doesn't have the strength to live.'

'And if it isn't?' His voice was unsteady. 'Do I simply abandon her to her fate?'

The Queen's face turned sterner. 'We don't interfere in the affairs of the Twelve, Drake. The dragons don't come sniffing us for truth in our beds, judging our every thought, but wait for us to go to them. The same way, we leave the twelve tribes be. Now put aside your thoughts of the girl Nina, tell me about the tribes. How are their laws, their lives?'

'Things are worse than we realised. They barely remember Kâo – we're no longer even a legend to them, barely a story to tell children, just a rhyme that everyone laughs at. They still have a spark of truth; they're very concerned about right and wrong, but it's warped – their principles have fossilised, so they follow that more than the truth. The courts all lie to each other and hide their hatred behind smiles. They spy on each other. The wedding ceremony's a farce, the bride doesn't make any vows, they value her virginity but dismiss her truth.' He shook his head in frustration.

'I see.'

'Aren't you worried?'

'I take the long view, Drake. We watch their quick lives come and go so fast, we keep perspective. But I remember even more . . .' Her eyes darkened dreamily. 'I see it all. So much history, so much drama, but it all balances out – what must happen will happen.' She focused on him again, shaking off her thoughts and smiling. 'Don't worry. Now off you go.'

He lifted her hand to his lips, his blood pulsing at the exquisite contact, and bowed deeply. As he turned to leave, she said, 'Drake, if I sent you out flying again, would you go to the fort and check for Nina?'

He considered thoughtfully, and said, 'Yes. I would try very hard not to, but I believe I would.'

'And, if you thought she needed help, would you help her?'

He closed his eyes in pain. His own heart and his own nature whispered the answer to him and he repeated it. 'I would. Despite myself and the law.'

'Then, my finest of fliers and bravest of lords,' said the Queen sadly, 'I forbid you to fly.'

When Drake didn't come to the dragon lairs or her rooms, Tanya went to find him. She checked his rooms first, which stood as empty and untouched as they had over his long absence, then went to the dining hall. She stood by the gallery balustrade, looking out through the fluted arches that rose dizzyingly above, scanning a thousand heads for the one she would recognise instantly. Voices babbled, cutlery clattered and glasses chinked; those who'd gone out riding held forth with the stories of their adventures. Drake was nowhere. She wandered up and down the corridors, checking rooms randomly, until she found herself outside again in the warm dark air. At the entrance to the halls, torches burnt and their light sparkled on the gems which encrusted the terrace and entry. She walked beyond them, to the edge of the shadows. A tangle of branches in the forest glimmered faintly with white phosphorescence, where they had been recently brushed and bruised. Following their dim trail into the absolute blackness, even the stars blotted out overhead, she made her way through the forest. She walked for hours, her feelings bubbling in confusion and pain that he hadn't come to her, then concern for what he might have suffered on his journey. When at last she reached the end of the forest, she saw him sitting in the starlight against a tamla tree, its smooth trunk rising in concentric ridges behind him. This was the edge of habitable ground; beyond this, was the wasteland. He was staring out at the pale corona, slowly ripping a leaf to pieces. Between his feet, a pile of torn slivers shone, the older ones fading and the new shreds still bright.

He looked up, but didn't speak. She crouched beside him and kissed the side of his mouth. He gave her a small tight smile.

'Was it very bad?' she asked.

He threw a piece of leaf in front of him. 'No.'

'Were they cruel?'

'Oh, they laughed at me and didn't believe me, but that doesn't matter. They don't know better. It's been so long, for them.'

She leant into his warmth and waited for his arm to encircle her. Something had gone wrong – it must have been severe if he hid even from her. Just his upper arm brushing hers made her ache. A thought flashed, half fantasy, half expectation: him turning to her, making love to her here at the edge of the fertile land, by the light of the corona, savage with his suffering and frantic from their long separation.

'What is it?' she said eventually.

A man from the twelve tribes would have answered, 'Nothing', but the lords and ladies didn't lie.

'I may have found her. And I've been forbidden to fly.' He took up another leaf and split it.

'Did you –?'

'Yes. Of course. Are you jealous?' He glanced sideways.

She shrugged. 'Yes. I'd hoped you might not find a candidate. But getting a new queen is more important, I know that.'

He nodded and looked away. When he didn't speak for several minutes, she asked why he was banned from flying.

'The Queen thinks I'm too involved. I can't be trusted to check without interfering.'

Tanya was quiet for a while. 'Oh.' She nestled her head against his shoulder, but he didn't shift to accommodate her. Unseen by his glum eyes, her face slowly hardened. When she rose to her feet, he still didn't move. 'I'll see you in the halls.'

After a pause, he glanced up. 'Yes. OK.'

Both remained locked in the polite option of silence, then she walked back through the forest, her jaw set. As she passed, some of the giant leaves showed jagged luminous marks like lightning, where she lashed out.

Nina's dreams wouldn't leave her alone. From unconsciousness, she rose to dark dreams of lust. She woke, every time, with her body begging for more. The pain inside was so bad that she couldn't yell her repentance from the windows, but she prayed in tears for purity. It only worsened. When the copper basket of food clanked against the wall, she scrabbled over to it. She gulped down the water; the food, however, meant only one thing: she could set fire to something besides her own flesh. The need to burn outweighed the need to eat. A handful of bread, steak and fruit was almost nothing, when she could've sent whole forests up in flames, but it eased the agony for a moment. When it became too much, she flung herself on the mercy of the hard stone floor. As she weakened, it became easier to fight the reflex to catch herself and the periods of blankness extended. From a dawn jump, she might open her eyes to black night, or see pale light and not know whether minutes or a day had passed.

The two guards camped on a hillock near the fort, bored and patient. They'd drawn this duty by the simple misfortune of having been there at the time and when the winter winds cut across the ground they missed the warm smelly fug of the guardroom. With a fire blazing, it wasn't too bad. They had each other, and no captain clouted their heads if they drank too much. One day Hugo would win all Vario's pay for the month, at cards; the next day Vario would win it all back. Every week, one rode back to the castle for fresh food and liquor. The quartermaster gave them supplies in two parcels – the best quality for the Princess and run-of-the-mill goods for the guards.

'It doesn't seem fair,' said Vario, unwrapping the parcels. 'She only burns it all anyway.'

They met each other's eyes and that night they ate rump steak while the smell of burning offcuts drifted through the mist.

'This is the life,' said Hugo, leaning back after his meal and uncorking a fresh bottle of liquor. He took a deep swig and passed it to Vario.

'Yeah.' His eyes rested contentedly on Hugo, then he frowned. 'But what about our careers? What's the captain going to say to the King – they're good at camping?'

'We're showing our mettle,' said Hugo comfortably. He patted Vario's shoulder and took the bottle from his lap. 'Guarding the Princess – that shows we're trusted.'

'How long do you reckon we're here for?'

'I think till the fires stop.' Hugo scratched his chin thoughtfully. 'She's quieter, at least.

'Thank God.'

The next week was Hugo's turn to visit the castle. When he returned in the early evening, Vario was standing at the base of the fort gazing up worriedly. Hugo reined in next to him and looked down at the copper basket. For the third time in a row, it had come down with the food untouched.

'She hasn't burnt it, at least,' he said uncertainly.

'We don't even know when she last ate,' said Vario. He bit his lip. 'She's still our Princess, Hugo.'

'I know.' He dismounted and followed his friend's gaze up the silent darkness of the fort. 'Raise it up again. She might take it tonight.'

As they led the horse back to their tent, Hugo said quietly, 'I have a sister the same age.' He glanced at Vario, whose eyes were unnaturally glassy, and punched him lightly on the shoulder. 'Come on, you old softy, toughen up. She'll be fine. The fire will go and the Princess will be OK again.'

'Everyone has to eat,' said Vario stubbornly. 'If she dies . . .'

They looked at each other grimly.

'We should fetch the King.'

'And if she's already dead? Hi, here's your daughter's corpse, safe and sound. Can we have our pay now?'

'We'll give it one more night. If she hasn't eaten in the morning, we'll go up.'

That night, the party atmosphere of new supplies eluded them. Without a word, they set aside the Princess's parcel and ate their own inferior food. The bottle passed back and forth in silence, as they drowned their anxiety in deep draughts of liquor. When it was empty and the fire dead, they crawled drunkenly into the tent and slumped together on a bedroll. Above their stupor, a strange wind gusted over the ground, tugging at the tent pegs. The sky's black deepened as monstrous wings sailed overhead, circling in towards the fort.

As Tanya's dragon glided over the dark forests of Kâo, she saw Drake in the lamplight on the terrace. She landed smoothly and he ran forwards, his usually stern face bright. Her heart twisted, wishing she could believe his impatience was for her, and she avoided his eyes as she dismounted.

'Alexis!' she called to one of the nearby lords. 'Will you tend Xylar? I need to speak to Lord Drake.'

As Alexis bowed to the dragon, Drake followed Tanya to the tree-line. He caught her elbow in his hand – it was the first time, since his return, that he'd touched her voluntarily. A pang ran through her.

'Tell me, Tanya, please – did you check?'

'Yes.' She twisted away to stare into the trees.

'How is she?' He was breathless; he wasn't even bothering to hide how much he wanted news of her rival. 'What did you see? Tanya, why won't you speak?'

'I don't want to tell you,' she mumbled.

That was the closest the people of Kâo ever came to evasion, but a straight question demanded a straight answer and he said again, 'How is she?'

Tanya lifted her head to the stars, blinking frantically. When she turned to face him, she was masked with grief. 'Drake, she's – I'm sorry.' She put her hands over her face. She couldn't watch him hear this. 'She's dead.'

He stood motionless. 'Dead,' he echoed.

Tanya nodded and wrapped a hand tightly over her mouth.

'In the fort?'

'Yes,' she whispered through her fingers.

He looked away, into the darkness. His jaw twitched. 'Then she wasn't the new queen,' he said rigidly. 'Then she was just a child with too much of the true blood – too much to ignore her true nature, not enough to break free. Then, if I hadn't kissed her, she would still –' His voice shook too much to continue; he stopped abruptly and stared at the ground.

Feeling sick, Tanya watched his mouth working as he fought for self-control.

'She said herself – honour be damned,' he murmured, and repeated, 'Honour be *damned*. If I had gone back . . .'

'We don't interfere with the ways of the –'

He spun so fast that she leapt back, her arms rising to shield her face. He lowered his hand slowly. 'Honour be damned,' he said again. 'Honesty is all that matters. Not rescuing her is the most dishonest I have ever been.'

'Drake . . .' Tanya laid her hand on him and he jerked away.

'You've brought me this news,' he said unsteadily. 'I can't look at you right now.' He turned on his heel and strode away, down the long corridor that wove into the vast halls and stone rooms underground.

That night, when she crept into his room, the complete dark meant he still didn't have to look at her. She could hear in his breathing that he was awake, but he lay rigid as she crawled in next to him, then spun around to flatten her against the mattress. His hands pinned her wrists, his weight crushing her. He was naked under the sheet. Through her thin night-dress, his packed muscles chafed her.

'You can't want this,' he said hoarsely. 'Not like this.'

'I do.' She parted her legs under him, the nightdress rucking up as he shifted. 'I want you – regardless.'

His rod shoved hard and blind, clumsily looking for entrance, her trapped hands unable to help him. His head turned away from her, his breath ragged. When the round tip nudged against her lips she gasped, opening wider. Her need for him stung – even if this was all she got, even if he lay on top of her in the dark and thought of Nina, nothing could take away the reality of his body. His cock was gliding into her at last, his clenched buttocks beneath her heels, and his chest was squeezing down on hers. He moved fast, slamming deep, sending waves of gold and showers of sparks through her. Within a few strokes she was screaming; he was silent, pumping furiously, until with a strangled sound he was still. They lay panting. Before she'd caught her breath, he withdrew and rolled on to his side, facing the wall.

'I'm sorry,' he said dully.

He didn't move or speak again and at length she left as quietly as she'd come.

The next day, he avoided everyone and Tanya left him to his solitude, but at night she came to his bed again. This time, when she slid in next to him, she was already naked.

He lay on his back, staring up at the dark. 'Don't do this, Tanya.'

In answer, she ran her hand up his torso, his cock stiffening as her arm brushed it. He pushed her away. She lay quietly, then slid over him, rubbing her breasts on his chest. He froze for a moment, his shaft twitching against her belly, before pulling himself out from under her. She stayed face down on the mattress, her despair growing. He needed to reconnect with life – his dismal pride, his so-called honour, kept him locked in a cage of grief. How else could she reach him again? Then he was on her, his knees parting her legs.

'Is this what you want?' he demanded.

'Yes,' she whispered.

He hauled her hips upwards and, one hand guiding his cock, drove into her. He fucked fast, tugging her backwards against him as if to get it over with, but again she was coming almost instantly, each rough shove a fresh ecstasy. The sound spurred him on and for the space of a few minutes pure lust drowned out the grief in his heart, then it was over. The sadness came back with a wave of self-disgust.

Day after day he absented himself from the halls, preferring to walk alone with his misery through the black forests. Night after night she came to his bed, soft-skinned and willing. Some nights he refused to touch her. More often, he tried to resist but took her anyway, burying his pain in her yielding curves. He hated himself for touching another woman, when all he wanted was Nina – blinding beautiful Nina, dead because of him. He also hated himself for thinking of Nina while he screwed Tanya. Sometimes, when he heard her bare feet skimming the floor, he hated Tanya, and those nights he always had her. It was her own fault, he'd think, plunging savagely in and out – if she didn't want to be used like this, she should leave him alone. One night, he stood up when she came in and bent her over the side of the bed. As he slammed harder and harder into her, the pain didn't ease; the lust didn't cloud it. His movements grew jerky and slower. He pulled out wretchedly and sat on the bed. Sobs ripped from his throat. His shoulders heaved. For the first time since he'd heard the news, he cried, and she curled her soft body around him, rocking him gently.

The clumsy stone and mortar gave way beneath the guards' mallets, exploding inwards. The hardwood door that had stood behind it was long since burnt away. The floor was smeared with dust and old blood and at the centre lay Princess Nina, her naked body wasted, white as ash, and motionless. Her forehead was discoloured and grazed. Hugo and Vario looked from her to each other and back again. Hugo swore softly. Vario picked his way over the rubble and crouched next to her, one hand reaching out to touch her cheek. He snatched it back, his eyes huge.

'She's warm!' he whispered. His fingers reached out again. 'She's alive, she's hot. Feverish.'

'Is she breathing?' Hugo tiptoed forwards.

The Princess sat bolt upright with a death-rattle gasp. Her fingers dug into Vario's jacket. 'Fuel,' she croaked, her eyes rolling upwards as she tugged at his clothes. 'Take them off, take off your clothes.'

He stared at her, terrified. The fever had given her strength and she ripped one sleeve off. As it came free, she opened her mouth and billowed white-hot flame, the material combusting in midair as she threw it aside.

'More!' she demanded. He hesitated. Her eyes were on him, but unseeing, as her hands fought to strip him. 'Fast – I don't want to burn you.'

'Do what she says,' said Hugo, white-faced. He was already unbuttoning his own jacket.

Piece by piece, they threw their clothes to the Princess, right down to their boots, and she snatched everything greedily, spewing fire. Her glazed expression turned to avarice and she rose to her feet. She caught and threw the burning clothes around her, floating through the air, sparks showering.

'Yes!' she cried out, exultant. She turned rosy in the reflected firelight and she laughed, spinning around. She halted suddenly, facing them. The last threads shrivelled to black on the floor, but her skin still looked golden, her eyes clear and sane. Both guards cupped themselves hastily. She swayed and Vario caught her, lowering her tenderly to the ground.

'You're still weak,' he whispered, his throat so tight he could barely speak.

The touch of her skin on his was electric. Her eyes closed out everything else as he bent closer, reeling. Still in his arms, she arched upwards sensually. When his mouth met hers, she rolled naked against him and his tongue delved. He was losing himself in her kiss, a hand was shaking his shoulder and he was tugged backwards, dazed.

'What the hell are you doing?' said Hugo.

Vario ignored him. Only the Princess's slow smile existed and he leant over her again. Hugo yanked him and he sprawled backwards.

'Do you want to get killed?' yelled Hugo, staring at his

comrade in disbelief. He looked down slowly. The Princess's hand was winding around his ankle and stroked featherlight across his instep.

'Oh, God,' he murmured.

His cock unfurled, standing like a branch in front of him. Vario crawled back to her, her mouth parting under his, as Hugo sank to his knees. She was smooth and gold, her skin full again where minutes before it had been sunken. His hands ran disbelievingly over her naked thighs, up her waist, and cupped the sides of her breasts. It didn't bother him that Vario was kissing her – she deserved to be kissed and caressed like this. Her lips, rising to meet Vario's, were plump and perfect. He sighed with pleasure, just to be allowed to watch, and jolted when her pink tongue darted out. His palms moved over her breasts and she rewarded him with a moan. Their camp, their duties, the King's threats, the cold winter room – all were forgotten as her nipples crinkled between his fingertips. He took the tip of one breast in his mouth. His hair brushed against Vario's as they kissed her and the two men's hands entwined. She crooned, guiding Vario's mouth to her other breast.

Her hands were in their hair. Between them, her hips rose and fell. Hugo wriggled closer to her, her thighs hot against his cock, her body radiating warmth like the summer sun. Vario groaned and Hugo opened his eyes to see his friend suckling hungrily. Their eyes met.

Whatever tide of desire was carrying them, they were both aware of what they were doing, and knew it. They watched each other's mouth working softly at her nipples, which glistened and disappeared. Her hands pressed lightly on the back of their heads and they leant forwards willingly. Their lips, hot from her skin, joined. Their cocks bounded in unison against her as their mouths opened and their kiss deepened. Each slid a thigh between hers, shifting to rub harder against her as their tongues delved. When they pulled back, their breath was short, their eyes dark with confusion. Her soft smile said it was all fine and they bent to kissing her again, moving more freely, their hands clasping and unclasping, brushing over each other as they rolled and wound around her.

Vario's hard cock was nudging her breast, his soft mouth dipping between her legs. Hugo caught her gasp in his mouth, kissing her frantically, and her legs spread wider. Vario's tongue-tip twirled gently. She bucked and wrapped her hand around the shaft at her breast, then turned Hugo's head towards it. His eyes gleamed then clouded with shame, but her soft pressure moved him steadily forwards. His mouth closed hesitantly around the tip. His eyelids shuttered. He groaned and jerked forwards, devouring it hungrily, forgetting her watchful gaze, but not her small hand running shivers up and down his back. As the wet heat enclosed him, Vario wrapped his mouth desperately over her clit, his fingers sliding into her. His other hand clutched for Hugo's shaft, rubbery and stiff, and rubbed it slowly.

She lay under them both, feeling Vario's fingers and mouth fill her with gold, Hugo's chest crush her breasts, but mostly relishing the pent-up passion that rolled off them. Hugo was lost to everything now but the cock in his mouth, the expert hand manipulating his own cock. When Vario twisted away, he whimpered with loss, which turned to a sob as his friend's tongue touched his glans. He shuffled back until he knelt behind the Princess's head, stupefied, watching his shaft slide back and forth between Vario's lips. Again, Vario stopped, his eyes on Hugo's. His slick staff jerking, Hugo saw Vario slide into the Princess, her hips rising to receive him. Her eyes fluttered open and closed, her head rolling in bliss. Vario thrust steadily twice, then leant forwards to kiss her hungrily while

Hugo moaned, mesmerised. When Vario's mouth rose, it found his cock again and Hugo's head flung back.

The three moved steadily together. The Princess's shining hair brushed between Hugo's thighs as Vario's rhythm carried her and Hugo bucked back and forth. Her hands pulled him steadily downwards until her tongue slithered between his buttocks and he cried out in shock, shame and bliss. He capsized, cradling Vario's back, whimpering Vario's name, as she lapped and delved further into him. Sucking and thrusting, Vario moved faster, carrying them all further and further into ecstasy. Nina was wild, meeting every stroke, tonguing Hugo frantically. The air was dense with their steaming sweat, the soft slaps of flesh, the squelch and slurp of their wet places. Their groans became screams as Vario's beat became a gallop and in one instant all three strained, still bucking. Hugo's cream streamed down Vario's throat as Vario's jetted into Nina, who clamped around him.

Their pyramid collapsed slowly sideways, still entwined. Lost in a dream, Vario still nursed at Hugo's cock as his own twitched and died inside Nina. The cold draught through the arrow-slot was reviving them and returning them to their senses. Hugo was the first to disengage. He curled into himself, then turned away, then stood by the window staring out at the marshes. Nina's lips curved tenderly as she touched Vario's face and nodded. He crossed the room to Hugo and laid a hand on his back. Hugo shook it off.

'That was sick. We should be ashamed of ourselves.'

Vario's face fell. Nina's eyes narrowed. Hugo turned, folding his arms across his chest.

'It's disgusting and unnatural.' His voice shook.

The Princess growled deep in her throat, her green eyes turning gold.

'Hugo –' Vario reached out and Hugo flinched.

'Don't touch me!'

'So now he mustn't touch you?' Nina spoke in a dry rasp. 'Now that he's finished drinking your come?'

Vario's head hung down. 'He's right – what we did was a terrible thing.'

Her lips parted. Her breath, in the cold air, was white as smoke. 'How easy to repent after the act,' she said witheringly. 'Now you're sated, you're oh-so-sorry – and when you want it again? What then?'

Hugo's eyes filled with hatred. 'I will never do that again. I don't know what came over –'

Before he finished his sentence, flames erupted from Nina's mouth, knocking him back with heat, stopping just short of burning him.

'Never lie to me!' she yelled. 'You're a filthy liar and that's *all* that's filthy about you!'

'I'm not like that!'

This time her fire scorched his face and singed his hair. He backed against the wall, beating it out.

'I said, don't lie to me. When you lie, I flame. Next time your skin will catch fire. Do you understand?'

He nodded, horrified.

'Now. Did you like what Vario did to you?'

He spoke so softly it might have been a whisper of the wind on the reeds. 'Yes.'

'Have you thought before about him doing that?'

The same tiny noise of assent came.

'Does it feel wrong?'

'Everyone knows –'

'Does it *feel* wrong?'

'No. It feels amazing.' His voice was strangled.

'Will you want to do it again?'

He cringed. 'Yes.'

'Do you want him more than you want women?'

Hugo covered his face with his hands.

'Do you?' she demanded.

'Yes.'

'Vario.' Her voice softened. 'Take him in your arms.'

As Vario's arms wrapped around him, Hugo shook. Vario's grip tightened. Slowly, he leant into the embrace, relaxing against him. Vario's head ducked, looking for Hugo's lips, and when he found them they responded. They stood together, bare, clasped, kissing, and, when they reopened their eyes, the Princess had vanished.

Drake took Tanya out on the vast terrace to watch the next contingent of dragons and riders come in from their search. None of the trails had yielded a new queen and every day the dragon-queen was weaker. Her heat was fading. She still inflamed them, tethering to her the lords, ladies and dragons alike. Their bodies responded helplessly to that force by surging with lust; their hearts rushed with love. Most importantly, their spirits obeyed meekly. She was the link between the people and the dragons of Kâo – without her, the people would lose their way. Without her, the dragons would turn wild again, hunting down every last shred of dishonesty in the world with their terrible purging flame. She was dying and they hadn't found her replacement.

A dragon wheeled downwards from the sky, its rider small as a doll on its colossal back. The people scattered to make way for it. Far above them, three dragons turned slowly. Their wings blotted out the stars. Awed, Drake watched two more dragons twisting in to join them, effortlessly manoeuvring their bulk around each other. If he couldn't ride, he could at least be near them, watching their scales glitter in the light of each other's flames. Tanya tugged him backwards towards the shadow of the forest and he followed, looking back reluctantly. She slammed him against the tree trunk; he responded instantly, even with his eyes on the circling dragons. Since his return to Kâo, his need for sex had been unbearable. Before, visiting the Queen had always left him blinded with lust, but now that heightened state persisted all the time.

'Tanya!' shouted a voice across the terrace. 'Will you tend Karatar?'

She froze. Her hand inside Drake's trousers clenched his shaft and he groaned quietly.

'I'm busy!' she snapped.

Even from this distance, she could see the rider's shock, his mouth making an O. Tending a dragon was an honour one didn't refuse. Drake stared at her. Her palm ran up and down the length of his cock, which spasmed in her grasp, and his head tipped back. The rider turned slowly away and someone else advanced towards the dragon, bowing.

'You shouldn't have refused,' said Drake, strained.

She was tugging him rhythmically, his need mounting.

'Are you sure?' she whispered slyly, kneeling.

'Oh, Spirits,' he muttered, as she took him in her mouth.

He tried to stop himself driving in, tried to let her set the pace, but his hips bucked impulsively. Soon he was holding her head, juddering back and forth, senseless with need.

Nina walked through the marshlands, heading nowhere but away from Navarone. The last of winter still held the land in its icy grip. The dress and fur in which she'd left the castle were cinders; all she carried was the chunk of éolith. Her skin was exposed to the knifing winds, but she wasn't cold. When she waded through pools, the water foamed and boiled. Steam rose from the ground where her bare feet touched it. She thought of the scene in the fort room, amazed that she felt no guilt and didn't try to summon any up. She barely understood how it had started. She'd risen from blank unconsciousness to find fuel and flesh, and knew she needed both. As she'd caught and burnt and threw away each garment, she'd thrown away what they all said she was supposed to do. The flames weren't her 'problem', they were in her and part of her. The petty rules and rituals of Navarone weren't the right way to live – they were a desperate by-numbers attempt to know what the right thing was, a crutch for those who had no idea where the truth lay. She already knew. She'd *always* known. Only, when she'd tried to believe their way, her flame had turned against herself.

The scalding pain inside was gone, though her skin still burnt and itched. As she walked, she used the rough éolith to scratch her arms, shoulders and belly. She bent to scrape it over her calves until the irritation became pain. She twisted her arms over her shoulders and backwards behind her, struggling to reach the spot on her back where it was worst.

The dreams, too, stayed with her. At night, she curled up on the mud, closed her eyes and was launched into that world of perpetual darkness and passion. The same scenes played out each time, changing subtly, layering new elements. The mud under her became forest mulch, into which Drake's hard body pressed her, and she slithered back and forth as he pounded into her. Figures emerged from and disappeared into the shadows, and gradually she was aware of them even when they stood invisible in the dark – she felt their needs and passion as clearly as she'd felt Vario's and Hugo's. Other ties, heavier, burning and stern, dragged her down into the ground and up into the sky. She was splayed in them all, caught in a golden web in the dark, while Drake sank repeatedly into her. What had been complete dark, the first time she dreamt it, was brighter – distant fires erupted and vanished. By their light, she saw his face. It shone with the same fierce ecstasy as when he'd first thrust right inside her. She always woke before the peak, shuddering, her legs wide apart, her slippery passage clenching around sudden emptiness. The mud, each morning, was baked to hard rock beneath her.

Drake sat cross-legged on his bed, a lute cradled on his lap, plucking lightly at the strings. The halls, deep underground, weren't even lit by the starlight that faintly illuminated the surface. Torches stood in brackets along each corridor and in each room, but he let his burn out and played in the dark. Forbidden to ride, he was filling the empty days as best he could. Nothing chased away his thoughts of Nina. Phrases from her letters spoke themselves unexpectedly in his head. Turning a corner, he'd be abruptly revisited by how she'd stepped close to him in the corridor. He thought of her fingers tracing the letters on his ceremonial breastplate, the first time he'd spoken to her. He remembered that touch as if the metal were his skin. His plucking fell into a rhythm and he sang softly, the oldest song of Kâo.

'Karayeethra ga Karayu . . .'

The door opened. A slice of light fell over him from the corridor, bisected by Tanya's wavy silhouette.

'Don't stop,' she said, closing the door behind her.

His fingers hesitated above the strings. 'I thought you were riding – weren't you in the next wave, to find the Queen?'

'I was ill,' she said casually.

The mattress shifted as she sat on the foot of the bed.

'Are you better now?'

'I think so. I'm not sure.' She chuckled, low. 'In some ways, yes.'

'This is no time to shirk your duties, Tanya – not with the Queen so desperately ill. We need people searching. I'll go myself, as soon as she lifts the ban.'

Tanya was silent.

'You did report to her, didn't you?'

'Not yet –'

Frustrated, Drake laid the lute aside. 'Do you really mean you haven't told her? That I'm banned from flying because of your laziness?'

Tanya flared up at his accusation. 'I didn't think it was a good idea, with me unwell! I might be contagious – and with her so weak . . .'

'How long have you been ill, then?'

'Oh, it's nothing serious – probably just one of those mild flus the twelve tribes are so susceptible to. I must have picked it up when I went down there, the last time.'

'You've seemed fine.' He frowned.

'Just a bit weak and headachey.'

He could hear her moving across the mattress.

'I didn't want to worry anyone,' she said softly, closer to him. Her hand brushed between his legs and she giggled. 'Where's the lute? I meant to pluck the strings – weren't you playing?'

He gulped. 'I stopped.'

Her fingertips fluttered over his groin, as if she were picking out a tune, and his cock stiffened.

'Tanya, please,' he said desperately.

The constant coupling was beginning to weary him, even though his body couldn't resist. She ignored him, her fingers dancing, and he wondered whether she were suffering the same heightened lust as him. She flung herself on him at every opportunity, as if time were running out. Now, she sat over him, her long dress open down the front. Her breasts massaged his face. Despite himself, his hands moved to her bottom, massaged its rounds and tugged her closer to his shaft. His teeth grazed her breasts.

'Do you never get enough?'

'I could ask you the same . . .'

She moved to give him the tip of her breast and he devoured it, his pulse accelerating. He could see nothing, only feel her curves writhing in his arms as she ground into him. With one hand he freed himself hurriedly. She rose, wiggling, and with a groan impaled herself. She rode him; their breath came quicker and uneven; his hands clutched her hips to heave her up and down faster. The dark was his friend, like this. He thought of Nina, and imagined it were her sliding on his cock. He'd lingered so much with her in the fort, delaying and teasing, wanting to give her the most perfect crisis. Instead, he'd only just penetrated her when the King and his soldiers arrived.

Moving slower, he laid Tanya on the bed, telling himself it was Nina. His ecstasy rose pure and hot at the thought. He held himself up on his arms, gliding stiff and steady into that soft sheath, grateful she didn't speak and destroy his pretence with her words. She moaned, though, frantically, and he told his ears it was Nina's voice, Nina he was patiently bringing to ecstasy. Up and in he surged, again and again, holding back by the skin of his teeth, making her howl and thrash with joy, until he could bear it no more and it was all he could do not to scream Nina's name as he came.

Whether Nina scratched or not, the itching worsened and her skin flaked. The éolith was rubbed smooth on one side, from rasping it over her rough skin. The rash entered her dreams, in which her skin became unnaturally smooth and glassy, covered in diamond patterns. In the firelight, as Drake made love to her, it was lustrous copper, silver and gold.

The dreams stayed with her as she walked. The marshes were behind her and she had no plan of where to go or what to do. Still naked, she avoided the roads and paths that might be used by other people or lead to towns, and struck out across the hills towards the mountain range. High ground seemed a good idea. Close to Crewer, the terrain was rocky. With the dream ribboning through her mind, she sometimes saw that dark world instead of the ground and tripped over stones, shaking her head to clear it. As soon as she fell into a steady pace, the dreams swarmed back. She found herself detouring around trees that weren't there and plunging into unseen rivers that were. She rubbed her palms in her eyes, trying to see straight, and wondered if starvation were making her hallucinate. She hadn't eaten for weeks, but she wasn't hungry or losing weight and even thinking of food disgusted her. She was strong without it – except that she still burnt with itching.

She used the rough side of the éolith and the constant scratching made her back swell. At the top of the swelling, the skin felt broken but it wasn't raw to the touch and her fingers came away clean of blood. She decided not to scratch it again, then couldn't help herself, and soon skin was hanging like leathery flaps down her back.

Without the dreams, she would have agonised about it and fretted over what to do next, but she was too bewildered to think straight. Every night, she fell straight into the dark forest world. Drake led her through the trees, down echoing tunnels, into lofty halls, and wherever they went they made love. Every day, she lived half there and half in the real world, the balance tipping inexorably towards the delusion.

One night, she sat on the lower slopes of the mountainside, turning the éolith over in her hands and trying to think clearly. The smoothest side of the stone reflected the moon and she smiled faintly at its familiar face in mirror-image, then turned to look at the real thing. It wasn't there. The mountain's black bulk blocked her view and it hadn't yet risen over the peak.

She rubbed the éolith with her hand. The moon still floated in it. She peered closer. Underneath the round coin of the moon, in dark black on pale black, she saw the outline of the mountain ridge behind her.

That's where I must go then, she thought. It was the first clear thought she'd had since the fort. From then on, she headed in the direction of moonrise.

Too weak to walk, the dragon-queen was carried to the balcony of the deepest hall. Its ceiling soared hundreds of metres, high enough for dragons to enter it, but today the floor was filled with the lords and ladies of Kâo. The Queen's shrivelled body was a distant dot above them and a lord stood at each side to help her stand, but she still found strength to unfold her huge wings. A whimper stirred through her people. Once her wings had gleamed like diamonds and her skin like polished metal – now her sheen was clouded and greying.

'I am dying fast.' Her voice was still clear. 'We have tried to find the new queen quietly, without alarming the twelve tribes, but time is running out. We can't afford to be secretive any more, sending riders out in twos and threes – tomorrow, you will all go, *en masse*, and you'll show yourselves, everywhere.'

Drake felt her looking directly at him. The silence was breaking into shocked whispers and muttering, and she spoke over them.

'*Everyone* must go. Whatever effect that has on the twelve tribes, it is nothing compared to what will happen to them if we don't find the new queen in time. I am holding on to life by a thread. I have spoken.'

She raised her hands and all the assembly knelt. As the two lords lifted her back to her room, babbling talk broke out. The Queen's nearness animated everyone and they argued, shouted, sobbed or grabbed each other to discharge their emotions in kisses. Drake wriggled between the knots of people, looking for Tanya, but she was nowhere to be seen. He forced his way out the crush, into the corridor. He looked in her room, on the terrace, in the smaller halls, and found her at last in the little tavern. She was sitting by the bar, her shoulders hunched, her eyes gazing deep in the goblet. When she saw him, she brightened abruptly.

'Where were you?' he said sternly. 'The Queen called an assembly.'

'Did she?' she said vaguely. 'I didn't hear.' She turned back to her goblet.

He scowled. Her laziness and irresponsibility insulted everything Kâo stood for. 'You'd better not drink any more – you'll be riding tomorrow.'

'I can't,' she said quickly. 'I'm still not well.'

'The Queen has spoken. There's no more time. Tomorrow, everyone rides. Tanya – what is it? You're pale!'

She'd swayed in her seat and swung her face away from him. 'I'm fine! I'm just ... dizzy. I told you, I'm not well.'

He crossed the floor in three long strides and grabbed her jaw in his hand, twisting her to face him. Her face whitened, her eyes huge and full of fear.

'We *all* ride,' he ground out.

Her eyelids flickered. He let go of her and stepped back, one hand rising to his breastplate. She caught her breath.

'Lady Tanya,' he said loudly.

Two people nearby glanced over curiously.

'Drake, no,' she hissed frantically. 'Drake, please, I'm begging you – don't do this!'

'Lady Tanya,' he repeated.

People turned, watching.

'I accuse you of dereliction of duty and ...'

Her eyes begged him to stop, but he closed his own and went on.

'And of lying. Who'll bear witness?'

'I will,' said a woman's voice.

He opened his eyes to the fury and hatred in Tanya's. From the crowd, two people stepped towards each of them, as guards. Both accuser and accused were under arrest and both would be tried. The woman who'd offered herself as witness was Jenna, the rider of Katara, whom Tanya had refused to tend. She slipped out of the bar and slid the bolts behind her.

Two hours later, they were taken to the huge hall where again the Queen was on the balcony; this time, they'd carried her bed, too, and she lay feebly against the cushions. Two dragons, Zenerith and Xylar, were crouching, filling most of the hall, the tops of their heads level with the Queen's. Drake's and Tanya's hands were closed in manacles and each of them chained to stand in front of their own dragon. The galleries were crowded, the onlookers safely above the watchful beasts.

'Let us hear the charges,' said the Queen wearily.

The dragons swung their heads towards Jenna, standing by the Queen, who repeated Drake's accusation.

'The most severe charge first,' said the Queen.

Jenna bowed. 'My Lord Drake, do you believe your accusation that Lady Tanya has lied?'

Drake looked up at the huge snout of the dragon a few feet from him. 'Yes.'

'Lady Tanya, have you lied?'

She swallowed. Xylar let out a wisp of smoke and she lowered her eyes. 'Yes.'

'Are you willing to tell us what your lie was?'

'No.'

Jenna sighed. A lie could be anything – narrowing it down with questions was an art. 'Tanya, our Queen is dying! We need to ride! We *will* uncover your lie, but it'll take time we can't spare.'

Tanya looked defiantly at her. She'd already given her answer and the dragon's quiet vouched for her honesty in that, at least.

'Very well. Lord Drake, do you know what the lie is?'

'No.'

Jenna turned back to Tanya and began to pose questions. Tanya, her eyes fixed on the dragon, answered in monosyllables. As long as she answered honestly, it wouldn't harm her. Jenna ranged through the options, floundering, uncovering nothing, until the Queen touched her sleeve and whispered in her ear. Jenna faced the hall again.

'Did you lie to Lord Drake?'

Tanya was silent, her head bowed. Xylar raised her head. Drake stared.

'Lady Tanya –'

'Yes.' She started crying.

Jenna looked at Drake. 'It's your right to take over the questioning, if you want.'

He nodded. She wouldn't look at him, still.

'Are you ill?' he said, across the hall.

'No.'

'Did you say that to get out of flying?' His voice was gentle.

'Yes.'

'Tanya . . . Tanya,' he said soothingly. 'We've all been less than perfectly honest, sometimes. On Navarone, I couldn't approach Zenerith for weeks.'

The galleries buzzed and he grimaced. So much for his unsullied reputation. But honour be damned, honesty was all. A sick suspicion formed in his mind and his voice shook as he framed it.

'Is this – is this about Nina?'

She cried harder, tugging at her chains as she tried to cover her face.

'Answer me!'

'Yes!' she yelled.

'Is Nina alive?'

'I don't know.' Her tone was almost insolent. 'Probably, yes.'

'She wasn't dead when you checked on the fort?' The blood was roaring in his ears and he understood why he, too, was chained – he could have torn her limbs apart.

'No, she wasn't!'

His heart ripped. His face wet, he screamed his questions across at her, yanking at the chains. 'Was she flaming?'

'Yes!'

'You *lied* to me! You let me think she was dead – you watched me grieve . . . you've put us all at risk – all so you could keep me for yourself?'

'Yes!' she screeched back.

'Damn you, why?'

'I would rather die than see you fuck that slut!'

But at that lie, Xylar raised her massive head, opened her jaw and billowed flame at her rider. Zenerith's snout knocked Drake off his feet as she pushed herself protectively in front of him. In the galleries, people reeled from the heat. Drake clung to Zenerith, his streaming face against her hot scales. With one claw she raked across the chain, freeing him. When he rose unsteadily to his feet, Tanya was nothing but ashes.

Nina scrabbled blindly up and down the paths of Crewer. The éolith only ever showed one peak now, the highest mountain in the vast range that composed that country. Steep paths led down and halted abruptly at cliff edges. Towering outcrops rose up from the valleys like inverted cones, the softer stone between them eroded. Some had ropes and bridges slung between them, houses perched precariously on top, but she shunned those and only crept close enough to steal some rope. With the éolith lashed to her stomach, her hands were free. She was forced to slither down scree slopes, where she could find them, or climb steep cliffs. Her itching skin was tougher, no doubt from having the harsh stone scraped over it. She used her hands as grips, shoving them into cracks and clenching a fist, letting the skin of her knuckles rip as it supported her weight. Nothing mattered but following the stone's guide. The harsh pain of her skin tearing was almost pleasurable, like pulling off a scab, and she grunted with effort as she forced her hand into another gap. Far beneath her dangling feet, the trees were as small as children's toys, the river glinting thin as a snake in the canyon. As she made a fist, she realised she'd misjudged – but her weight had already shifted as the weak sandstone crumbled. Her hand shot out and she fell.

She woke at the bottom of the canyon, her head full of dreams and her body unharmed. She stared around her, trying to see the real world through the visions of dark forests, then stood anyway and went on unquestioningly. She had to reach the peak and she'd lost height. She moved faster, swinging her weight rhythmically, using the momentum and not giving her grips time to fail. When she reached the top, she dusted her hands on her bare thighs and without pause hiked upwards, zigzagging the steep slope. The peak was near enough to deceive her – every rise promised to be the top, then as she crested it more would come into view.

The sun fell, the stars came out and the moon was hidden by the mountain peak. It was harder to differentiate between this world and the dream world, when neither had moons and both were black and starry. She walked blindly on, trusting that uphill was the right direction.

The terrace outside the halls of Kâo was only big enough for three of the massive dragons at a time, but an endless procession of the huge beasts slouched up the tunnels from deep in the belly of the ground, their riders falling in beside them. As each dragon emerged, it extended its hind leg. The rider ran and leapt, nimbly finding footing on the scales, then darted the length of its back to settle behind its head. In threes, the dragons rose to their feet, their wings beating, and launched themselves up to join the massive flock already circling in the skies. As they leapt, more were already crawling up behind them.

In her room, the Queen turned her head to her two attendants. 'Go.'

'But, Your Majesty –'

'I will live or die whether you're here or not! But if I die before you find the next queen . . . just go!'

They raced out of the room to join the procession.

The air was thick with dragons. From the ground, the stars had vanished. The whole sky was mosaicked in precious metals as their hides shone by the light of each other's rippling flames. More dragons were still leaping into the air – the full force of Kâo would set out tonight. Zenerith dived and wove dexterously between the sinuous bodies and flapping wings as Drake shouted instructions from her back, to get the colossal flock into formation. At last the beasts' roaring and rushing wind from their wings drowned him out entirely, and the last of the dragons were in the air. Zenerith swung around, shooting ahead like a meteor, and as one the countless massive heads swung to point and rushed after her.

*

Nina lay on the hard rock, staring numbly up at the bright moon. She'd reached her destination. The air here was thin and she inhaled slowly and deeply. Aching, she rolled on to her front, then on to all fours, and her stiff fingers unravelled the rope around her waist. The éolith fell on to the rock and she collapsed next to it, straining for air. Her eyes drifted closed and she jerked them open again. Fumbling, her hand found the rock and dragged it up to her face. Its glossy surface mirrored the moon above it. She ground her knuckles into her eyes and blinked hard, peering at it again. It reflected nothing but what was there, no hint of her next destination.

She rolled on to her back again. The stars were dazzling from here, high above the mists and clouds that clung closer to land. The moon stung her eyes. Her weird dreams echoed in her mind and she watched in fascination as blackness slid across the moon. '*Karitta go karew karack*,' she sang to herself. 'In the land of Kâo, the moon went black.'

No, those weren't the words – how did it go? '*Karayeethra ga Karayu . . .*'

She stared at the sky. The moon had vanished completely. Slowly, she turned to the éolith, in whose depths it still shone brightly, and she realised she wasn't heading in the direction of moonrise. She was heading for the moon.

Far above her, the swarm of dragons twisted and dived, their formation spreading outwards. It no longer mattered who saw them and how much terror they inspired in people's hearts, just as long as the new queen also saw them. She would recognise her own. Like arrowheads they shot through the sky, to skim through every city, town and village of the twelve tribes. As they neared the ground, they belched fire, calling their queen. The smell of deceit was everywhere, but the link still held.

On her rocky pinnacle, Nina stirred in her sleep. In the deserted halls of Kâo, the dragon-queen croaked and clawed at her blankets, gasping for breath. No one remained to help her sit up as she hacked and coughed. Her wings flapped feebly against the ground, straining to support her. She rose a few inches and slumped back. Her hands unclenched. She was still.

The dragons' eyes flared as the rage erupted in their hearts. The world stank of deceit – the quartermasters who skimmed the stores, the merchants who hiked the price of their goods and mouthed rubbish about rarity, the husbands who came to their wives fresh from the bed of another woman and the wives who let their lovers out the back door, the spies who won people's confidence and betrayed them, the smooth diplomatic lies in the courts – hardly a soul was pure and clean. The sky exploded in flames. In mid-air, the dragons bucked violently, throwing off the little riders who dared to sit on their backs and presumed to direct their movements. The lords and ladies plummeted, their screams mingling with the shouts of terror breaking out below. Some were close to ground and landed softly; other smashed, killed on impact. The dragons spiralled downwards, indifferent to their riders' plight, intent only on purging the lies that polluted the world.

Drake lay on a cliff edge, whose rock had broken his fall and knocked the breath from his body. Zenerith had sped on, death in her heart. He struggled to his feet and fell over again, his hands scraping on the charcoal sticks of burnt bushes. By moonlight, he traced the circle where fire had been, but no ashes remained. His hand rubbed the ground to be sure: it was baked hard. She'd been here. He spun around, looking for traces of singed foliage, and found blighted grass. He began to run.

In all the cities of the twelve tribes, the dragons ducked and spun through the air. Their wings swept the roofs off houses, laying bare the cowering inhabitants, and blasted them to ashes. They landed, crouching, in the courtyards of castles, and with a slow twist of their heads sprayed flame all around them. In the streets, people ran for their lives, shoving each other out of the way and scattering, but then a huge lazy shadow would drift over them and, with a sudden flare, they were gone. Buildings caught fire; storehouses went up like dry tinder. The dark flickering air echoed with petrified screams and howls; a woman backed away from a malevolent snout – she sobbed, clutching her baby, begging for mercy, but the dragon was indifferent. With a scoop of its claw, the baby was whipped from his mother's arms, and then she was only ash falling through the air.

On the mountain peak, Nina stood tall, howling. The deaths ripped at her, but worse was the fury. From this height, she could see beyond the borders of Crewer and she whirled around in the light of burning cities. The sky glowed red; her own flame jetted high above her.

'Let them be purged!' she bellowed. 'Down to the last child!'

From the slopes, Drake saw the column of fire and ran faster, his legs pounding into the ground and sweat flying from his skin. Far below, behind him, people's screams echoed and he knew that Zenerith was among them. He didn't need to track the ground any more. He just raced, muscles throbbing and lungs burning, towards the bursts of light on the mountain peak. The dragons would kill everyone. They had no mercy, no compassion for flaws.

He heard Nina shriek – he was close. His body begged him to stop, to rest, but he accelerated, sprinting so fast that his hair streamed behind him. His face shone with her firelight; he could see her in the distance, storming and raging. She arched, her wings spread behind her, flames bursting from her mouth. Then she doubled over, wailing, as the new death hit her.

'Let them die,' she screamed.

He was close enough to see her face glistening with tears, contorted.

'They deserve it!'

'Nina!' he bellowed.

She spun around to face him, blazing. Her eyes were wild and thick with tears. 'My children are killing my children!'

He grabbed her waist and she flung him off.

'You have to have mercy!'

'I am Dragon,' she roared. 'I know no mercy!'

'Nina, you're us, too – you're us as well – for all your children . . .'

'They lied. They all lie.' She was sobbing. 'The dragons don't lie.'

'The dragons don't *love.*'

He pulled her to him, fighting her inhuman strength, kissing her neck and arms as she wrestled.

'We have love, they have honesty; you're *both*, you must love.'

Exhausted with running, his legs crumpled. He tugged her down with him, throwing himself on top of her.

'They stink of deceit,' she moaned.

'But you love them.' He was pinning her down with his weight.

'They mustn't lie, they mustn't lie to me; they must know what happens.'

'I will *never* lie to you.' In the heat of the moment, the word 'never' was a cold chill across him. The dragon lords and ladies didn't use it. It invited a lie from the future which could never be undone. She lay in his arms, her wings spread wide on either side, and didn't flame at him.

'You love me,' he whispered, waiting for the flame and certain death.

It didn't come. She inflamed him – his spirit obeyed, his heart rushed with love, his body surged with desire. This was the same wild lust that had pursued him since he'd first seen her, which he'd tried so many times to slake with Tanya, but which always came back with renewed strength. He groaned, and moved to let her feel how much he wanted her, then laughed because that was so simple and honest and who better to be honest with than the dragon-queen?

Her eyes dilated, her rage momentarily forgotten, as she became aware of his heaviness and how he throbbed against her. The human part of her was coming to the fore again, and her arms ran over his back. He lifted himself on to his elbows, dipping his head to kiss her, and, as her tongue swept over his, the lust was almost too much. He rippled with her. He slid down her, her legs splaying under him.

'This is love,' he whispered, his head ducking, and then his tongue was busy with a different kind of speech. It circled the little bead above her entrance and traced down, wiggling between folds, up again, lapping at the tip, then down on another exploratory foray. She was opening to his touch, arching upwards, her arms lying wide over her wings.

'Please – now,' she said.

His breath stopped. 'For you, no.'

He licked her again and took the tip in his mouth, his lips nuzzling over it as she moaned in higher and higher notes. Her arms rose above her head, shining in metallic colours. She'd been adrift in dreams for so long that she hardly knew what was real any more, except that this seemed the absolute core of reality: she had wings, she lay on a mountaintop under a bright moon, and the man of whom she had dreamt again and again was kneeling between her legs, turning her as bright and hot as the centre of a flame. Only the emptiness inside her said this wasn't a dream – in her dreams, he always filled her – then his finger slid inside and she bucked wildly.

Back and forth it pistoned, her muscles hopelessly trying to grasp him tight and hold him, his knuckles grazing her clit each time he pushed in. He moved up to cradle and kiss her while his hand worked; she smelt herself on his chin and that was no dream either. Her hands fumbled at his clothes, but then she flailed, her shoulders falling back, her hips rising. He was gone – her eyes flew open to see him standing above her, tearing his clothes off. His chest swelled and gleamed in the cold light and, as his trousers fell, his cock leapt up. He crouched; her hand reached for it. She remembered this, though everything in between was blurred. She'd taken this in her mouth, warm and swollen – she curled towards him again, her tongue tasting, her lips closing. One wing wrapped around him where he knelt. He rocked into her mouth, then back out again. His chest heaved with emotion. His hand caught up her flame-coloured hair as he watched her lips swallow, clasp, and release him. The sight of it, the way she inflamed him, the sensation, all threatened to burst over him. 'Nina – please – wait,' he said.

Slowly, she looked up at him; slowly, she withdrew. Her lips were still parted, her eyes full. Her breath was fast. He waited, swaying, for the throbbing to recede a little. As he moved over her, she lay back, and like her dreams he held himself up on his arms above her, the curves of his muscles glowing in distant flames. He moved forwards. The round head nudged between her lips, prodding her clit, then he shifted and pressed again, making the space he needed inside her. Their eyes clung to each other's; he sank deeper. As the reality and dream collided, he filled her, then drove in more. She cried out; he thrust further. When she was crammed with him, he pulled out gradually, letting her feel the friction, then bore relentlessly back in. As patient as the moon, he retreated and advanced, letting her sob, his torso shining, his face stern and intent. She cried more stormily, because she was coming home at last, was becoming who she should have been all along, after so long, and he didn't stop to comfort her – only moved faster. The wind was whipping erratically around their mountain eyrie, blasting and gusting from every direction. Her eyes were blinded, her neck straining backwards, her ears deafened by the roar of blood and the whoosh of wings. When his hips were slamming into her thighs, her tears turned to wails and his lunges turned to fury. Sweat clung to his forehead, his hair damp, his mouth wide.

'Nina,' he gasped. 'My Queen . . .' She could see him more clearly, in the white dawn light. 'I – I can't –'

He was trying to hold back, but she spasmed and constricted around him, her warm passage rippling up and down his length, meaningless sounds streaming from her lips, and he had no choice. His hips bucked into her of their own accord. He bellowed in triumph, mounted on his queen, pouring into her.

The first sunlight found them motionless. Thick red light crept over them, glinting on the damp skin on his back and bouncing in dazzling refractions off her. It wrapped itself around her tousled hair and turned its red to gold. He raised his head to look at her shining green eyes, then lifted himself off, to let her stand. She turned slowly on the mountain's peak, staring in wonder. From the tip to the bottom of its slopes, it was lined with dragons, crouched and kneeling, their wings furled, glittering like burnt gold. She turned back to Drake, and found him also kneeling.

'My Queen,' he said.

Enjoyed *Magic and Desire*?

Read on for a sneak peek at Portia Da Costa's scintillating

HOW TO SEDUCE A BILLIONAIRE

Also available from Black Lace

BLACK
LACE

Prologue

He was tall, dark and handsome. Always tall, dark and handsome. A romantic cliché, but who was she to argue with her subconscious?

Dream Lover didn't speak as he climbed into bed with her. He rarely did speak. Her fantasies were visual, not auditory and her own sighs and moans were all the soundtrack that she needed.

Falling back against the pillows, she let her imagined lover take the lead. His smile was enigmatic as he loomed over her, a subtle play of light and shade, but his eyes were vivid and dark with desire. Aquamarine and too brilliant to be natural, they almost dazzled her as he moved in close to kiss her. His lips were mobile and velvety, and the contact compelled her mouth to yield, his tongue demanding entrance, and thrusting fiercely.

Oh yeah!

Fantasy hands settled on her body, the contact firm but not rough as he explored her. He cupped her breast, squeezing lightly, thumb flicking back and forth, driving her crazy even though he'd barely begun his magic. She squirmed, every bit of her coming to life. Especially certain bits ... The touch of his fingertips was smooth and warm, sliding easily against her skin. It felt lovely and made her wriggle even more ... until an intrusive memory popped unwelcome into her mind.

A nearly-man, someone she'd once dated and hoped for great things with, he'd had callouses on his finger-tips when he'd touched her. They'd felt horribly rough against her skin when he'd tried to sneak his hand up her blouse, and it'd destroyed every chance she might have had of getting turned on.

I'm my own worst enemy. Everything has to be perfect when in real life it probably never is.

As she banished the thought with a furious shake of her head, her hair lashed against the pillow as if she were already in the throes of orgasm. Still without speaking her phantasm-man soothed her, gentled her. His touch both calmed her down and shook her up at the same time, and he stroked her breasts, one then the other, alternating, knowing just when to switch. Then, kissing harder, he drifted that enchanted arousing hand further down, cupping her crotch in a light grip that employed a pinpoint degree of assertion and confidence. Her legs lolled apart of their own accord, making room for his exploration. Seducing him...

Of course, it went right. Why wouldn't it? It was all idealised. Questing, he parted the hair of her pussy with those perfect fingertips, dipping in to touch her clit. She gasped, always astonished to be so wet at these times. Lost in her fantasy though, it was easy to get slippery and silky, effortlessly easy.

She cried out, her own voice sounded shockingly loud. Usually she was able to keep the noise down in a shared house, barely articulating any more than wordless Dream Lover did. For a moment, she worried that her house-mate Cathy would hear her, but then told herself not to fret. She'd never heard any sounds of erotic partying from Cathy's room, and her housemate led a happy, uninhibited sex life with a real, live lover. Cathy was normal, and shared good times with her steady man.

She's younger than me too.

No! Another intrusive thought . . . It was a weird night tonight. Somehow she was more turned on than usual, and yet at the same time less able to concentrate on making Dream Lover real.

What had got into her? Had she lost it completely, from all this incessant brooding on ... her situation?

Closing her eyes tight, she focused on the dream man who was making love to her. He was passionate and beautiful, and though she still saw no exact likeness of him, he was somehow clearer. She didn't force the issue though. She had other priorities. Something else she needed to keep from slipping away ... Sensations that could be as fugitive as they were precious and exquisite.

Stroking, stroking, stroking. The pressure, the pattern just right. No man would ever match her own fingers. No man would ever map her own body as she did.

No man had ever even had a chance to try, because no man was perfect.

Stop it! Don't go there. Focus, idiot!

Slipping, circling, swirling, Dream Lover banished her conundrum. His touch and the way it journeyed over the folds and dips and hotspots of her sex was matchless; dominant without being domineering, powerful without being rough. The gathering pleasure made her rock her hips, jerk and thrust against the contact. But Dream Lover was Dream Lover and he didn't miss a beat.

Gasping, she rose to him again, imagination finally taking over, the fantasy and the sensations becoming one. As if sure of her readiness, the man she'd conjured up moved over her, gracefully settling between her legs, his idealised cock pressing for admittance against the entrance of her sex.

The unknown country.

But it felt right. It felt wonderful. Hot. Solid. An iron-stiff rod pushing inside her, yet living and sensitive. Driving, thrusting, possessing, the rhythm divine and metronomic. The way he knocked against her clit with each plunge triggering pleasure that bloomed like fireworks, streaming up into the heavens and taking her with them.

Her teeth clamped hard together, keeping in her shouts, but inside she cried, *Oh thank you, thank you, thank you!*

Whoever you are . . .

Afterwards, she lay still and gasping. Wrung out like a dishrag, sweaty and dishevelled.

This was getting ridiculous.

You need to get a real man, you bloody fool. You need to find out what it's really like. Nobody but a nun is still a virgin at twenty-nine nowadays, regardless of whatever life 'stuff' happens to them.

Holding out any longer for some crazy ideal of a perfect man was stupid. There *were* no perfect men, and if she kept holding out for one, she'd find herself holding out forever, and end up as a dried up spinster with only her sketching and good works or whatever to keep her occupied. She'd bet good money that any normal woman would be prepared to sleep with more than a frog or two in the hopes that one of them might turn out to be moderately princely.

Waiting for desire was daft. The years were flying by. She had to go half way, and take a risk; *work* to feel passion. Just sitting around expecting lust to suddenly arrive, kaboom, was pathetic.

Next time a nice man with potential crossed her path, she had to give him a chance, and not keep turning away because he wasn't Dream Lover.

As long as he's just a little bit tall and dark and handsome . . .

Shaking her head, she sat up and smoothed down her nightgown.

Time to draw . . .

1

'Oh no! Why today? Why do you have to do this to me?'

Jess Lockhart stared up into the pouring rain and almost shook her fist. She would have done it if there hadn't been cars whizzing by, driven by people who'd think she was a loony; cars that flung up sheets of muddy spray that soaked her shoes and legs as they passed.

Why had this happened just when she wanted to look her best at work? She didn't normally dress up. Smart casual, in fact very casual, was her usual look. But today she wanted to appear a bit more polished, just in case, because of the mighty, exalted VIP who was visiting.

Not that the new owner of the insurance group she worked for was likely to descend from on high to tour the cubicle farm. Why would he? He was a businessman, a tycoon, a financier. He wasn't interested in what the lowly drones at the coalface were doing, just the monetary assets that Windsor Insurance, his new acquisition, represented.

'Why does nobody I know ever drive past?' Jess growled at no car in particular.

This was the busiest part of the city and not everybody was going in the same direction, but surely somebody else was heading for Windsor Insurance? But most likely they wouldn't even recognise such a rain-soaked and bedraggled mutt as their work colleague.

Now, if she'd got up in good time, she could've checked the weather forecast and known that sharp, heavy showers were on the way. But no, she'd been awake half the night, stupidly fantasising about Dream Lover, and then equally stupidly trying to capture his image on paper. Consequently, when it was time to get up, she'd slept in, woolly-headed and weary. If she'd woken up at her normal hour, she could have begged a lift from Cathy, but she'd left it too late. Cathy was an angel, and she'd offered to wait ... but that would have made her late for work too.

Now you're paying the price for your midnight shenanigans, dimbo, and as you didn't even have the foresight to bring an umbrella, you're going to get soaked to the skin between the bus station and work. Brilliant!

Blinking water out of her eyes, Jess realised that the hair that had begun as a chic and elegant up-do was fast collapsing, its structure undermined by the teeming deluge. With a muttered oath, she pulled out the securing clip, and slung it aside in disgust, to run her fingers through the thick straggles of her sodden hair.

So much for 'maple syrup' low-lights and a twenty-quid conditioning mask.

Just about to retrieve the clip, she darted back from the kerb's edge. Despite the double yellow lines and 'No Stopping' signs, a vehicle actually was pulling up beside her now, its slowing speed only splattering her with a light swish of rainwater this time. Her hairclip was crushed to shards beneath the wheel of a distinctive, retro looking powder blue car. A long, low, classic Citroën. An uncle of hers had driven one once upon a time, and she'd always loved riding in it, because of the way its suspension made you feel as if you were floating on air. Happy, innocent days those had been, when she and her sister had accompanied her uncle's family on sketching holidays to Cornwall.

But what was a vintage 'blue whale' like Uncle Mark's doing here in this neck of the woods, jostling amongst the school run

SUVs and the hot hatches and the occasional luxury saloon or hybrid?

Looks like I'm going to find out.

A figure within the blue car leant across the passenger seat and rolled down the window.

'Can I give you a lift somewhere?' said a deep, musical voice, easy on the ear, but very 'not from round here'. The accent was hard to pin down though – basically British, but with bits of other things – especially amongst the drumming rain and the honking car horns.

Jess blinked again. And not just from the water running into her eyes. It was like a double recognition. *Really* weird, making her feel weird too, as if she'd been whirled around several times, far too fast.

No, surely not . . . Surely it's not him . . . *or* him!

The man in the car was the spitting image of the pictures she'd seen of today's VIP visitor . . . and he could also have been Dream Lover at a pinch.

The familiar but unfamiliar man grinned, his face lighting up in a sunny, happy, amused expression, glowing somehow, almost dazzling. Eyes that were a bluish green – bluer than his car, but not as green as the actual green of leaves or grass – almost seemed to twinkle at her.

Dear God, it is him! *It's the VIP! The new big boss of all bosses!*

'Lift?' he prompted, making Jess realise that she must look a complete fool, standing there, wet and bedraggled, with her mouth hanging open, and was probably compounding that impression with every second that passed. Yet still she stood there, and time seemed frozen, apart from the ominous approach of an incoming traffic warden, heading along the street.

But what was this handsome devil, this mighty captain of business, doing cruising along, driving himself in an obviously ancient car when he should be riding in a limousine with a brace of PAs and a chauffeur to look after him? And the VIP's clothing didn't fit the surroundings either. He looked as if he was on his holidays. His suit was light-coloured, fawnish linen, stylish but slightly crumpled, and he wore his flower-patterned cheesecloth shirt with the tails out.

It's definitely him though. Handsome as the devil, but nothing like your everyday average billionaire tycoon. Definitely eccentric.

'Thanks, but it's all right. I'm nearly there. I wouldn't want to trouble you, and I'll get rain on the upholstery of your car. Thanks ...'

He laughed softly, cheerful and clearly entertained by her absurdity.

'Sod my upholstery, it'll survive.' He quirked his dark brows at her, and his smile was oddly entreating. 'Please won't you get in? You're getting drenched, and I'll never forgive myself if you end up catching a cold or flu when I could've prevented it. I'm not a pervert or a kidnapper, honestly.' He glanced quickly up the street at the approaching warden. 'I think I'm going to get a ticket any second if we don't move on.'

'Okay then. Thanks.'

Jess slithered into the passenger seat, embarrassingly aware of the slim skirt of her one good suit riding up her thighs. Her tights felt horribly slimy on her wet legs, but she'd wanted to look 'well put together' today and groomed, so she'd worn a pair. Normally she relied on a spot of fake tan.

'Where to?' The VIP arched his eyebrows at her again. And what eyebrows they were! Dark and very firmly marked, they were a perfect match for the near-black brown of his slightly tousled hair and the sexy roguish stubble of his semi-beard.

I don't think Dream Lover has ever had a beard.

'Um . . . Windsor Insurance. It's about two monoliths down, on the left. You can't miss it. There's this silly picture of a castle on the logo.'

And it's your latest acquisition, Mr Beach Bum Billionaire, I think you'll find.

'A silly castle, eh?' he observed, setting the car in gear, eyes on the traffic, yet still making her feel as if he was scrutinising her intensely. 'And what are you then, the lost princess?'

'Nope, just a serf. A minion. A lowly member of one of the claims teams.'

'Oh, not so lowly. Not from where I'm sitting.' Before Jess could even form a response to that, he gestured towards their destination, which now hove into view on the left. She hadn't noticed but he was driving quite fast in the wet and had navigated his way neatly through the hurly-burly of the morning rush hour. 'That it?'

Was he even going to mention who he was? Maybe not. Maybe he wasn't going to bother inspecting the troops, after all, and was just going to hang out with higher management echelons?

'Yes . . . Yes, thanks. You could drop me just here. That's the staff entrance.' She nodded to where some of her work colleagues, most of them considerably dryer than she was, were filing through the double doors.

As she put her hand on the car door handle, he stayed her, his fingers on her arm. It was the lightest contact, but she almost rocked in her seat, imagining the same lightness of touch in another context. A night-time context, slight and gentle, but the beginning of more, so much more.

Jess! What the hell . . . What . . .

Incredibly, her body roused. It was so sudden and so incongruous that she almost swayed in the seat.

Why now? In these circumstances? In the rain, with a man she'd met seconds ago, and would probably never meet again, other than perhaps a nod of acknowledgement as he swept through the claims department on some kind of royal progress.

And yet, it'd happened, shaking her in a way that had always seemed like some magic unknown, a state fantasised about and achieved in solitude, but never experienced out here, in the real world. How could one fleeting touch from this displaced beach bum catch her unawares and take her effortlessly to the domain of Dream Lover?

Staring at him, she could almost see her every thought mirrored in those tropical ocean eyes. As if he knew her. Totally. Understood her lack of experience, and comprehended that she didn't *want* to lack experience, but simply didn't want to throw away something precious in a meaningless act with someone she didn't quite care enough about.

'Are you okay?' He frowned. Looked puzzled. Probably not as completely bedazzled and befuddled as she was, but somehow, amazingly, affected by the moment. 'Do you have towels in there?'

'What?'

'Towels. For drying yourself.'

'Er . . . No, not really, it's mostly hand-dryers.' Now there was a point.

He leant forward, popped open the glove compartment, and fished out a box of man-size tissues, as yet unopened. 'Take those. They'll be better than nothing. Your boss should provide better facilities for his staff than just hand-dryers. Especially in this soggy climate.' 'Oh, I couldn't . . .' Easy for him to be Lord Bountiful. Nobody would get soaked to the skin by dank northern weather on his tropical-somewhere hideaway or any other parts of a billionaire's exalted world.

'Oh, go on. It's just a box of tissues.' He reached over, unzipped the top of her tote bag and shoved in the box of tissues. 'Now, off you go. You'll be late, and we wouldn't want that, would we?'

'No, we wouldn't,' she shot back at him, glad to have retrieved her backbone from somewhere. He'd given her a very brief lift – and the weirdest jolt of pleasure – but he wasn't the boss of her . . . even if he was.

'Thanks again,' she cried, opening the passenger door and shooting out before things could get any weirder.

Soft laughter rang in her ears long after she'd entered the building, echoing as if imprinted on her brain.

2

Portrait of a young woman as drowned rat. I wouldn't want to draw that!

Jess could still see her face in the ladies' room mirror. Her makeup had mostly gone to hell, as had her hairstyle, leaving her looking generally gobsmacked and waterlogged.

And the man who'd given her an almighty shaking up for a variety of reasons had seen that impressive look, and obviously found her a rich source of amusement.

Arrogant bastard! In your world there'll always be a nice dry car to take you where you want to go! No slumming it in the rain like us plebs...

Now though, at her desk, an hour later, she felt warmer, better, and at least slightly drier. His big box of tissues had helped with the blotting, and she'd set it beside her computer, like a talisman. She entertained silly, subversive thoughts about hanging on to it when it was empty, as a keepsake of their 'moment'.

Or at least your moment, Jess. Ridiculously bad timing. Couldn't have been worse.

Silly mare, she chided herself, yet, even as she went through routine tasks, she tried to reclaim the sensations.

Heat, even though she was shivering. Heart racing. The deep, slow, honeyed surge, low in her belly. Astounding ... alarming ... wonderful! Everything she could induce in her fantasies, yet never feel here in the real, living world!

Unfortunately, though, the man who'd induced those feelings would never know it. Hell, he'd probably completely forgotten her even before she'd reached the door to the building, even though the smell of his gorgeously spicy cologne was still powerful and exotic in her brain.

Those blue-green eyes. That sunny smile. They were still with her too. And she kept seeing his strong, lightly tanned hands, so relaxed yet sure on the steering wheel . . . and in everything they did, probably. Could this man be the full-on placeholder for Dream Lover? A face she could picture in her fantasies? An avatar to make do with until somebody real came along? If they ever did . . .

Banishing that grim thought, she felt her fingers itch to start doodling, and after a sly look around, she succumbed, pretending to jot notes on her pad, yet in reality pencilling the curve of that smiling mouth, that sexily stubbled jawline. Just elements. She daren't get absorbed in a full face sketch or she'd get no work done and somebody would notice. Not a good strategy at the best of times, but doubly unwise today. Everybody was supposed to look super-efficient, and wholeheartedly dedicated to insurance, for the 'royal' visit: the arrival of the group's new owner to inspect their very humble and fairly insignificant division. Which was weird, but apparently the VIP's eccentric habit.

And management doesn't know the half of it. She grinned to herself while she doodled the curve of his gorgeous lips on her pad. *That stuffy lot upstairs will have a fit when they see your flowered shirt with the tails hanging out.*

So, she'd actually met Ellis P. McKenna, international financier and general all-round filthy rich tycoon. One to one. He was the scion of a billion-dollar entrepreneurial family who'd bought out Windsor Insurance as part of a group along with a large number of other financial concerns, just like someone going out and buying three sweaters in different colours rather than only one. If actual whole companies were so easy to acquire and dispose of to him, it didn't bode well for the little people like her who worked in them.

We all might be just as disposable as cheap jumpers if you decide to keep this operation lean and mean, Mr McKenna.

Jess shuddered. She needed her job, because she didn't have any reserves. Ensuring that her gran had been comfortable at Baxendale Court in her final years had hoovered up every scrap of Jess's modest savings, and she was still gradually paying off the loan she'd taken out to make up the difference. She didn't regret a thing, and would do it again in a heartbeat, but it had left her finances since then a tad precarious, even long after Gran had passed on.

Impatient suddenly, she flung down her pencil, breaking the point and attracting curious looks from Jim and Michelle, who shared her 'pod' of desks.

Oh, come on, Mr McKenna, let's see you again. We'll all sit here tugging our forelocks for a bit, then we can get back to our normal drone activities . . . and I can be sure that Dream Lover is just Dream Lover, a man I once met for about thirty seconds.

Would he even acknowledge her? Or just swan past, barely noticing the faces behind the desks? She pushed his box of tissues to a more prominent place. Perhaps that might remind him?

Even as Jess was thinking that, there was a faint jumble of voices out in the corridor, a small commotion like a looming weather front. People around her sat up straight, fiddled with their ties or smoothed their hair. Michelle even pressed her lips together to refresh her lipstick. Ridiculous! The VIP would come blowing through the office barely breaking stride, a self-identified deity amongst them, hardly bothering to acknowledge the individual insects he now employed.

The minor hubbub intensified, still approaching. Unconsciously, Jess did the smoothing of the hair thing too. She'd drawn it back now in the best 'do' she could manage at short notice and with her clip smashed and gone, a ponytail at the nape of her neck, secured by a covered elasticated band she'd discovered at the bottom of her bag. She patted at her blouse too, the only part of her ensemble that had more or less avoided getting soaked. Unlike her skirt, which was soggy round the hem, and her shoes, which audibly squelched when she walked. She could have changed into her comfy shoes, but they were far too casual. Ah, the irony, considering that Ellis McKenna was more casually dressed than anyone here.

Jess's heart thudded. Some of those voices were distinct now – those of her bosses – but another one also sounded vaguely familiar.

Oh holy shit, you are tall, dark and handsome, Mr McKenna!

The potential candidate for Dream Lover met the height credentials too.

Flanked by the Windsor Insurance bigwigs in their best dark suits, stringently ironed shirts and sober ties, the man with the vintage Citroën strolled into the room, looking like a shabby but dazzling peacock god surrounded by a scuttling murder of crows. Sharp aquamarine eyes scanned the desks and the people behind them, registering, summing up, and passing by with the efficiency of a Terminator. It took but a split second for him to find her ... and smile.

Oh no!

Without any warning to his entourage, the newcomer abandoned them and strode towards her. Jess had the ridiculous urge to shoot to her feet.

God damn it, he's not a king or anything! I haven't even decided whether he's Dream Lover or not yet.

Sitting tight, she offered him a friendly smile. He had stopped and given her a lift, after all. 'Hello, Mr McKenna,' she said quickly, getting in there first, amazed that she suddenly felt both super-confident and quivery as a jelly inside. He was definitely having Dream Lover effects on her.

His gaze flicked to her nameplate. 'Hello, Ms J. Lockhart. Have you dried out yet?'

'Yes, thank you.'

His brow puckered as he took in her still damp hair, and then, as he peered around the edge of her desk, her wet-hemmed skirt and her sodden shoes.

'Fibber,' he said in a low voice, possibly audible only to her as he leant closer. Jess gripped the edge of her desk to steady herself, made woozy by a sudden waft of his intoxicating male fragrance. It seemed stronger now than it had been in the car.

Who the hell were you intending to impress that you needed to top up your cologne?

His Mediterranean eyes, and the way they flashed, supplied the answer.

I've told you before! Don't be idiotic, Jess, you're nothing to him.

But against all reason, that was wrong. The way he looked at her said she *was* something to him. Something she couldn't completely believe. She could almost imagine she was *his* Dream Lover.

He didn't say more, but his intent expression, and the little quirk of his firm, rosy, biteable lips said their conversation was merely postponed, not over. With a wink, he turned from her, his sharp eyes focusing elsewhere, this time on a step stool against the filing wall, close to her desk. Swooping down, he drew it out, and then leapt lightly up onto it, just a yard or so from where Jess was sitting.

'Right, everyone. I guess you know who I am, and if you don't, I'm Ellis P. McKenna and three weeks ago I took Windsor Insurance into the UK portfolio of the McKenna Group.' He beamed around at everybody. Jess didn't know what the men in the section were making of this, but she could feel a cresting wave of fluttering female excitement building in the room. *Stop showing off*, she wanted to say to him, even though every part of her subconscious and most of her conscious mind loved his display. His body was lithe, but strong-looking, and its proximity was like having some kind of sweet, heady alcoholic syrup bubbling inside her. He was inducing all the reactions that her fantasies managed to trigger, but which never occurred outside of them. Against her will, she found herself zeroing in on his waist ... his linen clad thighs ... his crotch ... Wondering and wondering.

Desiring ... At last. An actual living, breathing man. It was just like in the car. She was experiencing real female lust for a male who wasn't simply a figment of her imagination. All her adult life she'd wanted this to happen, and she'd believed she was weird and a freak because it hadn't. She'd never experienced the siren call. Never want to give ...

Blinking, she realised he was speaking again. But there had been a pause. A pause where he'd looked back into her eyes, and, yes, watched the birth of her physical attraction to him. Had he sensed its unusualness?

'What I just wanted to assure you all was that there won't be any redundancies or any cuts in salaries. Well, not at this level.' He winked again, to all the deskbound assembly in general. 'I haven't decided about this lot yet though.' He made an elegant sweeping gesture to the suits in his retinue, then beamed again, obviously highly amused by their discomfiture.

'Well, that's it really. I'm not one for speechifying. I just didn't want anyone to worry.' He leapt down from his vantage point. 'As they say in the movies, "Have a nice day."'

Yes, please go. I can't think. I need to settle down. Go away, Mr Dream Lover McKenna. Just walk out of my life so I can keep you in my fantasies.

A new emotion sluiced through her, as shocking and intense as the lust she'd felt. It was a black, aching sense of loss and despair. Why feel what she felt now, for a man she'd never see again? Why couldn't it have happened with someone attainable, with whom there might be a future? And more to the point, somebody that she liked, not this clearly supremely arrogant alpha male.

But Ellis McKenna didn't walk. He stayed where he was, scoping her, and frowning.

'You really are still a bit damp there, Ms J. Lockhart, aren't you?' The frown deepened, became layered somehow, as if his attention to her was operating on multiple levels at once. 'We can't have that. I'm not keen on the idea of an employee of mine coming down with pneumonia on the very first day I meet her. I think you'd better come with me.' Imperiously, he held out his hand, as if to draw her up from her seat. 'Please?'

And there it was again, that strange hint of entreaty in his eyes. That very human quality, a need for genuine interaction, however brief.

What the hell is going on? This is just barmy!

Still not sure whether she was succumbing to a consummate manipulator, or a man's real wish for her company, she took the offered hand, snatching up her bag from the side of her desk. His fingers closed around hers, firm and unyielding as if he thought she might flee if he let up on the hold. It was impossible not to follow him now as he led her the length of the desk farm, running the gauntlet of dozens of pairs of curious eyes tracking their every move.

'Where are we going? You can't just waltz me away somewhere,' she hissed, in the lowest voice she gauged he could hear without it carrying to the curious ears of her colleagues.

'I can. I'm the boss,' he said, twinkling at her over his shoulder.

'You're only the boss of me as an employee, not as a person. I ought to report you to my union rep for harassment.' And in any other circumstances, it might have been harassment, but this . . . this was something else entirely.

He stopped as they got to the lift, and released her hand.

'I'm sorry. I'm being a bit of an arse, aren't I? Do you want to go back to your desk?' His expression was still that curious blend of provocation and appeal. He was daring her to walk back between the rows of avidly gaping faces, yet hoping that she wouldn't call his bluff.

But what on earth is he planning?

Jess shot into the lift, and almost adhered herself to the far wall, about as far away from Ellis McKenna as she could get. After pressing the button for the top floor, he winked at her, and leant against the opposite wall. Why did she feel disappointed that he didn't lunge in her direction?

But, he didn't need to lunge. He just did it with his ocean-green eyes, scrutinising her from head to foot while a little smile played around his lips.

Jess wished, wished, wished she looked more impressive. She lifted her chin and eyeballed him back boldly, but she was all too aware of the soggy hem of her skirt, her squelchy shoes and the stringy wet strands of her hair. Still, pretending she looked fabulous, she stayed strong, trying not to be intimidated by his effortless, scruffy glamour and his sexual aura, an emanation so intense it was like a mist that filled the cabin of the lift.

Oh shit. Oh Lord. I want him. I've no practical idea how to do sex, but I want to do it with him, even if I will be the most hopeless lay.

Ellis tilted his head a little, his eyes narrowing almost as if he'd heard her. For about a fifth of a second, he caught his plush lower lip between his teeth, and looking at him, at that complex expression on his face, she could imagine that it wouldn't matter to him that she was inexperienced. Whatever happened, he would be good enough for both of them. He'd be sensational.

The 'ding' of the lift arriving at their destination made her jump, physically. They'd been in the lift less than thirty seconds but it felt like a lifetime.

'Where exactly are we going?' she asked, following him as he strode out of the lift, then paused to wait for her.

'I've commandeered old Jacobson's office for the day. He's slumming it, in with one of his henchmen.' Ellis winked at her again. 'He says he doesn't mind in the slightest but I can see he's really fuming inside.'

Jess had no idea what Mr Jacobson, the head honcho, looked like when he was fuming. He hadn't even been the one to interview her, and staff on her level never really interacted with senior management.

Looks like I'm interacting with a level of management way above 'old Jacobson' today. It isn't possible to reach a higher level than this.

'I hope he doesn't decide to take reprisals on people like me when you've flitted on to wherever you plan to flit to next,' she said crisply, as Ellis ushered her into the Executive Director's office suite. Jacobson's secretary gave her a curious glance, but only momentarily. The woman barely seemed to have eyes for anyone but Ellis McKenna.

'No interruptions please, Ms Brown,' he instructed, pausing at the older woman's desk to bestow a brain-melting smile.

'Of course, Mr McKenna,' she replied, sounding suspiciously breathy.

You make all women crazy, don't you? Jess accused him silently as he held open the door to the inner sanctum for her.

The way his beautiful mouth quirked seemed to suggest, once again, that he'd heard the thought.

It was a large office, with a very fine leather-topped desk, banked computer workstations to one side, and an 'informal' area over by the floor-to-ceiling windows that looked out over the busy street below. Across the rooftops, in the distance, there was a tantalising view, between two high rises, of the city park, a bit of breathing space amongst the built-up metropolis. There was even the faintest glint of the boating pond, the glitter of water.

Two long settees faced each other at right angles to the triple-glazed glass, with individual armchairs drawn up to the sides and a couple of small, low tables strategically placed.

But wasn't really the seating arrangement that caught Jess's eye. It was the collection of items assembled, some on one of the tables, some on one of the couches.

Ellis led her to the nearest couch.

'I think you should take your skirt and your shoes off.'

Jess gasped. What the hell?

The dazzling, roguish god laughed, his white teeth glinting.

'No, I'm not planning to ravish you . . .' He paused, and for a moment a more saturnine expression crossed his face. 'Well, not unless you absolutely insist. But really, your skirt is still wet at the hem, and I swear I can hear your shoes squishing as you walk.' He nodded at the offending footwear. 'It's bloody cold today, considering it's supposed to be summer round here at the moment, and like I said before, I'd never forgive myself if you ended up catching a chill.'

Thunderstruck, Jess said the first thing that came into her head. 'Why? It's not your fault.'

'Oh, I think it is, in a way. The big boss is visiting, so you chose to wear a smart but rather flimsy suit and insubstantial shoes. It *is* my fault.'

'That's nonsense. I always dress smartly for work.'

He narrowed his sea-blue eyes.

'All right ... Yes, this isn't my usual work suit. It's my interview suit. And these are my best dressed up shoes.'

'Well, take them off for a while then. I've had the heating turned on, so we can slip your skirt over the radiator and your shoes beneath.' He leant over and patted one of the curious items on the nearest settee: a thick, fluffy bathrobe in navy blue. 'You can wear this while they dry off, and we can have a nice little chat and drink some hot chocolate. That'll warm you up.' He nodded towards a tall vacuum jug standing on one of the tables, with china cups and saucers, and a basket with what looked like home-made cookies nestling in a white table napkin. How had he assembled all this stuff in just an hour? Had he decided the moment he'd first seen her that he'd hijack her from her desk like this?

'I can't take my clothes off just like that. It's ... um ...' She clasped her bag, as if it were a weapon with which to defend herself from him. 'I mean ... you're like the super duper boss of me. I only met you for a few minutes less than an hour ago, and this is an open office, for God's sake!'

'Who do you think is going to ogle you? It's just storage across there, as far as I can tell, and I don't think the birds are particularly interested in us.' He gestured towards the building across the road. He was right; the only living creatures that could overlook them were a few pigeons roosting on the windowsills across the way. 'I'll turn my back, of course.'

The situation was hurtling into the surreal. Jess shook her head. It was as if she'd stepped through a magic portal at some time since the blue Citroën had drawn up beside her. Or maybe that was the event horizon, entering his car.

'Okay then, if you don't trust me not to look, Jacobson has a small executive bathroom.' He waved towards a door at the end of the computer bank. 'You can change in there instead.'

Stop acting like a ninny, Jess. Just treat this like a game, a hoot. Pretend it's all a big giggle and an adventure. He'll be gone in a few hours, and he'll most likely never come back. You'll laugh about this afterwards and he is fabulous fantasy material . . .

'I trust you not to look, but I think I'll still change in there.' Kicking off her wet shoes, she swept up the thick, luxurious robe and then hurried off towards the door to Jacobson's bathroom.

This was the weirdest situation she'd ever found herself in, and she needed a moment to regroup. To think and to look at her reflection in the mirror and convince herself she wasn't in an extended and augmented version of one of her own erotic fantasies. A freaky dream that she'd wake up from in a minute, and then have to drag her half-asleep body out of bed, to go to work.

And she needed a minute away from the challenging, macho aura of Ellis McKenna . . . The only man she'd ever met who actually honest to God turned her on.

3

Ellis pursed his lips as the door slammed.

What the hell are you doing, man? Being Mr Impulsive and playing up to your reputation for eccentricity is one thing ... but this, this is different.

She's different.

Jessica Lockhart. What was it about her? Everything about her initial impression upon him had been unpromising, and yet, oh dear God, he'd been aroused the minute she'd slid into the Citroën in her soggy suit and her waterlogged shoes, and with her dark, saturated hair hanging in thick, wet rat's tails.

Frowning, he retrieved her shoes, imagining the shapely feet they'd protected. He wasn't a foot fetishist, but it was easy to imagine the lovely legs those feet were attached to. And the luscious thighs. And the lithe yet curvaceous hips.

His mind flashed a vision to him of those enticing legs and hips naked, and the mysterious grove of her sex, fully revealed to him. If she were a natural brunette – as he had every reason to believe – she'd be dark-haired down there too, the contrast against her creamy skin stark and stunning.

But great legs and an enticing little pussy were character-istics of a thousand girls. What was it about this particular girl ... this woman ... that had hooked him? Still musing, he placed the shoes close to the radiator, but not close enough to ruin them by cracking the leather.

Maybe it was the fact that he *did* perceive her as a girl?

But she isn't one. She's a woman. Later twenties. Not all that much younger than me, if truth be known.

But his journey through the valley of grief had aged him prematurely. Not physically, but emotionally. He felt as if he was a thousand years old in loss and regret, but in reality, thirty-six was no age at all. And he'd found a way to deal with his life as it was. A set of workable parameters...

But even so, that still didn't explain why Jessica Lockhart shook him up like this. She didn't remind him of Julie. Not in the slightest. They were entirely different types, except perhaps for that elusive quality; that of being untouched, yet curious. The way his wife had been at the dawn of their relationship.

A sudden image of Julie in her wedding gown pierced him like burning spear, hitting so hard he almost cried out, his excitement and arousal instantly forgotten.

No. No. No. That's the past, a paradise that can never be revisited. That state, that love that I once had ... That's a closed book now, and never to be reopened.

He turned away from the window, and the vision of the waterlogged metropolis and its unknown humanity, all hurrying about their business. Not that he'd even been seeing them.

The room, for all its sterile utilitarianism and lack of real character, was warm now, both physically and in an obscure, discreet sense that had everything to do with the woman he'd brought up here.

Perfection was a thing of the past for him now, but he could still have something different, something distracting. The pleasures of the flesh in all their delightful forms were still available to him, and some amenable company for a strictly limited while would be welcome.

Hmm ... flesh. He was back to musing on her thighs again, and back to considering the mouth-watering curve of her bottom as she'd walked away in her trim but damp skirt. His fingers flexed, anticipating soft skin and firm musculature, as he imagined touching and squeezing, not to mention exploring and perhaps even a bit of judicious spanking, should things develop along those lines. She hadn't ever played any kinky games, he'd wager the entire income from this rather mundane company on that certitude.

What will your cries of surprise be like, Jessica? Will you moan with pleasure when I touch you? Will you whimper and cry out my name when I'm between those silky thighs of yours, thrusting?

Ellis McKenna smiled to himself. Life still had the potential to be good, even for him, and as he unscrewed the top of the vacuum flask, the hot, rich cocoa smell only added to his excitement and the gathering thrill.

His cock leapt, as he imagined those deeper pleasures, better even than the luscious taste of chocolate.

He always felt better when he was planning a seduction.

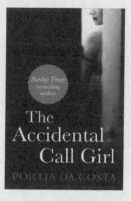

The Accidental Call Girl

It's the ultimate fantasy:

When Maria checks in, an attractive older man in the bar of a
luxury hotel, he mistakes her for a high-class call girl on the
look-out for a wealthy client.

With a man she can't resist . . .

Maria finds herself following him to his hotel room for an
outrageous liaison where she feels the pleasures of illicit
flings to the fullest extent but what will happen when she
discovers that there is far more than she seems . . .

Sexy, thrilling erotic romance for every woman who
has ever had a 'Pretty Woman' fantasy.
Part One of the Accidental trilogy.

BLACK
LACE

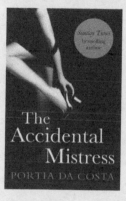

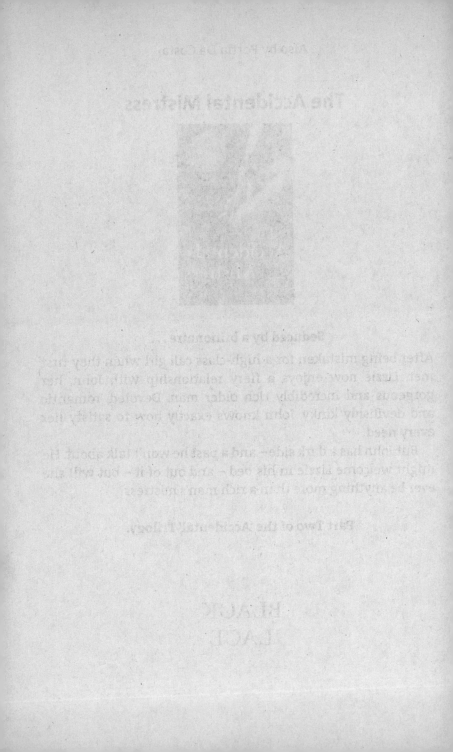

Also by Portia Da Costa:

The Accidental Bride

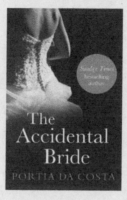

Marrying a billionaire?

It's every girl's fantasy but ever since meeting brooding sexy tycoon, John Smith, Lizzie has never been entirely sure of his true feelings for her.

Has he proposed marriage because he truly loves her or just to keep her in his bed?

Part Three of the 'Accidental' Trilogy.

BLACK
LACE

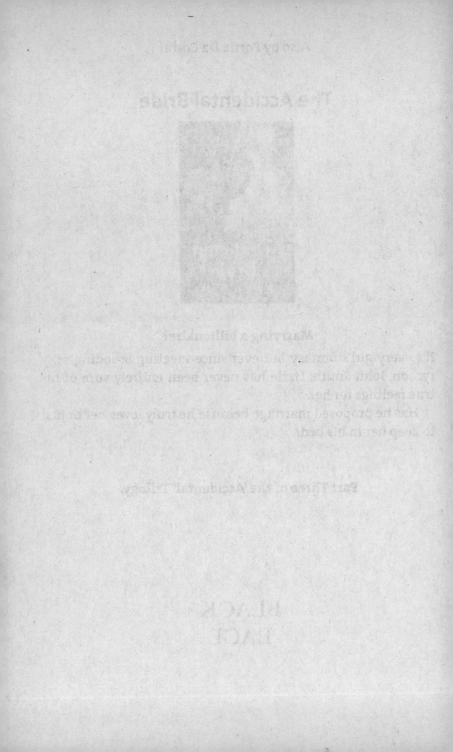

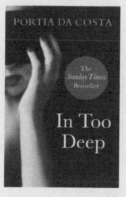

Also by Portia Da Costa:

The Stranger

Once she had got over the initial shock of the young man's nudity, Claudia allowed herself to breathe properly again . . .

When Claudia finds a sexy stranger near her home she discovers that he has lost his memory along with his clothes.

Having turned her back on relationships since the death of her husband, Claudia finds herself scandalising her friends by inviting the stranger into her home and into her bed . . .

BLACK
LACE

Also by Portia Da Costa:

Entertaining Mr Stone

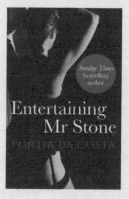

She's a good girl gone bad ...

When Maria Lewis moves back to her hometown, the quiet life she is looking for is quickly disrupted by the enigmatic presence of her new boss, Robert Stone.

A sexy, powerful older man, he seduces Maria into a deliciously erotic underworld. But will she ever be more than Mr Stone's plaything?

BLACK
LACE